Michael J Buckingham was born in Wokingham, England and educated in Buckinghamshire before joining the RAF. Following service in the United Kingdom and the Middle East he embarked upon a career in journalism and became an intrepid international adventurer in pursuit of 'truth'. For 26 years he was a fearless and often controversial columnist and features writer on a South Wales daily newspaper.

An experienced pilot he holds the dubious distinction of recently landing his aircraft upside down on a bare Welsh mountaintop. Classic. Uninjured, though his pride suffered somewhat.

Thus does life imitate art.

Luck
be a
Lady

Michael J Buckingham

GG Books

ISBN 978-1-905967-46-9

Published in the UK by
GG Books , an imprint of
Glimpses of Gwent Books
Cwmbrân, Gwent, UK
Website: www.glimpsesofgwentbooks.com

Made and printed in the UK
by J.R. Davies (Printers) Ltd.
Distributed by Old Bakehouse Publications

British Library Cataloguing in Publication Data: a catalogue
record for this book is available from the British Library.

The last act is bloody, however charming the rest of the play may be.

Blaise Pascal
17th-century French Philosopher

ONE

MALEFACTION. Now, there was a word.

He rolled it pleasurably around his tongue.

Poetic, and with a smack of the Bible. 'Wrong doing' and 'crime' didn't measure up even to the level of its first syllable.

The malefactions of Blaendiffaith had not been great of late, Sergeant Aneurin Hughes mused lifting the kettle from the hob and wafting a smell of scalding tea with which the other office aromas, polished linoleum, the tarriness of a coal fire and pungent pipe tobacco mingled.

When this last cup of tea of the day was drunk he rinsed the cup under the cold tap and left it to drain, placed his helmet on the shelf which had been its off-duty home ever since he had taken over at the village's police station sixteen years earlier, shook a gabardine mackintosh from its wooden hanger and adding a rather raffish touch placed upon his head a grey fedora with silken band, the brim extravagantly curled up at the back and snapped rakishly down at the front.

At six o'clock on the dot Sergeant Hughes lifted the telephone receiver in the manner of one obliged to pick up something very unpleasant and reported to divisional headquarters that the day had been without incident … without malefaction.

A short while later he entered the snug of the Colliers' Arms in which for years beyond recall good ale had been drunk and conviviality nourished in the glow and warmth of a coal fire.

'Very poetic you look. Like Lord Byron in his middle years,' Talfan Evans the landlord observed as Aneurin settled himself into his usual fireside seat.

'I think though, you should do something about the boots. A touch hobnailish and constabularial for such a devotee of the muse Calliope, if you do not mind me saying so.'

'I often think, Talfan, it would be better had you finished your degree at Aberystwyth University instead of being sent home for wickedness.' Aneurin responded gruffly but not unkindly, picking up the copy of the *South Wales Argus* which always awaited him and trawling it evidentially for the items which had a bearing upon local literature or the performing arts.

1

'Men of true erudition carry it lightly. Now, a little drop of the good stuff if you would be so kind.'

Talfan swept up the four pennies Aneurin had placed on the bar and reached under the counter for a bottle of Islay single malt, pouring a generous measure.

Actually, Aneurin mused, Talfan had a point. A man who had published poems in *Y Cymro* and was in possession of a fine collection of silk cravats and ties should have footwear similarly proclaiming his artistic status. Brogues or suede, perhaps, of the finest quality to be had in Wales. The thought brought a wistful smile which transferred itself to an *Argus* item about the Pontypool Thespians and their production of Noel Cowards's *Private Lives* with Mrs Patricia O'Malley as Amanda and John Jones as Elyot, a casting he thought must have made for a love scene as erotic as the couplings of two amiable, but immensely inelegant farmyard beasts. This thought in its turn was evaporated by the whining of a lorry's gears somewhere outside followed shortly by shouts and thumps as men began to unload barrels.

'I thought your beer deliveries were on a Tuesday.' Aneurin's seat was so placed as to give him a good view both out through the Colliers' front window and, over the other shoulder, into the public bar.

Talfan, who was knocking a wooden spike into a barrel, affected not to hear.

'Today is Wednesday.' Aneurin glanced at the October 18, 1944 dateline printed at the top of the page for confirmation. 'I saw a brewery dray arrive here yesterday. Now I observe an Army lorry also delivering beer which you must admit is a strange thing,' he persisted, sniffing possible malefaction.

'There's suspicious you are, Aneurin. The Army at Ponty borrowed a couple of barrels from me for a do they were having. This is merely the Navy, Army and Air Force Institute returning what it owes. Little favours, you know. They make the wheels of life go round.'

'Indeed I do know. We must all do what we can to help one another during this terrible war,' Aneurin said, relenting.

'Just so, Aneurin. Just so.'

The war. The damned war, Aneurin thought bitterly. He would have been retired on a tidy pension and him and Mary might still have their son had it not been for the war. But with the young and fit men needed for either the pits or the forces it was the old ones who had to form the thin blue line. His gaze turned back towards the fire. David, his son; brightest boy in the maths class at Pontypool Grammar who had once explained how it was that aeroplanes flew through the night sky and all the time knowing where they were going. Only two years before he had sat in the seat next to the one in which he now sat, drinking his first beer with his father, face glowing at the compliments and proud of the navigator's half-brevet stitched above his tunic pocket. Talfan had managed to find something a little bit special under the bar that night, too.

Nothing in the Colliers' or indeed in Blaendiffaith had changed since that rollicking evening. The polished brass colliers' lamps gleamed in the same low wattage lamplight which was making the fox's head over the bar glower balefully down and the old grandfather clock which had been there since Aneurin's grandfather was a boy still ticked and wheezed the quarters. Familiar but still inscrutable, the old clock had been ticking away at the instant David's body had been torn apart by cannon shells somewhere over Germany. The prickling on his eyeball was not the heat from the fire, but tears.

Talfan, again exercising a landlord's prerogative, feigned not to notice and busied himself at the far end of the bar.

'The armies of Marshal Zukhov continue to repel the Germans, I see,' Talfan said when once more conversation became appropriate.

'Stop sounding like the *Daily Worker* and serve me a pint of beer.' Aneurin Hughes, now composed, counted out more coppers and began to stuff the pipe which was his favourite accompaniment to ale, one bowlful only, but variable in the length of time it took to smoke according to the size of the bowl and the density with which it was packed and therefore indicative of the intended length of his evening in the Colliers'. This was a large bowl and well tamped down.

Through a shifting veil of smoke Aneurin observed three young men one of whom, a youth with carroty hair, was tapping on the bar with the edge of a coin. The faces of all three were shining with the cold, the brightness of their eyes indicating that they had probably come by way of the Drum and Monkey. One of the youths Aneurin recognised as having stolen a bicycle four years before, for which misdeed he had been hauled before the juvenile court. A second lived in one of

3

the council houses in which he happened to know they were fattening a pig for slaughter. The three played two games of darts and each drank a pint before jostling out beerily into the night.

'Who was the ginger nut?' Aneurin asked Talfan after the sound of the threesome's raised voices had faded into the evening. 'I have never seen him before.'

'Nobody special. Just a lad who's been in a couple of times.'

'Not in the forces, though.'

'Give it a bloody rest, Aneurin. Neither are you. He's a perfectly ordinary lad who I expect is due to go in the army any time now but in the meantime is hewing coal because otherwise there'd only be silly old buggers like you and me to do it.'

'Bloody Hell. Did you hear that?'

A dull seismic thud of the kind which in South Wales sends women weeping to the pithead and fills chapels shook the china jugs hanging over the bar. Habit ingrained since his time as a young constable made Aneurin look at the grandfather clock which said six-fifteen and check it against his own pocket watch. Two thoughts come when such a sound is heard in Wales, the first; God have mercy on the souls underground, and the second more selfish and secretive: O God, let it not be a brother or father or a son of mine.

Talfan shook his head, for he knew what Aneurin was thinking. 'No, it wasn't the Little Pit. I thought I heard a plane. Then a bang.'

People were running from the council houses on the Pontypool Road and spilling out from the Drum and Monkey and the Workingmen's Institute. In the direction in which others were pointing, high on the beetling ridge overlooking the village, he could make out a speck of flickering light. The air was beginning to fill with the acrid smell of burning bracken.

A Sergeant of Constabulary should make his way to even the gravest incident in a dignified and stately manner. Even so it was at a smart lick he proceeded towards the police station, unlocked the door with his heavy key and picking up the loathed telephone's hand piece dialled divisional headquarters.

'Yet another aeroplane has flown into the mountain,' he said to the faint and scratchy voice at the other end.

'You had better telephone the air force or the army to come quickly. The residents of Blaendiffaith are apt to acquire by dubious means the Government's property unless temptation is put beyond their reach.' Aneurin spoke slowly and clearly, reading off the map reference for the crash site from an Ordnance Survey map occupying the wall near the telephone.

Were the truth to be told no aeroplane had actually crashed within ten miles of Blaendiffaith but Aneurin had heard crashes were common not all that far away on the Northern flank of Pen-y-Fal, the shark's-fin shaped crest of which mountain had scythed half-a-dozen from the sky within the last two years and it seemed quite wrong for his village to be wanting in the matter.

'What? What are you saying?' Aneurin glared at the receiver and shook it, as though this simple act might in some way stimulate the brain cells of the constable on the other end of the line.

'How would I bloody know what sort of plane it is? Do you want me to run up the mountain and ask the pilot? ... What? ... Dead or injured?' He breathed deeply, letting the sarcasm flow with his exhalation. 'Well, there has to be a possibility, doesn't there? I imagine that more than your pride would be hurt if you flew headlong into a mountain.'

'The Inspector says you'll have to go and watch over the wreck until the RAF recovery people arrive.' The constable's voice dripped with prim satisfaction, aware of the fact that its owner was at the centre of authority and control.

Aneurin removed the instrument from his ear and regarded it with hatred.

'Buggeration, bloody buggeration,' he muttered as with a click the line went dead.

Elsewhere in the village, in the part known as The Posh, where the mine managers and those of the professional and business caste lived, Mr Jeremy Parr-Gruffydd, retired headmaster and formerly of the Army Education Corps was metamorphosing into Captain Parr-Gruffydd, company commander of the Blaendiffaith and Ironmasters Row Company of the Home Guard.

He had already donned his tailored and carefully pressed battledress tunic and was casting around for his service pistol and webbing belt when the telephone trilled.

The orders were from further up the chain of command and more detailed than Parr-Gruffydd expected them to be. Whilst placing himself at the disposal of the civil authority, in this case Sergeant Hughes, he was by any means necessary to see that no unauthorised persons approached the crash site.

This large dollop of responsibility completed the transition from schoolmaster to soldier. Parr-Gruffydd felt his chest grow an inch and his waist contract into ridges of muscle.

'I don't suppose that means shoot them if necessary, does it, Sir?' he said hopefully to the Lieutenant-Colonel on the other end of the telephone.

'That would be a little drastic, I would have thought. But I suppose ... in an extreme case ... ' the sentence drifted away and with it further talk of on-the-spot shootings.

'Anyway walls have ears and all that stuff but I can go so far as to say there's something fishy about this one. It's the RAF's baby of course but the powers-that-be at our end don't want any more people poking around than is strictly necessary so I'd jump to it if I were you.'

Parr-Gruffydd was about to ask the officer what 'fishy' might possibly entail when the line went dead. He lowered the handset back onto its cradle thoughtfully. When on previous occasions the Blaendiffaith company had been called out it had been a 'leave-it-up-to-you', 'do-the-best-you-can-old-boy', 'use your own initiative' sort of thing. This time his orders had been far more precise. He was to go to the site of the crashed aeroplane and secure the area at whatever cost which, he mused with a hint of anticipation did not preclude shooting at looters should it become necessary.

Having found the pistol and taken up a small box of cartridges which he placed in a pouch on his webbing belt Parr-Gruffydd shivered slightly at the realisation that shooting someone was something he secretly relished.

His rediscovered sense of importance was punctured slightly when he saw to his dismay that Pongo the Labrador pup had seized one of his master's officer-pattern brown leather gloves and was busy gnawing off the thumb. With a howl he lunged towards the puppy's basket but anticipating the move by a split-second Pongo scampered through the French windows that had been thrown open at the sound of the crash and retreated to a spot near an azalea to continue the thumb's messy severance.

After some tussling and growling on both sides Parr-Gruffydd retrieved the chewed scrap of leather from Pongo's jaws and turned back into the room. Helena Parr-Gruffydd, who had been disturbed by the mild excitement and who had come to see what it was about regarded the object thoughtfully, through a cloud of cigarette smoke.

'It looks like a pygmy's scrotum, darling,' she breathed with a theatrical rasp that had once excited him.

'Which is probably the only sort of scrotum you haven't minutely examined,' he replied softly, but with rancour.

'Never mind. You could put brown boot polish on your thumb. After all, your tongue got nice and brown obtaining your commission in the Home Guard.'

Her voice was slurred slightly with drink. God, the words formed themselves just below the threshold of audability; she was incorrigible. And desirable in a perverted sort of way. Parr-Gruffydd buckled on his service revolver feeling a tingling hatred he had come to recognise as sexual. To Hell with the woman. He'd see to her later, the bloody provocative little trollop. The job now was to get the men moving and snatching up the telephone with his ungloved hand he carefully dialled Blaendiffaith Workingmen's Club and Institute where those who were not down the pit would be drinking and playing billiards.

At the police station a mile away Aneurin had exchanged his constabularial footwear for rubber boots and heavy woollen socks and was in the process of removing his gas-mask from its haversack and replacing it with the sandwiches and cake Mary had prepared for him. A full-length greatcoat was too cumbersome even for the time of year, but the pockets were handy for a few squares of chocolate, a whistle, a large rubber torch and a flask of Talfan's Scotch.

It was dark by the time Aneurin came near to the Old Rectory just below Tump Path, named for the ancient mound to which it led.

A sheep which had tucked herself into a scrape in the old house's garden bleated softly at his approach and he wondered how long it would be before the Old Rectory once more had a human inhabitant. He had liked the young woman artist who had come to the village with the American and whose exoticism had lingered like a heady perfume. Despite his labours and the urgency of his task he smiled at the prospect of some Bohemian spice in the village's life to shake up the chapel-going buggers more than somewhat.

When the London painter had first shown an interest in buying the Old Rectory he had smiled inwardly.

The chain of thought was broken by a rabbit's scream.

All over the mountain there must be creatures living and dying, Aneurin pondered as he continued past the scene of the small death.

An instant of self-loathing struck him the way a sudden cold wave might strike a hesitant swimmer making him speak out loud. Christ, your own boy dead in an aeroplane and up until now you haven't thought of the other fathers' sons who could be dying up there on the mountain. Is this what happens with grief? Does a person become insensitive to the pain and loss of others? Perhaps there was a man up there whimpering in agony, terrified and cold. A screaming man was by definition conscious and could be comforted but it was the moaning of the wounded and dying he could not bear. A moan came from the boundaries of consciousness, a persistent and animal sound designed by nature like a baby's cry to force the hearer to act. Perhaps it was the beer and Talfan's enormous whiskies taking effect, but he began to wonder whether he would have the courage to put such a man out of his misery. He shuddered, hitting out with his stick at the wet bracken as if to drive the very thought away.

Lights and shouts ahead and above indicated that Parr-Gruffydd's Home Guard company had reached the crash site sooner than himself.

It was the smell that struck Aneurin first; scorched heather and bracken and the harsh synthetic stench of charred wiring and fuel and aluminium burned to white powder. A wind had got up, sighing in a minor key for the young men for whom oblivion had come on a bare and desolate mountain.

Two torches had seen his and were dipping weaving towards him.

'It's a Yank. A Flying Fortress,' a young man behind one of the torches volunteered.

'Unusual, that. It's normally RAF training planes trying to get below the weather to see where they are that end up flying into clouds with solid centres.'

'Aye. Cumulus Granitus,' another voice said lugubriously.

He recognised the speaker as David Cullen who had only just joined the Home Guard from the Air Cadets. Aneurin was riled by the flippancy of the remark but let it pass. Cullen was going in the RAF himself and perhaps within a twelve month would be one of the thousands of fliers sent to train among these hills and to die perhaps here or in mortal combat. It gave the boy some dispensation to talk in such a brutal manner.

He flashed his own torch into the boy's too-young face.

'Ah, young Cullen. You were first on the scene it wouldn't surprise me. You are plane mad, I seem to remember.'

'Aye, Mr Hughes. Me and my mate here.'

Aneurin turned towards the other young man who wore the single stripe of a Lance-corporal. It was the ginger nut.

'Raymond Williams is my name.' The Lance-Corporal introduced himself politely but without undue deference. Why should he stand in awe of my police sergeant's stripes, Aneurin thought, when he also might be dead within the year? The youngsters he'd first glimpsed in the Colliers' must have sobered up and changed into uniform a bit sharpish.

'We got here around seven, about forty minutes after the plane went in and started to look for bodies or injured. Crawled into the wreckage we did.'

Williams' voice was boastful and with the disdain the young have for the old.

Aneurin shone his torch back onto Cullen.

'And?'

'Six of them, all dead, Mr Hughes. Four inside what's left of the fuselage and the other two tossed out like corks from a bottle. We've covered them over as best we could. Only an engine that got knocked off caught fire. The rest is just mangled.'

Other torches were gathered around the mass of metal and shattered perspex that had been the front fuselage section of the big aeroplane. One point of light separated from the others and moved towards Aneurin.

'Good evening, Sergeant Hughes.'

Parr-Gruffydd greeted him with the touch of a swagger-stick to the peak of his cap. Aneurin did not return the salutation. Discomfited, Parr-Gruffydd followed the line of the sergeant's gaze before quickly concealing the savaged glove.

'The front and middle sections of the fuselage are pretty smashed up but generally in one piece. That's where most of the bodies are.'

There was a forced casualness in the voice. For all his pistol and uniform and air of bustling authority Parr-Gruffydd wasn't used to being around death, Aneurin thought.

'I've put my men to beating out the fires which are small and scattered. Nobody here burned to death.'

'I thought these aircraft carried more than six?' Aneurin asked sharply.

'They very well may do, but that's all we've found after as good a search as you can make on a mountainside in the dark.' Parr-Gruffydd seemed aggrieved at not being given the respect he thought his due.

'The RAF is coming to take them away as soon as it's daylight,' he coldly stated.

Aneurin shone his torch onto the machine's shattered nose. Just below the cockpit window on the left side had been painted a scantily-clad blonde holding four aces with the name Luck Be A Lady in flamboyant letters.

'Not very lucky for those poor devils. I'll take a look inside the plane.'

'I don't know … '

'What is it, Captain?' Aneurin said, allowing a full second to elapse before enunciating the man's rank. 'It is perfectly normal procedure and quite within my jurisdiction.'

'Oh, it's probably nothing. It's just that my orders seemed a little, well … precise.'

'If it is nothing, then I shall get on with my job, Mr Parr-Gruffydd,' Aneurin cut in, hardly bothering to conceal the contempt men who are used to exercising authority on those who buckle it on with pistols and badges of rank.

'It's just that I've been told to secure the site against civilian intrusion,' Parr-Gruffydd responded glumly.

'Which is as it should be. Although as an officer of the law I like to think my duties have more significance than mere civilian intrusion,' Aneurin said stiffly.

'Of course. I don't mean to be obstructive in any way at all. It's just that my people seem to be rather more worked up about this one.' Parr-Gruffydd picked at the ragged fringe of leather from which the thumb had been torn.

'Normally we're told to wait for the recovery crews and keep souvenir hunters away but the local brass seem more than usually concerned about this one. I thought it might have been carrying some special kind of bomb which it couldn't have otherwise it would have gone off.' And then with a change of tone 'I'm sorry to have sounded a bit officious. No offence intended.'

'And none taken Captain Parr-Gruffydd.' Aneurin allowed a note of conciliation to enter his voice. He'd probably be protective of his own dignity if like Parr-Gruffydd he had a mad and lecherous wife to contend with.

'Now, if you will excuse me.'

The aeroplane was indeed a B-17 Flying Fortress of the United States Army Air Forces. Perhaps in some desperate attempt to make a controlled landing, Aneurin considered, it had gouged through rock and turf for over a hundred yards before stopping on the edge of a small ravine at the bottom of which was the Tump Path. From the light of a still-burning patch of heather pieces of aluminium wing and fuselage glinted balefully back. The engine nearest to him attached to the fuselage by a stump of wing was still hot to the touch.

Aneurin's torch flickered round to the torn rear of the front fuselage searching for an entry point. A bulkhead door had been torn open. Beyond it, the pale probing light of his torch fell upon a jumble of wires and pipes hanging from the aircraft's roof and a litter of boxes, oxygen bottles, maps and navigational instruments and a thermos which he picked up and unscrewed sniffing good American coffee and still hot.

The first body torn from its harness and thrown to the side like a broken doll was some ten feet into the wreckage.

At first he had thought its hunched and screwed form to be the back of a seat or insulation material that had been ripped from the roof but as his senses adjusted themselves he realised he was looking at the back of a leather jacket. The dead man's head was slumped forward and bloodied, the arms lost in a jumble of metal and wiring. His lurching and uncertain movement forward made the wreckage sway, throwing him against the dead man's back making his torch fall from his hand and throwing him close to the body, forcing him to smell the sweet and sickly stench of warm blood. The dropped torch shone deeper into the fuselage onto the face of a watch strapped to a wrist covered in hair much darker than that of the first body.

Aneurin struggled to sit upright and to retrieve the light, rocking the fuselage once more and setting dead fingers trembling with the movement.

'Is everything all right in there?' He was momentarily blinded by Parr-Gruffydd's torch.

'It would be if you'd get that light out my eyes.' He could hear the peevishness in his own voice. He eased himself towards another bulkhead beyond which he reasoned would be the bodies of the pilot or pilots.

They were seated side by side; the man in the right-hand seat slumped forward over the control wheel and the body twisted backwards, dead eyes staring through the shattered windscreen at the rising moon.

Both had been wearing headphones, those of the man in the left-hand seat wrenched round so that an ear-piece almost covered his mouth with his dislodged cap covering most of the rest of his face.

He moved the battered cap with its cracked and stained leather peak to reveal a face he could have sworn he'd seen before even though it had been rendered mask-like by death.

No, it wasn't possible. He said the words out loud so as to fully expose the ridiculousness of the notion. There were tens of thousands of American fliers most of them as had been his own boy, with the bodies of men but faces not fully set in their adult mould.

A sound like an urgent whisper and a quick movement made Aneurin start.

A scarf draped around the pilot's neck had fallen in a cascade onto the scored aluminium floor.

Aneurin picked it up, feeling its smoothness and sniffing the heavy and sensual perfume with which it had been sprinkled.

He ran the scarf through his hands, recoiling when it touched congealing blood. Two hours before he had been sitting in front of the fire at the Colliers', his eyes moist with the memories of his only son. Who, when the sun rose, would be weeping for these young fliers? Memories yes, memories. Perhaps that very morning the man whose scarf he held had arisen from the bed of the woman whose scent still lingered in his nostrils. And tonight ... tonight, the bare mountainside would be his bed.

'Sorry, but I thought I heard you stumble,' Parr-Gruffydd's shout dispelled the last tendrils of the thought.

'Do you need me to come in?'

'No. It's all right. Thank you.'

Aneurin switched his torch to the other pilot's body which had been ripped apart as if by heavy calibre bullets. He then trained his beam on the cockpit roof which had been punched and shredded allowing a dappled pattern of moonshine to beam eerily through making blood as black as a lake in Hell. A fierce spewing of bullets rather than mere navigational error had caused the Flying Fortress to smash into the mountainside and yet no enemy aircraft had been seen anywhere over Wales for a twelve month or more.

Odd.

Not unfeasible and certainly not impossible but odd.

He was pondering the matter as something else when his light settled upon what was obviously a small notebook that had become wedged between the pilot's seat and the metal flooring. He dislodged it and as he habitually did with paper lifted it to his nose. Underneath the richness of the soft leather he could detect oil and sweat. The pages were not numerous and the book would have been slender had it not been fattened by their dog-earing and griming. The leather of the back cover had been curled back to form a sort of lip which betrayed the existence of a small pocket.

And inside that some photographs.

'Sergeant Hughes?'

His heart pounded and as the torchlight fell upon him some impulse made him slip the book into his greatcoat pocket. Slowly, so as to not set the fuselage rocking, he picked his way back to where the Home Guard officer waited.

Together they went to a gun turret that had been torn away from the main wreckage.

The body there was that of a dark-haired young man with smooth cheeks without the rasp of a beard. Sorrow and anger began to build up inside Aneurin. It was, or had been, a boy scarcely old enough to leave home and make his own way in the world. In a flush of emotion he imagined the lad's ghost fleeing the wreck of the Flying Fortress and under the wan, eerie light of the moon flying over Welsh mountains and the Irish Sea, across the Stygian waters of the Atlantic until it reached the Americas. In that setting although he had only seen America in films he imagined the boy with his mother with a father and brothers and sisters, living in a tenement in an immigrant quarter of one of the big cities, New York or Chicago, or another such place such as Witchita or Topeka that carried in their romantic name the sigh of limitless spaces. A waste. A bloody, cruel waste. The technical triumph of a modern plane and money that had gone into its construction, all so that young men could be crushed and mangled on the sacrificial altar of war.

Bloody, bloody, Hell.

He cursed out loud. Parr-Gruffydd looked at him curiously but bugger the man. He looked into the waxen face and muttered a prayer for the dead boy who in a strange way had entered his heart. Perhaps there was a way of communicating directly with the boy's family, consoling them as one who had been near at hand as his body grew cold.

Parr-Gruffydd having bustled off to see to something else leaving Aneurin alone with the dead boy and with two opposing notions rushed forward in his brain to clash like venegeful armies.

Everything he had been taught or believed, the inviolability of the belongings of the dead and years established police prodecure ran pell-mell into a deeper instinct.

He was alone with the dead gunner. Such voices as could be heard were at some distance. Surely there would be some personal documents; a scribbled will perhaps or a letter to be passed on to whomsoever must grieve for him?

To the very blazes with it. He'd already taken the diary and pictures. To Hell with regulations and procedures designed to soul-lessly tidy away wasted lives.

Here. What was this?

He felt the blood in his temple pounding.

In the sheepskin jacket's inner pocket. A fat brown envelope containing so far as he could see nothing in the nature of an official document. He took it, felt its weight, and with shaking hands jammed it into his own pocket along with the diary and scarf.

A dancing half-light from the torches and fires hid Aneurin's face as guilt swept over him in a hot rush.

Oh, God of his fathers, what had he done?

Perhaps he could slip the stolen items back inside the

wreckage and nobody would be the wiser but the fleeting thought was vanquished by his earlier resolve.

He had broken the very law he had sworn to uphold with great malefaction, but the need in some way to give meaning to the boy's death was too pressing and the loss of his own son too grievous.

Aneurin found Parr-Gruffydd and bade him goodnight before proceeding back down the Tump Path to the village.

Mary was sitting by the coal fire. A small pork pie with a couple of potatoes and some cabbage were on the scrubbed pine table together with a bottle of beer, glass and an opener. They spoke little, each knowing that discussion of the evening's events would be a portal for their own grief.

He drew her to him, kissed her head and went to bed where the hours passed fitfully and he recognised guilt as the thief of his peace.

Try as he might to fix upon a restful thought his mind was drawn back to the scarf, the diary and the package which he had thrust to the back of a drawer.

The moon had dipped from sight and an owl hooted as he slipped out of bed and went downstairs, the criminal returning to his booty.

The diary's varnished cotton cover had '1944' embossed in gold. The wedge of photographs had put pressure on the little book's spine causing some of the gumming to split. He would examine those later. The good-quality paper was peppered with entries many of which appeared to relate to the life of an airman in war; calculations and brief notes, the acronymics of war. Later, he would sift through it all for details, the reconstructed framework of a human life.

Next he picked up and weighed in his hand the packet taken from the boy. It was gummed shut but not heavy. Neither solid nor yielding. He slipped a kitchen knife worn thin with half-a-century's honing

He hesitated for a split-second. Still it might not be too late. He could still claim that he had removed the packet and the diary in case they contained important military information.

A vigorous flick of the blade severed the excuse.

Two more cuts and with trembling fingers Aneurin Hughes pulled from the package more money than he had ever seen in his life, an amount so great that for better or for ill, he knew his life would never be the same again.

TWO

CAPTAIN James Elmeyer raised his head from the pillow and groaned.

'You look divine.' Amelia drawled the words vampishly.

'I feel like Hell,' he answered and they laughed. He was of the opinion that if you could still exchange banter with a women the morning after sleeping with her she was probably worth sticking with for a while. It was the first test that daylight brings.

A strange mood had swirled around the Limbo Bar, the Soho drinking club where a shifting population of people, British and American, French, Canadian and Polish and all the other nationalities of the Allies' war, some in uniform others not, met to drink, laugh, forget, do business or a combination of any or all of these things, but always with sex in mind.

Last evening in this fervid atmosphere in which emotions were powered by lust and alcohol as surely as a Wright Cyclone aero engine is powered by high-octane gasoline, Elmeyer and the woman had argued politics. He'd drunk a lot and had argued with a passion that had some of the other Americans backing away in case tempers flared.

They had spotted one another at the same instant and every time she looked in his direction he sensed it and returned the glance. After the fourth or fifth exchange of looks he went over to where she was drinking alone and spoke.

The conversation about politics and art had been a lop-sided affair due to the amount of drink Elmeyer had put away. He'd been like a punch-drunk prize fighter unable to fully connect with his ideas and betrayed by his drink-thickened tongue. She had danced around him lightly, jabbing and feinting, until he had good-naturedly called a draw and bought some more drinks.

Then he had suggested they go to her place.

There was a deftness about his lovemaking which she had not expected. When they had got back to her studio she had poured drinks for them both and positioned him in the chair opposite her own so that she could study him. The play of her fingers on her glass and the adroit positioning of the hem of her skirt which usually with too-young men caused them either to remain stupidly transfixed or to make a clumsy lunge merely made Elmeyer smile, which annoyed her slightly.

'Are you laughing at me?' she had asked.

'Not at all,' he had replied. 'I am smiling as a man might smile who stands before a beautiful painting that frees some profound emotion. Your love-making is adorable because it is honest; without shame or guile.'

That had been the night before. Sex had been tender and voluptuous and after it they had listened to the leaves of the old lime tree brushing against her window sending patterns of dappled moonlight into the room. So many times before she had chosen men and in the morning sent them brusquely on their way. This one with his baritone drawl was different. Beyond the immediate passion of their lovemaking it was possible to feel that an easy familiarity might be established. That was something a part, but only a part, of what Amelia Kershaw craved. She regarded him keenly as she put her own light-brown hair into a roll. He was of medium height, or perhaps just a little above, with hair a shade darker than hers and hazel eyes which she had at first considered too serious. A moustache fuller than was fashionable aged him somewhat and suggested a latent bohemianism.

'I'm running off at the mouth. I guess I'm a little high from last night.'

He rubbed a hand over his face which felt gritty.

Amelia stopped brushing, holding her hair up so that he could see the nape of her neck and her playful smile.

'Would you like me to make you feel better?' her voice purred as she slipped from her stool in front of the mirror and into the bed.

Her hand found his member which had already begun to stir. Elmeyer tried to check his erection by controlling the lascivious thoughts that jostled in his brain like dark and dirty little imps. He summoned first a bleak inner vision of the airfield at Bassington on a cold, wet autumn day and absurdly, began to run through the pilot's checklist for a B-17G Flying Fortress.

'Oh, my God.'

Deft strokes were now being applied making the self-induced thoughts of work and the war fall away like a cheap pantomime backdrop. Now a moister feel that came with a reciprocating movement. He looked down to see that her little finger was crooked as though drinking a cup of tea. How English.

'You are an artist in more than one sense. Consummate. No doubt about it.'

In a last attempt to delay orgasm he fixed on the paintings all but covering the wall opposite, pushing and jostling right up to the window-frame with their vivid and sensual colours.

'You have a husband fighting the war against the Japanese and here you are in bed with me ... ' he managed to gasp.

'Having the sort of sex you expect from ladies who provide it for a living?' Her tongue probed the sensitive extremity causing a delicious pain.

'I didn't say that. Oh, that is just too damned good. Don't make me ... I want to save it ... '

'Go ahead. Live dangerously.'

'I do. Oh, my Lord.'

Amelia uttered a low moaning noise as Elmeyer's whole being was thrown into a space that was at once warmly enclosed but also a void from which all thoughts and other feeling had been expunged. She continued to work him and his body shook again. Only after another minute of exploration with her flickering tongue pursuing the last orgasmic ripple did she take her face away.

'Is that a little better?'

The full sex that came a minute later was quick and violent. Their parting in which she snatched herself suddenly away was part of the rough game he knew she liked to play. Amelia ran water into the sink and began unselfconsciously to wash herself before dressing. Elmeyer gathered his washing and shaving kit and put it in his Army issue haversack leaving half-hidden a tablet of good American soap for Amelia to find as a surprise.

'I can't get over how dull and miserable everything looks,' Elmeyer said half-an-hour later, turning up the collar of his three-quarter length jeep coat against the fine rain. 'It's like looking at things through smoked glass. Like you do an eclipse.'

It was a good comparison, he thought. He was witnessing the eclipse of the British Empire outshone by the gaudy and capitalistic glare of the American dream. London was inexpressibly drab, as dreary as had been Madrid six years ago, except that in Spain in the summer there was the sun to tease colour even from the blasted and splintered trees which had been stripped for firewood, the baked, crumbling buildings, the snow-capped mountain tops and ochre plains. In London, the sun, when it deigned to appear, served only to highlight the city's grey forlornness.

One day if he lived, and if they stayed in love, he would tell her about Spain.

'Come on. Hold my hand.' Amelia smiled softly, offering it. 'It won't bite. I promise.'

How could a woman be so horny in bed and yet colour up with the freshness of a virgin when he took her hand? He smiled his own smile and shook his head in mock-resignation. She looked good enough to eat though, when she gave that little smile.

It was an hour to noon but Nina the resident lush was already in place at the Limbo's bar with a newspaper and large gin. A string bag propped against the leg of her bar stool contained straggly carrots and something bloody wrapped in newspaper.

'Lovely summer's morning! And how are the sparring partners? You haven't been arguing politics all night is my bet,' Nina chirped in a voice that once had been smooth and refined before being being forced to run the gauntlet of four decades of gin and cigarettes.

'Henry won't be a moment. He's out the back doing a bit of business.'

Nina exhaled, appraising Elmeyer through a haze of cigarette smoke.

The Limbo Bar had variously been described as blowsy, garish, sensual and providing the same sort of lewd satisfaction as gazing at a dirty picture. It was a place that thrived in the dark, retreating from the daylight like a vampire from a phial of holy water. Henry, his dealings complete, waddled past them without a greeting and opened the door which led out onto some steps and up to the street.

Such sunlight as dared to enter formed a small rectangle illuminating a carpet of incredible filthiness, so drink-sodden that it was said that cigarettes dropped upon it extinguished themselves. Nina was the tipsy mascot of this little republic of the damned, sitting on her seat at one end of the bar like an all-seeing and malign goddess, viewing with leering amusement all the frailties of which humans are capable.

Even if not actually engaged in nefarious activity the Limbo's denizens were contemplating it. Men in snazzy suits and camel-hair coats would walk in off the street, trailing cigar smoke through the bead curtains beyond which lay the stairs and Henry's flat. Lorries pulled up in the side lane while watchful drivers whisked boxes or crates into the club's tiny yard. Minutes afterwards the whisper would go round that coffee or cigarettes, Scotch whisky or perfume, silk stockings or tinned meat were for sale. Sometimes after a Chinaman had paid swift and silent visits a special clientele, the most hopelessly damned and dissolute of all could buy the white powder they craved, or purchase the black, sticky balls of opium that for a time lifted them from the abyss on wreathing coils of thick, sweet smoke.

From her perch Nina would cock an eye at the silk stockings and the Max Factor make-up as they passed from supplier to Henry and think of the days long gone when such gifts might have been for her. Occasionally, much less frequently these last few years, a young drunk half-gallant, half-teasing would make her a present which despite her decrepitude she accepted with boozy outward grace but shallow gratitude.

'Can I get you a drink, Nina?' Elmeyer offered.

'Don't mind if I do.' The glass had already been drained in anticipation. 'Henry's coming back.'

There was a slight stirring of the stale air and a waft of expensive cologne as Henry heaved his bulk behind the bar and served himself with a large Scotch, the light reflected in the mirror behind the bar glinting on his dyed and brillianteened strands.

'What's your pleasure, eh?' The small, high voice escaped from the great bulk like that of a plaintive geni locked inside a lamp the size of a freighter. It was as though some petulant minor deity had decided to mock Henry for his size.

Elmeyer ordered a gin-and-tonic for Amelia and a Scotch for himself, not even bothering to ask for the ice because he knew such a request to be pointless. Amelia and Nina had struck up the smiling conversation of women who do not know one another well. Over the previous few months Elmeyer had become a regular at the Limbo, favoured by Henry with special nods and winks when a delivery of contraband came. The fact that the American smiled good-naturedly but rarely took advantage of the dubiously-acquired goods was put down by Henry as an eccentricity which went in tandem with Elmeyer's left-wing views. Frenchie, Elmeyer's tail gunner who often accompanied him on his forays into the club had no such scruples. Elmeyer liked Henry for his stoicism. It must be tough on old queers, he thought, who half fell in love with young men who were then snuffed out at the most intense moment of their lives. When the war ended they should put up memorials and have parades for men like Henry, too.

'One of those doodlebuggers crashed near me last night. Frightened the life out of me,' Nina rasped by way of acknowledging the gift of a drink.

'Doodlebugs, Nina. The flying bombs are called Doodlebugs,' Amelia gently corrected.

'Doodles are what I do for a living and buggers are what we get a lot of in here. Anyway there aren't any more doodlebugs. The RAF can shoot most of those down, or bomb their bases. These new ones are rockets called Vee-Twos.'

'Hey, you seem to be up on the latest German weapons. Are you sure you don't work for British intelligence?' Elmeyer half-joked, it having occurred to him that she might be the type.

He scrutinised her reflection in the huge, flyblown mirror behind the bar, taking in her gestures and expressions and imprinting them on his brain. What was she really like? What did the expressive curving of the mouth as she spoke to Nina mean? The seemingly carefree laughs, shrugs and hand gestures were like emotion wavelets on the surface but what moved in the depths of the ocean of her soul? In wartime all you ever saw was the surface. He lived on the surface, too. In the bad days of the year before when Luftwaffe fighters were chopping American bombers from the sky he'd stopped trying to know anything about the young replacements for the downed aircrews, the eager, frightened innocents who in their turn became fighter fodder. As with lovers so with comrades. It was not wise to invest too much of yourself in a person. When the worst period for casualties had passed he had allowed himself to believe that it might just be possible to once more make plans; to have a life that did not proceed simply from day to day. Survival seemed not only possible but - dare he even think it? - probable. For the first time since 1937 when he had gone to Spain there was a vision of peace and

21

contentment on the far horizon. Was the woman he now studied so intently in the mirror the one with whom he would find such bliss?

'Frenchie should be in around now,' Elmeyer broke from his reverie.

Staff Sergeant Norbert 'Frenchie' Hayes was Luck Be A Lady's tail gunner, an irrepressible boy from Illinois who was called Frenchie on account of his being short and Mediterranean-looking.

They needed short men to crouch in the gun turrets particularly the ball turrets in which Frenchie sometimes sat, a rotatable sphere slung under the belly of a Flying Fortress with only a half-inch of perspex between the gunner and four miles of sky.

The tail gun though was Frenchie's favoured place.

Tail gunners in particular were prey for German fighters, particularly when a plane dropped out of formation having taken battle damage. Then the black-crossed Messerschmitts and Focke-Wulfs would study their quarry from afar, as often as not planning an attack from the rear. Frenchie though, was a born warrior, his reactions welding him to the twin M2-50 calibre machine guns that had already hosed two dozen attacking fighters from the sky.

Maybe Frenchie too would make it Elmeyer mused. He hoped so. Frenchie had been a member of a weird religious sect, but excommunicated for unspecified but not wholly unguessed-at reasons. That Frenchie believed his continued survival to be wholly due to the Almighty was to Elmeyer as rational as wresting with rattlesnakes and speaking in tongues. For himself Elmeyer preferred to thank the superior defensive firepower of the Boeing B-17G bomber. The funny thing about Frenchie he considered was that the boy was an incorrigible and enthusiastic crook, a dealer on the black market immersed in a dark miasma of theft, deceit and violence.

Elmeyer had once pointed out that crime and a belief in the Almighty weren't the most compatible of propositions but Frenchie had simply shrugged disarmingly and said 'Heck, Cap. Doesn't all legitimate business start off as some kind of a scam?'

There was still enough of the communist left in Elmeyer to see his point.

'Here comes Frenchie. Right on time,' Henry piped. The

first livener of the day had brought Elmeyer back to something approaching normality.

'Good Morning Staff Sergeant Hayes. I take it you've been engaging in extra-mural activities?'

'Say that again, Cap?' Frenchie said, using his own irreverent abbreviation describing both Elmeyer's job aboard Luck Be A Lady and his rank.

Elmeyer pointed to the bulging pocket of his gunner's unseasonable greatcoat.

'You've been doing business other than army business.'

Frenchie returned Elmeyer a mock-hurt look. 'Cap how could you? I shouldn't have to explain the obvious to a man of your fine Eastern education. We're fighting this war for the freedom for citizens to buy and sell legally acquired property, ain't that right?'

'Ah,' Elmeyer smiled. 'The validity of that statement turns on the word 'legally'.'

'Now you're hurting my feelings. I'm just one jump ahead of other people when it comes to acquiring things is all. 'Unto everyone that hath shall be given, and he shall have abundance. But from him that hath not shall be taken away even that which he hath'. It says that in the Bible. What do you think about that, Miss?'

Amelia turned towards Frenchie with a look that was both warm and amused.

'I think that's the bit of the Bible Karl Marx had trouble with,' she laughed.

'You don't say?' Frenchie's brow furrowed for an instant before brightening once more. Elmeyer could tell from his talk that Frenchie liked the woman.

'Hey. Get a feel of this,' Frenchie said, veering away from the baffling matter of politics. 'This is something really special.'

From within the depths of his overcoat pocket he withdrew an emerald green scarf, holding it out towards Amelia. She took it, pressing it to her cheek and feeling its smoothness.

'It's lovely, Frenchie.'

'Real silk, Ma'am. Straight from the bug's ass.'

'Green scarves are supposed to bring bad luck,' Elmeyer cut in mentally counting the English pounds left in his pocketbook and wondering how and from whom the scarf had been acquired.

'Not this one,' Amelia said. 'It flows through the fingers like a dark and secret stream. I'm an artist, remember? It will bring you luck, I promise. How much is it, Frenchie?'

'For you, because you're a lovely lady, ten English bobs.'

'I want to buy it for you, James.' She turned towards him her face lit by a smile.

'It will make me feel that I'm with you when you're flying. Here. Take it. Please.'

Frenchie beamed, folding away a ten-shilling note as Elmeyer took the scarf in return kissing Amelia on the cheek.

'Now I gotta see Henry,' Frenchie said.

'He absolutely adores you,' Amelia said after Frenchie had gone.

'He thinks I can make you happy. Do you think that will happen?'

Elmeyer took a long swallow of his drink.

'I just hope there's enough happiness left over for Frenchie to enjoy. He's got a little daughter back home who has some kind of disease affecting her body and head. They're dirt poor so he works the black market as a way of paying the medical bills. The richest country in the world can't even buy the kid good health care, yet still he puts his life on the line for it. It's not only the Nazis who deserve to be bombed fucking flat.'

'So much anger. Yet you fight for freedom and democracy and all that.'

'The government was insistent upon the point.'

'I thought fliers were all volunteers?' Amelia countered, lifted eyebrows forming a question mark.

'It's complicated. Anyway, what did you mean about making me happy for a while?'

Elmeyer signalled a change of subject but Amelia persisted …

'Your political convictions must have been strong at one time. Nobody forced you to go to Spain and fly for the Republic. Not only that but it's common knowledge in here that you've volunteered to fly more than the usual number of missions. If that's right it sounds suspiciously like dedication to a cause.'

It wasn't a strict rule he'd made never to talk about Spain, just a general principle which he had breached last night. How badly he must have wanted to share something with this woman. His convictions in those days when he had crossed the Pyrenees and risked exile from his own country by joining in the fight against Franco's rebels were minted from the bright metal of youth and passion.

'The cause got mislaid. I just soldiered on.'

Amelia was showing Nina her new scarf as Elmeyer's thoughts wandered back to a high-ceiling bar at Aix-le-Bains on the French side of the Spanish border. It was there in a café bar with tall, peeling shutters and a dark wine-stained bar he had whiled away the days waiting to be taken into Spain. Each day before going there he'd buy *Le Monde* and sit with his feet dangling in the heated water of the town's outdoor Roman bath half-hoping that nobody would come to collect him.

But come they did.

On the third day more young men had arrived to paddle their feet in the blood-warm sulphurous water. They had been loud and optimistic and certain of the battle's outcome and to escape them he had gone into the adjoining chapel where typed-out prayer slips offered supplication to St Jude, patron saint of lost causes who given the way things turned out should have been able to offer some comfort to Republican Spain.

Then a guide had come and taken them to the civil war.

'Come on Cap. We've got a train to catch.' Frenchie's voice brought Elmeyer back to the present and another war. In Spain he had felt trepidation and, yes, fear. The brutal routine of bombing had taken most of the terror away but now the fear was one of separation.

He took Amelia in his arms and kissed her, eliciting a wink from Nina and an embarrassed shuffle from Frenchie.

'I'll come back as soon as I can. I promise.'

It was all he could think of to say but what more was there?

'Will you telephone? I've put the number in your bag. Write it in your diary.'

Perhaps one day there would be no more parting. Just three more missions and they could begin to lay their plans. They kissed once more but she did not offer to walk a part of the way to the station with him. Why should she? he thought. If he wanted to be at the centre of her world he would have to earn the right and one night, no matter how ephipanal for them both, wasn't going to cut it. He smiled a smile he did not feel as she waved, and turned back into the Limbo Bar.

Their uniforms guaranteed them a taxi to Liverpool Street where they boarded a train crowded with bodies smelling of stale booze and wet woollen uniforms, a persistent rain having by now dislodged the earlier bright spell. Elmeyer had been drunk the night before when he'd met Amelia but the couple of drinks he'd had that morning had perked him up. Now, with the dirty rain running streaking the carriage windows and the grimy North London suburbs slipping by a deep alcoholic depression began to bite.

Frenchie caught his mood.

'Have you ever wondered why these guys, the British I mean, put up with this?' He asked the question softly, making sure there were no British uniforms nearby. 'It's so damn' poor and dirty and grey. Like an old mule back home we had to shoot.'

Elmeyer watched two runnels of water shiver and eventually unite before the bottom of the carriage's window frame, the progress of the train so slow that they were barely blown backwards.

'They put up with it and fight on because they hope for something better.' Elmeyer too kept his voice down even though no British were within earshot. A surprisingly large number of Americans he had found despised the British.

'To be more like Americans, you mean?'

'I expect some want that. Most just want to be allowed to muddle through in their own inimitable fashion, I guess. They're a tired people. Tired of running an empire, tired of war and tired of this constant fucking rain.'

'You think about that kind of stuff quite a lot, don't you, Cap? Sometimes I think you might be a commie.'

The words had cheerful inflection but Frenchie's eyes searched for a reaction.

'You don't say?' He grinned despite himself. 'Well. I'm fighting in an American uniform and not a Russian one.' He forced a cheerful look and patted Frenchie's shoulder.

'All you need to know about me is that I'll get you and Luck Be A Lady back in one piece. The war will be over soon and we can all go home and none of this will matter.'

Except that it would matter in England even more than in America.

At Cambridge they were met by hostile, bored military policemen who had been leaning and smoking against a line of trucks. Elmeyer turned up his collar against the rain. A few short hours ago he had been in Amelia's bed. Maybe she'd had a couple more drinks and was now back in it, catching up on the sleep she didn't get last night. He saw with his mind's eye the old stove and kettle, the gas fire, the paintings and the tree which, when it waved in the wind, made it seem as though Amelia's studio was floating on a rustling green sea.

Two damp guards, water dripping off the rims of their helmets watched impassively as the line of trucks splashed past the entrance to the base. Shit. Didn't it ever stop raining? Even the half-round huts looked like giant bean cans half-swallowed by mud.

Smoke was coming from hut chimneys and melding with the low, grey sky.

The Solitary Cyclist squeaked by on his ancient bicycle.

The Solitary Cyclist was only ever seen on his machine and it was said that no two people ever saw him at the same time. Elmeyer thought about asking Frenchie whether he could see him too, but decided against it. Summer and winter the Solitary Cyclist wore a greatcoat with the badges of a sergeant. Nobody knew whether he was - or had been - aircrew and because he had his collar always turned up as if against some devilish wind no mortal could feel the keenness of. Where he had come from and where he was going none knew. Some people said he was a ghost and crossed themselves if they saw him before going on a mission.

Elmeyer shuddered. If not tomorrow, then sometime very soon, he would be shaken awake by an orderly and after the briefing climb into Luck Be A Lady and fly off on his forty-eighth mission. Two more and they would pin the Distinguished Flying Cross on him and send him home. He would then have completed fifteen more missions than the standard tour of duty that the month before had been raised to thirty-five, because they said 'survivability' had increased. That only held true if you hadn't been a part of the earlier air fighting. What had made him stay the extra length of time in the ETO - the European Theatre of Operations - risking both his health and his sanity?

Certainly, in the early days, it had been the fervent anti-Nazism which had sustained him during his Spanish days. The slogging, murderous fight of the bomber war, so unlike the swift, violent fighter engagements over the Jarama front and at the battle of the Ebro had, he confessed to himself, knocked most of the idealism out of him. And now there was

Amelia; beautiful, dangerous gorgeous Amelia.

As he jumped down from the truck Captain James Elmeyer made a big decision; ranking along with that which sent him to fight in Spain and to volunteer for extended combat with the Army Air Force. He would fly his fiftieth mission and ask Amelia to marry him. He'd have to go back to the States he guessed, but as soon as he was demobilised he'd come back to England where people were already saying there would be a new left-wing post-war government. Yes, that was it. He had fought for democracy in Spain and in the skies over Europe. Others still with their youth and innocence and with the incandescent optimism of his early days could carry the fight. Like Voltaire's *Candide* now was the time to cultivate his own garden. Politics and war did change the world, but behind it all was luck. Being in the right place at the right time, or for most people, the wrong time or place. Fate. Luck. Same damned thing.

'There she is, Cap.' Frenchie pointed towards Luck Be A Lady, her olive green paint given a greasy sheen by the drizzle, fat and heavy on her tyres like a creature that had hauled itself from the primeval slime under some ancient and terrible sky.

'She looks like a sad old whore. Yeah, that's it. Like one of the Piccadilly Commandos.'

Hunched and chilled mechanics none of whom even glanced at the passing trucks trudged around her. A servicing bench and some other pieces of ground equipment including platforms for the engine fitters were scattered haphazardly around.

'You don't look too good now old lady, it's true,' Elmeyer said softly. 'But you'll be a regular sweetheart when we fly. I'll treat you gently and fly a tight formation to keep out of the way of the fighters and I'll land you real gently and I'll always, always wear my green silk scarf for us both because, if you're a lucky plane then those you take to war will be lucky too.'

As the thoughts processed through Elmeyer's mind a British air force car splashed past.

That's right, he thought, as the little blue-grey vehicle swung round a big aviation fuel bowser and, receiving a salute from the MP at the gate, busied itself off in the Cambridge direction. Get on with organising your war British, American, German, Japanese or eskimo or what the fuck. Just three more missions, just three, and you can count me out.

THREE

ELWYN Creed slowly lowered his hand to touch the document as though obliged to pat a dog with fleas. It was his professional way of signalling that the affairs of Aneurin Hughes had finally been put to rest.

'He was a grand age. Yes, indeed.'

No warmth lay behind the words. The will had been read to its sole beneficiary and a fee extracted. Dead as he was, Aneurin Hughes had now joined the only class of people from whom solicitors could not find a way of squeezing more money.

'Pompous little arse.' The words were exhaled softly by Mair Huws as she regarded Creed without affection or gratitude. The solicitor had handed her the cheque in settlement of her father's affairs as if it were *his* personal gift.

'Your father left you a very considerable amount.'

'Yes. Isn't that gratifying?' It was said without the required degree of solemnity and caused a discernible pursing of Creed's lips.

'He made some wise financial decisions. Very adroit.'

Wise for a dense copper is what you mean, you obsequious little prick.

'He was always careful with money,' she replied with her police voice, a touch the right side of bald hostility.

'Now if that's all ... '

Creed spread his hands and smiled as if releasing her into a benevolent and assured future of his own creation. She took the proffered hand and allowed Creed to see her to the door.

Aneurin Hughes' final act had been to tell his daughter how much money he was leaving her. She had gasped when she heard the enormous sum. In fact the estimate was over fifty thousand pounds short having failed to include the latest tranche of interest. Mair had kissed her father on the forehead and held his hand until, with a thespian wink, Aneurin Hughes, former policeman and persistent poet, amateur dramatist and man of many of financial secrets, died.

She left Creed and gone to her building society with the cheque, preferring to handle the transfer of the money herself. The building society manageress with whom Mair had been at school was, possibly because she had heard of her lesbianism (or could it have been desire?) usually rather correct and distant. This afternoon she was bright and attentive.

One million, nine hundred and twenty-three thousand, six hundred and twenty-four pounds and forty-seven pence had that sort of effect, Mair was beginning to find out.

Later that same day the huge emotional forces of grief at her father's death and knowledge that she was a millionaire crashed like two violent weather systems, causing an occlusion of sorrow, and guilt contrasting with an elation that now and for the rest of her life money would cease to be a worry.

Such pleasant thoughts managing to survive this tangle of emotions was dissipated by the police station canteen's gloom and the approach of Chief Inspector Patrick O'Driscoll.

'Hi. Mair. Can I join you?'

O'Driscoll had pale grey eyes that never smiled and lips that rarely did anything else.

'I was sorry to hear about your Dad. He was a copper of the old school. After him they broke the mould.'

Mair inwardly grimaced, but managed a thin smile. O'Driscoll had come to the South and Mid Wales Police Force from the Northern Ireland Police Service where his indulgence of the semi-psychotic republicans had earned him rapid promotion. As had the Sinn Féin leaders to whom he had found it easy to 'relate'. O'Driscoll had kitted himself out with an easy and jargon-ridden style and language.

'There weren't any schools in his day, Sir. Just coppers,' Mair said evenly. 'But thank you.'

O'Driscoll would take that as an 'off-message' reply. Mair detected a shard of hostility, quickly concealed as he slid into the seat opposite, nodding apologetically at his coffee.

'Decaff. I've been told to keep an eye on my blood pressure.'

'We owe it to ourselves, Sir.'

O'Driscoll allowed his eyes to wander over her face, searching for the minute signs that would indicate whether the remark was sincere or sarcastic.

'I thought we could have an informal chat,' he continued, carefully selecting a cosy tone. 'Perhaps you've had the time to think about the RACE initiative.' He raised his eyes to the ceiling so as to suggest that Government-inspired initiatives and targets aimed at social engineering were an irksome extra burden to the policeman's lot.

Mair knew that for O'Driscoll immersing himself in the committees and procedures of political correctness was like a bath in asses' milk for a Pharaoh's queen.

'Just because we are police officers and have a ... uniform.' O'Driscoll pronounced the word as though it should be in inverted commas, 'Doesn't put us above the community. We have to be able to interface with cultural minorities and gain an intimate knowledge of their perspectives. Inclusivity is the key word.'

'Put into plain language, Sir, the Government wants to suck up to minorities at the expense of police impartiality.'

'I think inclusivity should mean inclusive, don't you, PC Huws?'

'What else could it mean, Sir?'

This time he picked up the thin shaving of sarcasm. Residents Against Cultural Exclusion had in a languid fashion been set up a couple of years before O'Driscoll's arrival but it was he in his own words who 'had given the idea wings.'

'You're asking me because of what you know about my private life, but as it happens I don't roar around on a Harley-Davidson or get dressed up in lumberjack shirts and boots and hang around in dark bars. I like gardening and local history and simply staying at home with a good book. I'm sorry if that sounds too un-lesbian.'

O'Driscoll sipped his decaffeinated coffee slowly, blowing over the top.

'You are fully committed to the idea of multiculturalism, I assume?' The voice was level and hard and without the rising note of a question.

'My feelings are my own, Sir. I know that I am expected to police a multicultural society which is what I do.'

O'Driscoll ignored the reply.

'Because as you must know the force has working towards a multicultural society as the core aim of its mission statement. You remember the trouble after the Libyan hostage crisis? How do you think we managed to stop the local yobboes throwing litter bins through kebab shop windows and torching Asian-owned shops if it wasn't by constructively engaging with the Muslim community?'

'Wasn't that just before you arrived here, Sir?' Mair pushed the tray to one side, fingertips resting on the edge of the formica table and ready for open confrontation.

'In fact it must have been about the time you were constructively engaging with the Irish terrorists.'

Look your enemy straight in the eye Aneurin had always told her. Face it down. Play on your adversary's uncertainties.

A tiny pulse had begun to beat just below O'Driscoll's severely-cut grey fringe.

'Are you a racist?' It was almost a growl.

'No. But I can see how somebody like you might think I am.'

He swept up his tray, his mouth set hard. That was it. All she could hope for now was the polite, impersonal letter pointing out that she was approaching the age at which one normally retired from the police service, and did she know that provisions for early retirement were available etc ...

'I have work to do, as I am sure you have.' O'Driscoll's voice was as thin as a honed knife.

'We'll speak again.'

What the Hell, she thought. With two million pounds as fireproofing she would never have to worry about the O'Driscolls of this world ever again. She watched him working the room as he moved toward the canteen entrance stopping twice to exchange a word with more favoured officers and once to pat another on the back.

It was now Tuesday. A week's leave began the following day. After her father's death she had been offered compassionate leave but had decided to take the time from her annual leave. What had to be faced was adding the last touches to the funeral arrangements. Only after Aneurin was snug in the ground would there be time to take full stock. Two million pounds bought a lot of options the most obvious of which was retirement. She would be able to live comfortably on her police pension using only a fraction of the interest her money would earn. Why then, did the prospect of settling down with her books, her music and the study of local history bring her so little pleasure? She tried to analyse her unease. Most obviously it was due to her father's death. How could she even think of the life that was to come when the only man she had ever really loved lay unburied?

That night Mair went to bed with the uneasy thought that much of the day had been consumed by anger and revulsion directed first against Creed and then O'Driscoll. From where had such a lack of ease come? Was it age, or the feeling that she had failed in her police career? Perhaps it was grief expressing itself as anger. Or her parting with Angela the year before.

The split with Angela had been protracted and painful and had cost her something in the way of self-respect but she was over it now, the only residue being a small addition to her reservoir of bitterness.

Mair's comfort now was in the cottage her father had bought before the war when he had been married to Mary who had died before she was born, and before he had married Ursula, her mother dead these past ten years. Aneurin and Ursula had bought another small house the other side of the village, less than a mile away. Mair had been christened with the Welsh form of Mary but had adopted the 'Huws' for herself, the last remnant of an early enthusiasm for Welsh nationalism. Her father had not disapproved. He was a loving and gentle man who had tenderly held her when she had confessed the secret nature of her first love.

Tears came, dampening the pillow as she thought of her father. It was just as the veil of sleep began to fall like a theatrical curtain that a small thought crept out from under it, the tiniest wisp which had her sitting up and looking around as if the answer were to be found in her bedroom's darkened corners.

Since as long as she could remember, right up until Aneurin's death, she had never wanted for the necessities and small comforts of life. Sometimes this had led to mildly embarrassing situations as when she had been a Guide with a better uniform than the others apart from the Parr-Gruffydd girl and always the right equipment. The confident air she was generally thought to have sprang from this, she supposed. It was always David Morgan in Cardiff rather than the Co-op. Aneurin's legacy had made her a millionaire. How had that happened?

Slithering and clawing in the mire of her darkest fears was the thought that her father might have been corrupt. That would explain the holidays and good clothes and the fact that they were the first family in Blaendiffaith - apart from the Parr-Gruffydds again - to have a new car.

But petty corruption could not be made to explain two million pounds. Aneurin had not been a secretive man but he had been a man with secrets. She recalled how with shining eyes and a kiss she had thanked him for a gift. Now she could read things into the smile, and the fond little pinch administered to her nose. It was his way of saying 'I have my secrets and you, my pretty, shall never know them.'

She thumped the pillow, snuggled her head into its downy softness and tried to chase away the troubling thoughts. Could she ever comprehend the mind of a man who had lost first a son and later a wife? Heaven alone knew how he might have saved and invested to protect her, the last of his blood.

A picture of David her half-brother who had died in the war and which she kept on her bedside table mingled with images of her father as she eased her way into sleep.

At ten o'clock the morning post arrived, a package with Bishop, Evans and Creed stamped on it and just small enough for her letterbox.

Mair carried the package to the table gingerly as though it were an unexploded bomb, an anxiety taking shape that something had gone badly wrong; that the money wasn't hers after all and that the will was being contested and would she please call into the solicitor's office at her earliest convenience to discuss matters. The letter slipped in with the contents of the package would be polite ... 'Bishop, Evans and Creed realised that considerable disappointment had been caused and in consideration of it might therefore be able to negotiate a small settlement. In the meantime some small personal effects belonging to her father were enclosed ... '

Mair's hands trembled slightly as she slid the blade of a penknife under the well-sealed flap.

A diary for the year 1944 was the first thing she eased out. Holding her breath with anticipation she opened the little book, smelling the mustiness of the pages. Tucked inside the diary were three photographs which she laid side by side.

The first picture was of a group of men dressed in a haphazard collection of flying clothing standing by the nose of a large aeroplane with other planes in the background

The second was of two people, a young woman with a striking rather than conventionally beautiful face and wearing a beret, her face lit with laughter and her hand resting upon that of a moustachioed American Army officer was placed around his waist. She studied the American's face, trying to make it tally with one of the airmen in the group picture but could come to no firm conclusion.

The third picture was of the same woman, this time standing by the side of an RAF officer. This she examined for some time, puzzling as to what elusive notion or memory made her eyes go time and time again to the RAF man's face.

She dug her fingers back into the package, touching something soft which seemed to warm as her fingers lingered on it.

Silk.

Green, and as she pulled it out, cascading like a mountain rill running between mossy banks and five feet long at least.

A scarf, patinated with oil, and the stiffness of dried blood.

FOUR

UNBLOODED replacements stood smartly to attention and old hands groaned and coughed to their feet as the 391st Bomb Group's commander accompanied by his intelligence and meteorology officers moved under a low stratum of cigarette smoke towards the podium above which hung a large map covered with green cloth.

Everyone in the room, no matter how much time they had spent joking or greeting always returned their eyes to the rectangle of baize.

The word had already gone round the base that the mission would be deep into enemy territory.

'I have the strangest feeling that we are not going to like what is under that cover,' the pilot seated next to Elmeyer, a boy from Kentucky who flew The Louisville Slugger which had a red jay bird with a baseball bat hitting a swastika for six painted on its nose, said softly. 'No, sir. Not one little bit.'

The senior officers were now on the dias. Colonel John Jessop, a short, tough, angry Arizonan, called for the mass of aircrew to be seated.

'It's my last mission before they send me home. I could sure have done with some nice milk run without the fighters and the flak and all. Hell, I would have been home by now if the bastards hadn't upped the mission count to thirty-five,' the Kentuckian said from the side of his mouth.

Elmeyer said 'Look on the bright side. Think what it'd be like if you were only five missions into your tour like some of these poor kids. You know the ropes. Fly a nice, tight formation and trust the gunners to do their work.'

'Aren't you the guy who volunteered to do more missions?' the Kentuckian said out of the side of his mouth all the time watching the men on the platform. 'I heard about you when I was posted here. You must be real lucky to fly with.'

'Don't say that,' Elmeyer hissed back. 'Never, ever say that.'

Elmeyer had never tried to explain to anyone why he'd insisted on doing fifteen extra missions.

'I've got a good crew. That's all.'

If Luck Be A Lady's luck was down to anything it was the gunners, especially the warm, generous Frenchie, who turned into a killing machine the moment he switched on his gun sights. B-17s flew in high, low and middle formations with the wingtips only yards from each other, each ship covering its neighbours with a zone of fire. Elmeyer often thought of the poor bastards in the RAF flying at night with only pathetic .303 machine guns for protection. Flying in the dark, not knowing, apart from the possibility of seeing his glowing exhausts, whether the other guy was on your wingtip or twenty miles away. Blundering through the sinister and hostile night was his idea of a personal Hell. If he had it coming to him he wanted it high and clean and in daylight.

A taut silence fell as the intelligence officer took hold of the baize cover and yanked it aside. Elmeyer noticed that the Kentuckian's pencil was trembling over his notepad.

Red ribbons stretching from Eastern England to the target ran out over the North Sea to Denmark then down into Eastern Germany and a point in Poland 1,200 miles from base.

'Poznan, gentleman. In Poland. A long way to go, but with targets worth bombing to Hell when we get there, that I can guarantee,' Colonel Jessop exclaimed with the enthusiasm Elmeyer had noticed was often displayed by men who were not themselves going to war.

'Poland. Jesus.' The Kentuckian moaned, making Elmeyer nervous and angry. It was a long haul but he'd done ones like it before. Fly accurately, trust the other members of the crew and believe in your luck was the thing to do.

They would be at almost 30,000 feet with the hard early morning light glittering on their aluminium skins and contrails flaring behind them as they rode like pennanted knights into battle. The battle formations had a great and terrible beauty. Up there, in the refrigerative cold and the vaulting blue of the heavens, death seemed like a visitor calling at an inappropriate moment; a brash and sullying intruder into the realm of high, cold purity. Many sorties into that vast arena had provided Elmeyer with a sort of unwanted six sense. He could generally tell the combatants who would be scythed from the sky by ripping cannon fire, flak or collision.

The Kentuckian was an old stager posted into the squadron for whatever reason right at the end of his tour of duty, and jumpy. Elmeyer could almost smell the fear but fear was of itself no bad thing. It was part of the mechanism you needed to survive. In Spain he'd drank with a man who'd shot big game in Africa and believed that lions could smell the most fearful individual in a herd of kudu.

'Believe me,' the old man had said, 'That old lion will seek out the most frightened for his supper. He may be as fit and as fast as the hundreds of others surrounding him, but it is upon the one that stinks of fear the lion will dine.'

As with kudu, so with men.

Attention to detail was something else that kept you alive. Elmeyer busied himself taking down notes about formations, radio frequencies and fighter briefings.

A priest was on the stage now, saying something about God's work. Elmeyer never questioned God's existence only his judgement. If he was so damned sure America was on the right side why hadn't the Krauts been finished off by now? He turned back to his notes.

The Louisville Slugger's captain had closed his eyes and was praying silently. He should be praying for his gunners, Elmeyer thought. People like Frenchie from the wrong side of the tracks. Oh, Frenchie, who art not in Heaven and I hope won't be for another sixty years or so.

They streamed from the briefing room for the most part in silence.

While Hosbach the navigator and the bombardier Mike Wiggins attended their specialised briefings he and David Steiner the co-pilot went over Luck Be A Lady with her ground crew chief.

An hour later the gunners had set up their guns and and were seated at take-off positions. The first of the mighty Wright R-1820 motors started with a whine, a report and a cloud of blue smoke.

The thrashing, coughing sound as other ships started up settled down to a roar. In the briefing room Elmeyer had been aware of being among the press of humanity. Now they were alone. Co-pilot First Lieutenant David Steiner, navigator First Lieutenant Peter Hosbach, bombardier First Lieutenant Mike Wiggins, Engineer and top turret gunner Staff Sergeant Kelsey Hodgson, radioman Staff Sergeant 'Sparks' Cotterill, waist gunners Staff Sergeants Elmer Simpson and Joe Attercop, ball gunner Sergeant Guiseppe 'Gissy' Gionotta, Staff Sergeant Norbert 'Frenchie' Hayes in the rear turret and himself, Captain James Elmeyer of the 321st Bomber Squadron of the 391st Bomb Group, at twenty-five years of age the old man of the crew whose greatest realisation was that he was no longer living for a cause, that of Marxism-Leninism which had absorbed his life up until now, but for a woman.

Elmeyer pushed up the revolutions while Steiner ran through the power checks, looking for the right pressures and checking against magneto drop. That done, he gave her another gunning with the brakes off to get the inert mass of the aeroplane moving, taking her place in the tempest of noise and whipped-up dirt and grass, rocking in the prop-wash of the Fort in front and gradually working her forwards in the queue.

Now she was on the runway threshold, straining at the brakes.

From his side window Elmeyer could see dozens of other ships, the early light catching the bodies of the newer ones which had been left in their natural, bright aluminium, the older Fortresses dull olive green and battle-scarred. Amelia's face floated into his consciousness and he touched the edge of the green silk scarf before a split-second later ramming the throttles fully forward.

'She gets off the ground like an old whore heaving her panties up, real practised and professional,' Hodgson, the engineer, bawled into the intercom as the speeding, bumping rush gave way to smooth flight. Hundreds of tons of fuel and bombs, men and machinery, bomb sights and cannons and wiring and switches and knobs, all contained within her alloy skin. It was a damned miracle conjured towards a malign end.

To Hell with thoughts like that and to Hell with worries about the distance to target. The problem now was the formating; finding their place in the bomber stream. All over East Anglia the B-17 Flying Fortresses and the Consolidated Liberators of the Eighth Army Air Force would be swarming before knitting themselves into a a glittering shoal and heading eastward.

Formating was always tough, and collisions common.

When he had been a pupil pilot back at the training field in Georgia, Elmeyer had delighted in plunging his Stearman biplane trainer into cloud, as if he were exploring the inside of some magical mountain. But when the air was full of aeroplanes jostling into their positions cloud was a death trap hiding ghostly bombers which at any time might roar out of the mist and tear into his own machine. With the American bombing effort at full stretch and pilots only just out of training being thrown into the fighting accidents were frequent. Elmeyer snapped an order to the gunners to look for other B-17s closing on them and continued his climb up through several hundred feet of stratocumulus.

The sight which presented itself as Luck Be A Lady broke through the cloud had a mesmeric quality, as if the normal senses had been ensnared by opium. All around, Fortresses were throwing off the embrace of the mist, the last skeins of it whipped and torn apart by their propellers.

No matter how many times he saw it he found the spectacle reassuring and he found himself slipping into the state of relaxed vigilance which is the mental territory of the true pilot.

The job was now to make formation and steer a track for the Danish coast. He made a thumbs-up signal to the co-pilot of the ship on his port wing, noting that the mid-upper gunner was already rotating his turret and quartering the sky. Above and to each side he could see the fighters, called by bomber crews the Little Friends who were the first line of defence.

It was fifty-five minutes into the mission since formation.

'Here they come!' A voice crackled.

A German plane had almost certainly been shadowing the bombers for some time, reporting back to the fighters who probably hoped that a swift, short attack early on in the raid would force the defending fighters to drop their auxiliary fuel tanks and thus limit their range. It was a neat trick which if it came off would make the bombers much more vulnerable when they were deep into the mission and without fighter escort.

'Come on you bastards.' The voice was Simpson's, high-pitched with tension.

Elmeyer was intent on keeping his position and had not noticed that the ship on his left was The Louisville Slugger. He waved to the Kentuckian's co-pilot. The Slugger was being flown accurately and the gunners were on their targets and she looked a tight ship but he remembered what the pilot in the bar had said about the kudu and the lions. Everything could look right about the victims but they were the victims just the same, picked out by fate.

A quick movement above and to the left sent adrenalin rushing into Elmeyer's head. Several Messerschmitts had broken through the defensive screen of American Thunderbolt fighters and were screaming towards the B-17s, now so close that Elmeyer could see flame spitting from their machine gun ports.

'The bastards must want to commit suicide!' Frenchie shouted as Luck Be A Lady's gunners opened up in a swearing, clattering crescendo. In the waist gun positions, Elmeyer knew, conditions would be hellish. Here, Joe Attercop and Elmer Simpson would already be up to their ankles in spent cannon shells, sweat running down their backs and faces despite gun positions that were open to numbing cold. Even above the gunfire Elmeyer could hear Attercop laughing maniacally as he loosed a burst into a German fighter which fragmented in a dirty orange explosion.

'They've got guts, the bastards. You have to admit they got guts,' Steiner, who, despite the racket appeared to be cocooned within himself, was scanning the skies all around the Fort. Steiner was sparing with his conversation having the detached air of a man sitting through a movie without ever getting caught up in the action. Elmeyer had never liked Steiner's clinical self-control; his seemingly mechanical indifference to the world around him, but he had to concede that it made him the almost perfect co-pilot. Steiner never made a mistake. It was creepy, though, the way the man could remain impassive even in the Hell of war at the edge of the stratosphere.

Elmeyer had some time ago realised that his dislike for his Steiner was reciprocated and that it mattered not a damn. Eventually he had stopped thinking about him as he had stopped thinking about his previous crews before he came to Luck Be A Lady. The way to be made sad or angry was to think about what happened to other men. Sad or angry fliers became, sooner or later, careless ones and the careless ended up dead. Those, and the ones already picked out by fate. It was a rule with Elmeyer never to invest too much of himself in another crew member. Except Frenchie.

Anyway Steiner was good at his job and would soon get his own ship to command and would become just another flyer in another plane caught up in the routine murder of industrialised warfare.

The attack cut off as suddenly as it had started leaving them all slightly surprised like when the lights are turned on at the end of a movie catching the audience dazed and feeling slightly stupid.

'We got through that little encounter lightly,' Steiner said in his strangely remote voice.

'They'll be coming out to play again once they've been home for milk and cookies.' Elmeyer wriggled in his seat in an attempt to dispel the clammy feel of his cooling sweat.

'And we've still got their playmates with the anti-aircraft fire around the target. Something tells me we are in for a very bumpy ride.'

'We just have to get through this one mission at a time, isn't that what you always say?'

There was an edge of reproach in Steiner's voice that made Elmeyer wonder whether his co-pilot might be cracking up. He thought of the Kentuckian at the controls of the ship on his port side. One man with the mark of death upon him was quite enough for this day. He realised with a chill that Steiner was stark afraid, terror twisting inside him like a worm burrowing into an apparently unblemished apple.

'That's right, Steiner. One thing at a time and leave it up to Luck Be A Lady to get us though. We'll be OK.'

'This ship and you. They say you lead a charmed life together.' A manic edge had crept into Steiner's voice.

'You make it sound like we're married. We just work well together. Me, the plane and the rest of you. When you get your own plane you'll be lucky too.'

'I've got a mascot.'

'Jesus, Steiner. Do we have to talk about this right now?'

'What better time? Do you want to see it?'

'In the middle of a fucking battle. Are you completely nuts?'

A mile across the sky a B-17 was trailing smoke. A dirty red flame erupted from it port outer engine. In a few minutes the Fort would have to fall out of the formation to die under the Germans' guns.

It was all madness, the whole damned vile, bloody kit and caboodle. What difference that there was just one more lunatic in the co-pilot's seat? People had all sorts of mascots. Rosaries and holy medals were most common followed by items of intimate female apparel. He had his green silk scarf. Hodgson, the engineer who also manned the top turret when things got tough wore his girlfriend's knickers under his flight issue long johns. If he ever got shot down and told to strip by his German captors, a few guys in Wehrmacht grey would be laughing their cocks off. Before they clubbed him to death with rifle butts.

'Okay. Show me. And then shut up.'

Steiner fumbled in the inside pocket of his flight jacket, extracting a glass bottle containing something wrinkled and dead.

'It's my foreskin.'

'What?'

'Not attached to me, Captain. I'm not crazy. Nobody would have a part of themselves for a mascot. I keep it in a screw jar, see?' For the first time Steiner turned to face Elmeyer directly, his brown eyes beseeching over the rubber mouthpiece of his oxygen mask.

'Steiner. You are crazy. The thought makes me want to vomit.'

The look in Steiner's eyes turned to something as hard and cold as a distant planet. He had been shunned and now Elmeyer knew that Steiner would kill him if he ever got the chance. The co-pilot turned back to his duties, absorbed and meticulous and Elmeyer decided, completely mad.

Staff Sergeant Kelsey Hodgson had been rotating the top turret on the look-out for German fighters.

'Here they come. Three o'clock high. Time to go to work!' Hodgson bawled, dissipating the weirdness of the moment. Oddly, the moments immediately before the onslaught came as a relief to Elmeyer. When you were forging a way to or from the target with nothing hitting you there was always the apprehension of attack. Now, the German fighters hit them like a storm in a screaming, blinding attack of blood and cordite, ripped and punctured metal, screams and oaths and time moved into another dimension.

'How far to target?' Elmeyer rapped at Hosbach, the navigator, more for confirmation for he knew they must be close.

'Twenty miles. Seven minutes.'

Before Elmeyer could acknowledge the information a blast hit Luck Be A Lady almost wrenching the controls from his hands. A Fort in front and above had been hit and was dropping out the formation trailing smoke. One or several of the attacking fighters would follow him down and finish him off. A Messerschmitt flashed from right to left and another just caught the corner of Elmeyer's eye but it was part of a battle that had been relegated to a different part of his brain. His job was to keep the ship in formation, trusting to the gunners to lay down a lethal cone of protective fire.

A new sound came over the hammering of the guns and the vibrating roar of the ship itself; a sucking, puncturing sound which meant they had been hit. He glanced at Steiner who was looking straight ahead.

'Superficial damage. Temperatures and pressures are normal,' came from Hodgson.

'Time to do your stuff, Mike.' Although Mike Wiggins the bombardier positioned below and in front of him would know that.

Sometimes Luck Be A Lady flew lead ship with other less experienced crews taking their cue from her. This time the bombardier's role was merely that of a copycat, watching for the bombs falling from the lead ship before sending his on their way. There was nothing for Elmeyer to do except fly straight and level and ponder who on the ground four miles below had been selected for death, and by what twist of fate.

'Bombs gone!' From Wiggins.

Freed of her load Luck Be A Lady leapt in the air. Now it would begin again. They would pass out of the range of the anti-aircraft fire only to be bushwhacked once more by the fighters. The attacks were always more vengeful on the way back. He had never seen an American ship rammed by a German pilot but had heard of it often enough. Ten deaths in the stricken plane and probably more in ships damaged by the force of the explosion or the ensuing storm of debris. Good odds and an Iron Cross into the bargain. Posthumous, of course.

'Here they come again. Rising like feeding catfish!' Frenchie shouted from the rear turret.

'Come on, just a little bit further you fuckin' douche-bag.' His crooning voice was followed by a shattering burst of fire. A black cross seemed to fill the cockpit as a fighter shot by and for a fraction the Fortress rushed through its trail of black smoke.

From somewhere inside Luck Be A Lady's airframe came a tattoo of jackhammer thuds.

'We're hit,' Steiner said in a flat, strange voice.

'Badly?'

'It could get that way. We're losing power from the port outer engine.'

The attack was now at its most furious.

The Fort with the engine fire had been hit again and lost most of its tail assembly. Slowly, it rolled over like a dead fish falling to the bottom of a pond.

Luck Be A Lady's own engine must have been damaged either by a shell or shot-off fragments from another aircraft and was overheating enough to worry about. Elmeyer ordered Steiner to feather the port outer engine's prop to cut down on drag.

Good old Luck Be A Lady. Good old bus. Come on, do it for us, he mouthed. Keep flying and keep up with the formation and get us home to where there were real eggs waiting for us and thick rashers of Canadian bacon and most desired of all, Amelia. Damn it, Luck Be A Lady was a good old chariot who could keep up with the formation on only three engines, saving the damaged one for a last burst of power if necessary. Come on old girl; his teeth were gritted and his heart racing. You can do it.

Then, quite suddenly and almost as if in a dream, bright sky flooded the cockpit just as Elmeyer remembered it had when his pa had pulled back the sliding roof on their Packard what seemed like a hundred years before, except the air had never been as cold as this and then there'd been no blood.

Blood which had pumped from Steiner's shattered body had been whipped by the fierce slipstream into ugly criss-cross streaks over his flight jacket and inside the cockpit behind him. Where the blood was smeared thinly it had already frozen

'Get the poor bastard away from the controls!' Elmeyer screamed over the noise of the slipstream whipped to a howl by the hole's jagged edges.

Elmeyer wiped from his face a salt stickiness that was both sweat and Steiner's blood. Electrical flex and piping trailed and whipped in the slipstream and a ragged piece of aluminium skin thrashed wildly threatening to tear at his face and oxygen mask.

'Report damage and injuries,' Elmeyer shouted without being able to hear his words over the roar of the three engines, the jackhammering of the guns and the lashing of torn wires and ripped aluminium.

'OK down here, Skipper,' from chirpy little Gionotta in the ball turret. Hosbach dragged Steiner from his seat and with a few short savage strokes hacked away the flap of aluminium inches from Elmeyer's face.

'Upper turret okay,' from Hodgson.

'Waist gunners are fine,' from Attercop.

45

'Okay back here but can we go home now, please?' from Frenchie on the tail turret and then an eardrum-pounding noise as first Frenchie and then Hodgson loosed off at a Messerschmitt screaming down on the formation.

The fighting at the height of its fury had a nightmarish quality as if a mediaeval painting of sinners being cast into the torments of Hell had been thrust forward to the middle of the 20th century. Chunks of aeroplane and men, whole and in part plummeted to earth as if sprung from some infernal trapdoor and through this grotesque hail the Forts ploughed and black fighters were darting like malevolent angels bustling about their tormenting business.

Elmeyer flinched as a Fortress's severed main wheel went shooting by. Undercarriage assemblies and engines, escape panels and parachute packs and chunks of duralumin cartwheeled past.

And men.

The lucky ones already dead, their bodies whole or in pieces. Arms and legs and torsos and worst of all those doomed to fall, conscious until the last instant, until being pulverised by an onrushing Fort or, Elmeyer's personal dread, tumbling through miles of space, conscious for what must be an infinity of terror.

The really lucky ones were floating down on parachutes. All around them he could see their white blossoms. Elmeyer scanned the oil temperature gauges of the three good engines fearing that they might soon have to join the drifting, silken progress to earth.

Fixed in their formation the Fortresses continued to plough through the grim hail of guns and tools, thermos flasks and hatch covers and bits of engine and fuselage and bodies. A huge explosion punched the air as a Fort disintegrated completely and a few seconds after that a smaller one as Luck Be A Lady's gunners and those of neighbouring American planes zeroed in on a black-crossed fighter and ripped it to shreds with concentrated fire.

'Oh, no. Oh Christ,' Elmeyer muttered into his oxygen mask. A figure emerging from the shot-up rear turret of a Fort ahead and above them appeared to be fumbling for his parachute release handle as he spun away from the aircraft. At first it looked as though the man might pass between Luck Be A Lady's port wingtip and The Louisville Slugger's starboard wing but some freakish force directed him towards the neighbouring plane. The man's oxygen mask had been torn away and Elmeyer could see his face as he tumbled toward The Louisville Slugger's starboard outer engine.

For a second it seemed he might miss the thrashing propeller but the man was caught a mighty blow by its tip and at first seemed to have been knocked away, but was instead drawn inwards.

In a split second what remained of the body had bumped across the wing streaking it with blood fanned by the slipstream into crazy and obscene patterns.

Elmeyer looked away from the horrific tableau feeling the bile rise. Nine hundred murderous miles Luck Be A Lady would have to drag her ailing aluminium body with one motor gone and no co-pilot. With the deep ice-blue heavens over-arching where once there had been a comforting insulated cockpit roof he felt awfully, frighteningly exposed; colder than he had ever been before, his arms and back in torment from heaving at the control yoke. Through gritted teeth he growled aloud the advice he had given to others so often that it had become a litany: Steady old fellow. One step at a time. You are not alone. The crew is back there and and there are thousands of Americans in their planes all around, so close you could almost touch them. Real men from real places, with real wives and real sweethearts who they think about just like you think about Amelia. Luck Be A Lady was a tough old whore who had who had been through worse alley fights than this. One thing at a time. Get through this and there will be bed, food, the peace to write up your diary - and Amelia.

He touched his scarf.

War - whoops from the gunners greeted the demise of a Focke-Wulf fighter plunging like a marlin that has taken a hook. Their best chance, Elmeyer knew, lay in keeping up with the formation but with one engine shot and another on the way out she was dropping back and would soon not have the cover of the formation's guns. He looked over at The Louisville Slugger, running his eyes along its glittering flank.

'That ship's not going to make it.'

'Don't say that. It gives me the creeps.' It was Hosbach's voice.

'Look at her chin turret slapping like a barn door in a gale. The servo must've been hit.'

A Messerschmitt had spotted the weakness in The Louisville Slugger's defensive field of fire and was going for a head-on shot.

Elmeyer bawled at Hosbach to get on their own front gun and a second later there was an ear-splitting racket and stench of cordite as Luck Be A Lady spat fire at the oncoming German.

'The crazy bastard's going to ram!' Hosbach yelled as his bullets tore chunks from the German fighter but still it careered on. In a blinding instant the fighter and Fortress became a fireball. Luck Be A Lady bucked in the force of the explosion and Elmeyer felt his guts press down on his seat and the sky through the torn cockpit roof slant crazily as he wrenched and stamped at control yolk and rudder straining to get her under control once more.

And then, in an instant, calm.

Only the beat of Luck Be A Lady's engines and the roar of rushing air through the torn roof and the beating of his heart.

The German fighter had hit with such force as to stop the doomed American plane in the sky. In a half-second the grim scenario was snatched away by the formation's onward rush.

Steiner's body shifted as someone back in the plane shouted in pain. Elmeyer called for a report from each crew station. Simpson, one of the waist gunners had been hit.

'We're losing a lot of power on number three engine, skipper,' Hosbach said. 'Take her home nice and low and nice and easy.'

'Watch out for any Forts underneath us. We're going down,' Elmeyer snapped as the altimeter began to unwind, past ten and then five thousand feet. Low and slow was the only way the old girl was going to make it. Christ, you are an old streetwalker, Elmeyer thought, swearing at the battering of the wind through the roof and the heaviness of the controls. Battered and ugly but still out there hooking. You smell too, you old bitch, of blood and oil and cordite but you're still flying and with luck the German fighters will go hunting somewhere else.

'We're out of it,' someone said.

'You should be where I am, Buster,' Elmeyer murmured, the screaming slipstream buffeting with a murderous cold.

'Come on, old girl. Turn just one more trick for me,' and he once again touched Amelia's scarf for luck.

FIVE

THERE she was. Laughter dancing on her face like sunlight on newly-cut marble.

Flying Officer Peter Dainty's eyes drank in the woman with earnest desire while his fingers played with the key to unlock his private fortune and which could make any woman in London his.

The symptoms of infatuation - dry mouth, beating heart and tunnel vision - were similar to those of fear Dainty mused. It was as addictive as fear too, and brought the same tingling in the stomach.

A plan began to form.

He would leave his Zippo lighter and an unfinished drink on the bar as a mark of his intention to return. Normally, he would have walked straight up to her and offered to buy her a drink, positioning himself for the kill with flattery or, as with some women who liked it that way, a glimpse of the edge of danger. This one though, was special. It was more than just the thrill of the chase. Something urgent and which left him breathless.

But first he would have to see off the Royal Engineers captain to whom she was talking.

The army officer had taken a few drinks and looked as though he might be laying his plans for the night with Amelia and bed as the centrepiece.

Swank and arrogance might, just conceivably, carry the day. Wait until the soldier went to the toilet then move in and take over. Dainty was a Flying Officer which was a rank lower but he wore the wings of an RAF pilot.

Bribery had worked in the past, too. He'd offered potential rivals a good deal of money not to make a fuss although sometimes men stood on their dignity and then there was trouble.

Trouble though might be the quickest and simplest solution. Clean. Final. Dainty looked round towards the toilets and to the Limbo Bar's entrance. The woman had caught his eye. God, how she made his insides churn. Maybe he could play the outraged suitor; march up to the captain and call him a blighter and make up a cock-and-bull story about the woman being spoken for and watch her surprised countenance or he could just get the business over with quickly with a few smashing punches.

A couple of queers, a Guards officer and a naval rating were eyeing him up. The young sailor had a sulky, insolent look. Dainty was attractive to that type.

The Limbo Bar. Well named, Dainty smiled. A place for the exhausted, the cynical, the lost, the perverted and those marked for death. Artists and writers frequented the Limbo Bar along with opium smokers and cocaine addicts and lushes and frowsy sad old queens. Some of the habitues wore uniforms; others not. Some affected efflorescent and billowing cravats and scarves, tight-waisted suits and hats with generous brims dragged into swoops and curls from beneath which cigarette holders lolled and hard, lustful looks darted. It was a place for outcasts, a republic of the doomed of which he felt himself to be a citizen.

The problem of the army officer troubled him so little that his mind grasped at a passing notion.

Dainty fancied that after the war he might take up writing as a way of whiling away the lazy hours ease that he had already decided were his to enjoy.

He would continue to fly of course and enter writing at the gentlemanly end of the market. To Hell with dragging himself to his writing table each morning with only a crust inside him. A full larder beat a head full of dreams any time. Writers and thieves had in common a distaste for sustained labour.

The glass had to be emptied to just the right degree - about halfway down - otherwise she would think he had abandoned it.

Dainty put his *Daily Mail* next to his glass and his lighter on top of the newspaper risking it being stolen before his return.

Five minutes later he was feeling for the lock which opened the Judas door to his own little Aladdin's Cave, his treasure trove.

Wet tyre marks showed that the driver had done the job he had been well paid to do.

Boxes and cases were stacked neatly in the middle of the concrete floor and the envelope containing money was gone. The driver's key would be back with Henry to whom it was entrusted. The drop would have been made while he was on ops. Dainty smiled to himself. Killing for King and Country but making a killing for yourself on the home front seemed a fair arrangement.

Two years earlier the realisation had come to Dainty that a Distinguished Flying Cross would count for next to nothing in the world to come. Nobody in peace time paid a premium for glory, chivalry and honour. Medals won in battle would after a few years be mere sentimental tokens. Money would be the reality just as it had always been but with a new and harder imperative. He had seen the Americans among whom money talked. They were the future. One, a Staff Sergeant gunner in Flying Fortresses who went by the name Frenchie Hayes was always cheerful and efficient. Carelessness got you caught out and it didn't matter whether working the black market or flying a fighter in combat.

Dainty quickly made an inventory of the goods. Exactly what he paid for had been delivered. Not so much as a packet of smokes had been taken. Frenchie would have seen to that. The boy's chirpy inoffensiveness concealed the instincts of a killer.

For a man of no background Peter Dainty had a lot of money to spend. Only one person, a titled buffoon in an expensive regiment who came to the Limbo Bar to indulge a taste for cocaine had ever made a sneering reference to Dainty's modest origins and to his working-class accent. Dainty had been a Flight-Sergeant then and the beating meted out to the supercilious officer had been heavy and systematic.

He had been commissioned not long afterwards and had gradually honed his own voice to a monied edge. The revelation that all that really mattered in the world was money had been rapidly followed by a series of insights as to how to obtain it. It was marvellous, Dainty thought, how easily you could get want you wanted once you had decided to go to Hell with a handcart piled high with black market goods. His business philosophy was simple: only buy goods with a ready sale and buy as much as you could afford. Cigarettes, sweets and spirits were always a winner but tyres, underclothing and medicines were good lines too. RAF aircrews were stacking their planes with wine and and spirits either looted or bought on liberated Europe's black market. He'd cornered some of this action but the real money lay with the Americans who had legal protection from British customs. Business in that direction was booming and he intended to make it boom some more. Work with cash and play several hands at the same time never giving the people you're dealing with time to stitch up a deal behind your back. War and commerce were pretty much the same thing when it came down to it, he had decided.

Breaking one of his own rules never to use the stock for himself Dainty took a carton of Lucky Strikes from Frenchie's recent delivery and slipped it into his pocket before locking up.

The Guards officer and his sailor had left and the Royal Engineer officer was nowhere in sight when Dainty returned to his place at the bar.

'You took a risk with your lighter. This place is a den of thieves.'

The woman's voice was cultured, her movement assured as she picked up the Zippo and lit her own cigarette.

'Isn't that supposed to be my job?' he said.

'Lighting cigarettes, or thieving?'

The lighter's flare then showed up the sculpted fineness of her cheeks.

'My name is Amelia Kershaw. And yours?'

The look was cool and level but Dainty wondered whether she wasn't just another well-brought up young woman trying hard to prove a point.

'Peter Dainty.' He glanced at her wedding ring. 'Is Kershaw your married name?'

'No.'

She smoked with the ferocity of an opium addict, something that Dainty found unaccountably erotic. Her face was quite long, the nose also long and straight and the lips pulling at the Lucky Strike thin and firm. Her perfume at first suggested a cool Spring freshness but his nostrils sensed a deeper, primally exciting note which contained the faint but discernible rich, sweet smell of corruption.

'There was an army chap with you twenty minutes ago. What happened to him?'

'Oh, he left.'

'That's good. It saves me the trouble of thinking of ways of getting rid of him.'

Amelia now held the cigarette away from her, scanning his face.

'You seem to have everything worked out. You don't think I didn't notice the ploy with the lighter and the drink?' The infinitesimal relaxing of her features subtly signalled the fact that Amelia Kershaw had come to a decision.

'What do you fly? Fighters or bombers, or aren't I allowed to ask?'

'You can ask, but I'm not supposed to tell. Fighters. Spitfires, actually.'

'That's as I thought. Bomber people have brown eyes, or so they say. Yours are the most startling cornflower blue and rather chilling. Please don't take that as other than a compliment.'

'I won't. You seem to have given eyes and the sort of RAF chaps they belong to some thought.'

'I suppose I am something of a connoisseur. The little wrinkles around them smile but your eyes are as cold as those of a hunting animal.'

'Brown eyes are warmer, so I suppose I should like brown eyes more.'

'Well. Here's to brown eyes.' Dainty raised his glass.

'On the other hand lots of hunting animals have brown eyes. It must work only with people.'

'I thought tigers and such had yellow eyes.'

'You must be right. Brown-eyed tigers would be a bit cuddly. No native about to be eaten could take a brown-eyed tiger very seriously.'

Dainty laughed at the flippancy and watched her face closely.

How people laughed and the things they laughed at were clues to character and state of mind. He could tell when his own comrades were frightened almost beyond endurance from the sort of jokes they cracked.

'You're right. Tigers with warm brown eyes would be ridiculous. Or perhaps not. It might lull their prey into a false sense of security, which would make them clever and successful killers, wouldn't it?'

'How right you are,' Amelia exhaled.

'Having established that I'm not a steely-eyed killer, may I freshen your glass?'

'We have established no such thing. And you may.'

Henry polished glasses at the other end of the bar pretending not to hear what passed between Amelia and Dainty but actually picking up every word. He could smell trouble brewing. The woman was playing a dangerous game. The Yank, Elmeyer, was stuck on her and when they'd come back into the Limbo for a stiffener you could smell the sex. The Limbo Bar's place in the scheme of things was to accommodate lust in all its manifestations but trouble between customers was never a good thing.

When true love did tiptoe into the Limbo's dinginess it shone like a diamond on a dung-heap. Amelia and the Yank together were quite touching but if she wanted to sleep with the RAF pilot it was no business of his so long as the trouble happened outside. It was a shame for the Yank, though.

'What would the lady like, Sir?' Good old Henry's playing the game, she thought. He knew perfectly well gin-and-tonic was her usual drink.

'Steely-eyed killer or not, you must be good at what you do. You've got the Distinguished Flying Cross.' Amelia turned back to Dainty and away from herself as a subject for conversation.

'You seem to know something about air force decorations. It's not the sort of thing I take all that seriously. One collects decorations as the war goes on.'

'If you say so, Flying Officer Dainty. All sorts of things come one's way in a war.'

Including you, my beautiful, dangerous man, she thought, taking in the fair hair and fresh face young and yet ancient with the wickedness of war. So different from my American and yet equally necessary to me. Both like intoxicating drinks but one to be sipped and savoured, the other to be taken in mighty gulps. Both though necessary to slake a great thirst.

'You know a little about me and I know hardly a thing about you. Shall I try and guess?'

'Guess away.'

It was an excuse to run his eyes over her. The light fawn overcoat was of a good quality and the ochre-coloured jumper under it skilfully hand-knitted. Her slacks were cut rather mannishly and wide but not so long as to hide serviceable but expensive shoes.

That was another good thing about money, Dainty thought.

It lets you appreciate the finer things of life.

'Your knowing about medals is a clue. Something to do with the BBC or films or newspapers. Maybe you work for the Ministry of Information making those nauseous propaganda films, *In Which We Serve* and *Target for Tonight* and such tosh.'

Amelia laughed. 'Even if it's what you think you shouldn't call it tosh. People get very protective about their work. Actually, you're not even warm. I'll save you the trouble. I'm an artist. I saw you looking at my wedding ring. I thought you might have been able to tell from the flecks of paint on my nails.'

She held up her hand which upon impulse Dainty took in his own.

Hers was not immediately withdrawn.

'Now I can see. Do you paint all the time?'

'Almost all of it. I take the weekends off to allow for such dubious diversions as the Limbo Bar.'

'What sort of things do you paint?'

'Oh, landscapes and ordinary people including those caught up in war. Seventy years from now I want someone to be able to look at my pictures and feel that they know something about the people I paint and the time in which they lived.'

Dainty pursed his lips. Amelia wondered whether he was pondering her words or simply humouring her.

'Come in here any night of the week and look around you. Toffs and proletarians all mixed in and happily going to Hell together. You saw that couple of queers who left quarter of an hour ago? The Guards officer is the son of a viscount and the sailor the offspring of God knows who. Actually, the sailor is the brighter of the two. It won't last and it's not intended to. Grab what you can while you can is the watchword.'

She took a long sip at her drink.

'Something about you that typifies this war. It would be easier to paint than to put into words.'

She hadn't offered him a cigarette, he noted. Wartime had taught people to be frugal. He slit open the pack he'd brought from his lock-up. She took a cigarette the instant it was offered.

'Try anyway.''

'I'm not sure that would be a good idea. I'd probably offend you.'

He smiled. 'You know the old saying about sticks and stones.'

'All right but don't say I didn't warn you.'

'You have an officer's rank but you are not from what we still think of as the officer class. The clues are in your voice. You're an officer because you are good at what you do and ambitious. I look at faces for a living. There's hunger in those blue eyes of yours.'

'You seem to have found me out.' Dainty smiled, kissed her hand with a playful gallantry and slowly let it go.

'Don't you want to know about my husband?'

'That might upset me.'

'I doubt it.'

He's a Lieutenant-Commander in the navy attached to the Yanks in the Pacific. As a fighting man yourself I imagine you think it's not the done thing, hanging around in Soho bars chatting to handsome young pilots while one's husband is thousands of miles away, fighting for King and Country.'

Her voice was getting louder with a defensive note. Dainty wondered how much she'd had to drink before coming to the Limbo Bar.

'I don't altogether believe people who say they're fighting for King and Country so that part of it doesn't bother me. If you want to hang around in bars that's fine with me. Anyway, I thought it's what arty types are supposed to do.'

Bitterness lay behind the easy cynicism she thought, but bitterness at what? Dainty had charm and good looks and an easy way with money suggesting he might have a fair bit of it.

From somewhere behind them sharp, querulous voices were being raised. Dainty had been absorbed with the woman and had not noticed that the Limbo Bar was filling up with drinkers, most of them in uniform, checking overcoats and military greatcoats at the shabby cloakroom which Nina staffed at busy times.

It was always the same. Drink, the social leveller and loosener of tongues set ties askew and hitched skirts above knees, made laughter coarse and hands fumble in dark corners. Whatever you dark heart's desire could be got in the Limbo Bar, girls or boys, drugs, contraband or alcoholic oblivion. It was a sweet swamp of corruption from which sometimes ugly monsters arose.

The thrill which runs through a crowd as a fight starts broke their absorption in one another.

Women were usually the first to detect the scent of impending battle. Tarts with hard, glittering eyes lusting for blood. It must have been like that since before we swung down from the trees, Dainty thought. From the furious flurry of teeth and fur the dominant male emerged to take his pick of the females.

A British major in the artillery had been getting morosely drunk by himself but was now squaring up to an American Staff Sergeant.

'You don't call me buddy. You call me Sir. And bloody well stand to attention when I'm talking to you.'

The major's voice was slurred and peevish. All eyes turned towards the two men. Women instinctively leaned into their men or sought their hands for protection but their eyes remained fixed upon the combatants.

'I'm just here to enjoy myself, that's all. Now sit down before I knock you down. Buddy.'

The half-beat before the 'buddy' was heavy with insolence. The American was tough-looking; the major tall and thin and lacking the demeanour of one accustomed to bar fights. Somewhere within himself though, he had found a reserve of headstrong resolve.

'What did you say, Sergeant?'

Even the darkest and most furtive corners of the Limbo Bar now fell silent.

'Shit, I'm going to have to cream this toffee-nosed Limey.' The words uttered in the direction of his friends were ugly in the American's mouth as he put his drink down heavily on the bar and without turning to look at the major lashed out with a curving right. Within seconds a ring of people was pressing around the men. Dainty had seen plenty of fights between Americans and British and had even been in a few. They were always the ugliest, as though a carapace of solidarity in the face of a common enemy had split to reveal a stew of guilt, resentment, and wounded pride.

'I think we'd best keep out of this.' Dainty eased Amelia towards the entrance but it was blocked by baying spectators.

Two young naval officers who had been trying to secure themselves a berth alongside the same amply proportioned and thickly-painted trollop broke off from their amatory endeavours to try to pull the artillery officer out of range of the American brawler's fists but the Staff Sergeant was on his feet and shouting for blood. The Major shook his would-be rescuers away and began to square up to the American but before he could fully gather his wits the American aimed a groin kick which the Major, twisting away, took in the thigh.

'You dirty Yank bastard!' one of the naval Sub-Lieutenants howled but was sent reeling back into the crowd when the American delivered him a mighty punch under the ear.

All Hell broke loose.

Dainty pushed Amelia into a corner where two women were squealing with fear and excitement while instinctively looking for the heart of the fracas and its likely outcome.

'Play something! Anything! Just play,' Henry screamed at the middle-aged musician with lank and thinning hair whose quartet had been dolefully attempting an evocation of New Orleans.

'Probably not the most appropriate choice!' Dainty laughed as the combo scraped and blew a rendition of *The Star Spangled Banner* only the shrillest notes of which rose above the hubbub.

'Somethin' you don't like about the music, fly boy?' A squat dark American infantry officer snarled before, exultantly, Dainty saw the man's nose flatten like a pulped tomato and realised that his own fist had done the damage. He looked over to where the fight had started and saw that with sudden sobriety the demeanour of the artillery officer caught up in the fight with the American had changed.

There was now something of the executioner about him. Something had hardened and quickened.

The American was burly but a rim of fat bulged over his canvas belt and sweat darkened his shirt under the loosened tie. The major's eyes now as cold and dispassionate as a snake's flickered over his opponent deciding where to land his blows. The mob had ceased to fight amongst itself and was howling encouragement at the combatants. The infantry officer Dainty had punched had retreated from the battle and sat nursing his bloody nose.

Too late the American had sensed the Englishman's killing mood. The first left jab snapped the American's head back, goading him to an undirected charge which the Englishman deftly side-stepped adding a punch which caught his opponent on the cheek thus aiding the momentum which sent him sprawling into tables and chairs. A brushfire fight that had flared up on the edge of things ceased in order that the Limbo Bar's denizens could concentrate on the central tableau.

'Do you want to call it a day?' the English officer snapped at the American wiping blood from his mouth.

A kick from the prostrated form caught the officer in the leg and made him wince. The American scrambled to his feet.

'Have it your way, old boy.'

'He's drunk, you snooty English bastard!' a sailor in the mob screamed lunging at the artillery officer but was prevented from reaching him by a British uniform. This was the sign for the general ruckus to resume. Whipped on by a frantic Henry the dance combo lurched into a ragged waltz in time to which a sailor went flying back into the shattered remains of a table. Glasses, bottles, blood and bodies flew as the battle reached a crescendo of screaming obscenity. A Highland Fusilier with kilt rucked up to his hips, a man of no great height but displaying a manhood which alone looked capable of securing the future of the Caledonian peoples was biting the leg of a bombardier in the Eighth United States Army Air Force while a jacketless Canadian, his identity mistaken by both sides, was retiring from the fray having been punched simultaneously by a British Merchant Navy first mate and a GI.

A clanging of police car bells and thudding boots in the lobby announced the arrival of the Metropolitan Police. United in flight, an ebb tide of khaki and blue figures rushed for the entrance and scrambled for toilet windows. Grabbing Amelia roughly by the arm Dainty forced their way through the jostling mass at the entrance, and were on the point of gaining the open street when he was roughly shoved back.

'You can't go yet, Sir,' a large red-haired constable said with a barely concealed sneer. 'Even pilots in the Royal Air Force sometimes have to yield to the civil authority.'

'Is that so, Officer?'

The punch came up from the floor and lifted the policeman off his feet. Others of the police contingent who had been struggling with the excited crowd turned to join the chase but were hampered by the milling crowd. Amelia and Dainty ran hand in hand until the corner of D'Arblay Street by which time they could hear only the occasional shout from behind them.

A wan moon flitted over the jagged rooflines of bombed buildings and stared sadly in through gaping window frames behind which only ghosts moved. Cats prowled among the rubble and every so often they passed blacked-out pubs from inside of which came singing and shouting and the strong waft of stale ale. A man vomited in the gutter outside as a military truck full of lolling heads rumbled by.

They stopped, panting. Amelia laughed.

'I do so love the moon,' she said after a while. 'People used to think that moonlight was the sunshine of the dead. It's so mysterious.'

The moon, friend and enemy to the night bombers, Dainty thought. Glowing softly from lakes and rivers and pointing the navigator's way to the quarry with seductive ease and then traitoress that she was, glinting along the bodies of the bombers and backlighting them from below, giving the fighters and anti-aircraft gunners their mark. Diana, the eternal goddess of sky and stars who hunts through the clouds a chap on the squadron who had been to Oxford University had wistfully called it.

'They also believed that all the things that were wasted on earth flew to the moon,' he said.

'Pots-full of unanswered prayers and broken promises, mis-spent time and wasted tears ... the courtier's promises and sick man's prayers, the smile of harlots and the tears of heirs. It's from Alexander Pope.'

The line had been used in an earlier seduction.

'The moon also represents limbo. Rather appropriate under the circumstances.'

Amelia grabbed his arm. 'Come on.'

A plane tree still with some shrivelled and persistent leaves stood guard outside the small doorway which led directly off the street and onto three flights of stairs at the top of which was Amelia's studio. Even before she inserted the key in the lock Dainty could smell paint and turpentine. In the dark her footfall and the hollowness of their voices made him think the room must be empty.

'Stay there. I don't want you to crash into anything.' Amelia launched out into the darkness. He heard blinds being pulled down and light from a single electric bulb high above made him give a low whistle like a small boy crawling into a rock crevice and raising a torch and seeing the sombre magnificence of a giant cave's art.

Many of the pictures were of sea creatures plunging and leaping in aquamarine seas and pterodactylian birds soaring in skies of searing tropical blueness, a hellish world from which all humans had been expunged or had never existed but against the wall facing the large window human figures beckoned from their frames and it was towards these Dainty turned. Several of the figures were set in seascapes but this time the sea was earthy and gentle, so much so that he felt he could hear the swishing of the surf and the laughter of children frolicking amongst the rocks. Other pictures featured adults, many of them in uniform, caught in informal situations. Some Sappers - members of the Royal Engineers - drawn with pen and ink in quick, busy lines were having a tea break by the side of their earth-moving machinery surrounded by the military bric-a-brac of map cases and haversacks, stripped-off shirts and mess tins.

One picture double the size of a foolscap page drew him as if by magnetism and kept him fixed in front of it. The central figure was a girl soldier, still wearing her rough Army trousers and webbing belt but with her back bare and three-quarters turned toward the viewer at whom she cast a smile both sensuous and challenging.

'It's taken from life, more or less. The War Office commissioned me as a war artist working on the home front. I spent a week with some ATS girls at an anti-aircraft site on the South Coast and saw her about to go skinny-dipping with her friends. Seductive, isn't she?'

Amelia had moved beside him.

'I should say. Are you meant to look at pictures in that way?'

For the first time since they had met Dainty sounded off-balance Amelia thought. It was obvious that he was not used to viewing pictures, yet he was drinking this one in with his eyes. Had her picture connected via his optic nerve an artistic streak of his own?

'You looked almost scandalised for a moment.'

'I don't know how to describe the way I feel,' Dainty said. 'The sea monsters were frightening. These are gentle ... did she really look at you like that?'

'Do you think she might have been a little bit in love with me? I think she was. She was a working-class girl from the North and would have slept with me without thinking anything about it. She was the most innocent person I have ever met precisely because she was the most openly sexual, without any sense of guilt, or shame or need to resort to intrigue.'

'I see. Would you have ... '

But there was nobody of whom to ask the question.

Somewhere else drawers were being opened in what Dainty could see was a tiny kitchen. Amelia emerged with some bread on a plate and matches.

'Goody. The gas is back on,' she announced, indicating that he should sit in one of two battered chairs. The fire facing the chairs lit with a little 'pop'. A memory of boyhood prompted by the picture was sharpened by the smell of the gas. Rain was beating against a caravan window on some low, sandy shore, with only spiky marram grass between themselves and the sea. His father was not present but his mother was holding a toasting fork up to the fire just as Amelia was doing ...

As she bent to her task his hand reached out to touch the nape of her neck.

Her back stiffened but after a couple of seconds she relaxed. By now the sexual inverts and the crooks, the fight at the Limbo Bar and the dash from the police seemed miles away and long ago and he was at home, a home comprised not of bricks, mortar, plaster and slates, but one which Amelia's pictures had helped furnish. He looked at the picture of the girl soldier again, and thought it the most wonderful and perfect picture he had ever seen in his life and completely at odds with the strangeness and violence of what Dainty had put down in his mind as the 'prehistoric' pictures.

The studio in which such a titanic battle of styles was raging was sparsely furnished, containing the two chairs they were occupying, a chest of drawers, a wooden kitchen table with three chairs placed around it and a large bed facing the big window. Several small tables held pots and jars. Canvasses hung cheek by jowl up to the level of the picture rail and were propped one against another on the floor. Two works on easels presented their unfinished state. The empty sound when he had first entered was because of the bare floorboards. Every flat surface was covered with paint-encrusted pots, jars and tins, even a lidless and spoutless teapot having been pressed into use. Almost used-up tubes of paint were a gnarled and leaden undergrowth through which rose forests of brushes in jars.

'I wouldn't change a thing in this room. This is what an artist's room should be like.' Dainty breathed in the delicious smell of the paint and the linseed oil which reminded him of the cricket bats he wielded as a boy, the warm mustiness of the gas and now the toast being smeared lightly with real butter.

'I'd like to see it on a bright Spring day when it glows with colour. I can imagine light filtering through the leaves that brush your window and making patterns.'

'That's a surprisingly sensitive thing for a warrior to say,' Amelia offered him the first bit of toast.

'Actually my reason for being here is less poetic. Because of the flying bombs you can get places in London at knock-down prices if you'll excuse the unintentional pun. It's cheap.'

'That's pretty.' Dainty indicated a small seascape in oils hung at eye height over the fireplace that the almost physical power of the mass of other paintings had caused him to overlook.

'It's Les Sables d'Olonne in the Vendée. I keep it there because it reminds me of a time when I was properly happy.'

'You sound sad when you say it like that but things will be a lot better when this war's over wait and see. All the production lines that are turning out planes and trucks will be making cars for ordinary people. There'll be passenger planes, too. You'll be able to visit the place in the picture pretty well at the drop of a hat and be happy all over again.'

'Goodness. You sound like a politician or a business mogul promoting a vision in which they had some sort of interest!' There was a hint of reproof in her voice as she pronged another piece of bread.

'It's progress. You can't stop it.'

'That's one of the things that makes me sad. It took us two days to get to Les Sables d'Olonne creeping across the South of England in our battered old Ford and on the ferry to France and staying at a sweet little pension and letting the feeling seep into us that we were well and truly abroad. Just getting on a plane and being there in a couple of hours takes the adventure out of it somehow.'

Dainty crunched his toast thinking of missions he'd flown so high that the English and French coasts spread below him like map. At that height and speed crossing the Channel seemed instantaneous.

'But suppose you owned the company that took people to wherever they wanted to be? You could afford to go wherever you liked and not just to France. Anyway,' he added as an afterthought, 'Why shouldn't ordinary people see the sights?'

Feeling the warmth from the fire and looking at her own teethmarks on the buttered toast she thought how intense small pleasures could be and how difficult to describe to others.

'That would be lovely for a time but then the world would begin to run out of unspoiled places.' She gave a little shrug and a wistful smile. 'Everything laid open to legions of airborne gawpers. Oh I know it sounds terribly snobbish, but I don't want to see everything packaged and standardised. But I suspect you're right. It's going to happen.'

Amelia shook her head slightly, by such a small movement signalling that the conversation was at at end.

The last couple of hours he reflected as he lay his plate to one side had been like the sampling of a fine intoxicating drink; the powerful sensation of first meeting followed by the raw, exciting, dangers of the flirtation and the warm smoothness of the consummation he knew would come. And, just like a fine wine or Scotch malt, there was the suggestion of an aftertaste. The paintings - in particular the one with the ATS girl - had released something hitherto hidden within him.

Without talking more they embraced.

In the morning Peter Dainty knew that Amelia Kershaw was the woman he would die or kill for.

He also realised when he felt in his trouser pockets that she'd kept his Zippo.

SIX

VEN was verbal shorthand for 'Venerable One' which was what Mair called Compton Picard when they were alone together.

The old man's house had once been the Rectory and was still so named but with an 'old' prefixed. It looked out over the village from under a brow of moss and lichen as thick as snow clumped on the Welsh slate roof.

Ven's old Volvo was not in the doorless and ramshackle corrugated iron garage.

Mair felt on top of the doorframe for the key (she had given up chiding him about keeping it in such an obvious place) and let herself in.

The fire was low enough to need a couple more apple logs. She eased herself into the chair which by unspoken agreement had been assigned to her and let her mind gravitate towards the photographs which had come to her by way of Elwyn Creed.

One of the men, the one in the RAF uniform she was sure was Ven.

At first she had dismissed the idea. At any one time over a million were serving men in the air force during the war. Compton Picard was for his age a strikingly good-looking man but in the 1940s he would have been one such among very many.

And yet ...

The face was bonier now, the swept-back hair thinner and the jaw line softened by age and indifferent dentistry but the essence of the man was frozen in a moment of time.

The eyes looking out of the picture were glittering, hard and confident rather than thoughtful but she had seen Compton Picard in all his moods, and anger could flash over his face like light striking a cold, hard surface.

Picard and the man in the picture were one and the same she was sure.

Mair watched the flames begin to catch the damp bark making little beads of fire at the edges which dried and caught first.

The effect was like the streams of tracer bullets she had seen on films and she began to think about the war.

Her conviction which was so firm only a few moments ago began to dissipate.

She knew Ven had been a pilot but then so had tens of thousands of other young men.

She was trying to impose a narrative which sense and experience could not sustain and yet the eyes reflected insolent detachment as if laughing at the world.

The logs sparked and flared and she let her thoughts drift with their sweet, blue curling smoke.

She and Ven had met twenty years before when he was in his mid-sixties after she had delivered her talk on Bronze and Iron Age sites in South Wales and he had emerged from the audience to shake her hand. 'Distance in time always dehumanises people somehow,' he had said in a soft but certain voice. 'But you turned those old Celts into living, breathing and thinking people. I thank you from the bottom of my heart.'

And with a theatrical flourish he had kissed her hand.

A month later an invitation came in the post to tea and as the years passed and by retaining the scraps Compton Picard let out about himself Mair built up a reasonable biographical sketch.

Some things were certain.

He had been born in Northamptonshire to a father who was a general dealer, a term Ven managed to imbue with undertones of roguishness. A seemingly random education (the details varied somewhat) had been followed by employment in a drawing office. He had them gone to Canada to work as a lumberjack, a hand on a Vancouver fishing vessel, a nightwatchman, a croupier in an illegal casino, smuggler of goods from the United States, and journalist. Somewhere near the outbreak of war he had joined the RAF. Any further than that he would not be drawn.

'Oh, I did my bit, you know,' was the usual response to questions about the war before he rapidly passed on to his novel-writing. Depending upon which version was current this happened to switch from journalism to novels came as a result of lurid but inspiring visions during a bout of malaria or as a result of Ven's flooring an editor after a drink-fuelled row. Mair had once tried a flanking attack by asking Ven whether his war experiences had inspired him as a writer but he had anticipated her and replied only that in those days he was too young and too busy to be 'full of bookish rot'. Gently persisting, she had pointed out that two of his books that had enjoyed a reasonable sale in the 1950s had been about the war.

'Well of course you can't go through something like the war without something sticking,' he'd said with an odd little sideways glance. 'Anyway, none of it biographical. It's all artfully contrived. It was Frederica who got all that nonsense out of me. She made me forget the war.'

He had met Frederica in the 1950s upon his return to Britain and shortly after the misery of the newspaper had been partially eased by the acceptance by publishers of his first novel, *The Damascene Sword*. His second book, when it came, had not enjoyed the critical acclaim of his debut work; indeed it had almost not been published at all.

In desperation he had taken his full entitlement of holiday and rented a caravan in West Wales where he had spent a cold and damp winter completing his third book, *The Rubbiyat of Homer Karshmann*.

It had caught the mood of the moment.

In his late forties just as any chance of literary fame and fortune seemed to be slipping from his grasp he got wildly drunk, turned in his newspaper job and bought a house in the relatively prosperous Cardiff suburb of Penarth with a fine view of Flat Holm and Steep Holm and across the Bristol Channel. This was what Ven called his 'cravat-and-suede' period around the time of Mair's birth. Sometimes he would show her photographs of the period, Frederica a fair-haired woman of medium height, tending to plumpness and seemingly never without the white sandals that seemed almost mandatory for women fifty-five years before.

From the fragments Compton had let slip ('I joined the local flying club for a while but I had to make up my mind - writing or flying') Mair was able to continue piecing together his story.

It was while they were living in the big Edwardian house with its onion-shaped copper cupola and large gardens set with bamboo and hibiscus that his beloved 'Freddy' had died.

A Place To Be, *Caspian Dreams* and *Beatrice's Ice Cave* were written in a storm of grief ('It was either that or the bottle, and my God, how the bottle beckoned during those long, cold days') until at some point Compton Picard took the decision to leave his seaside mansion for the South Wales Valleys ('To touch the grief of a people and to find a new voice').

By the time he'd introduced himself to Mair after his talk his celebrity was well established.

The fire was burning brightly when she heard the outer door open and close.

'Ah. A visitor!'

She rose and kissed Compton Picard on the cheek.

At eighty-six he was still striking. Once of middling height he had bowed slightly with age although his slimness and the fine cut of his tweed jacket and cavalry twill trousers largely corrected the deficiency. Except when he was deep in thought his high, curved eyebrows gave him a mildly startled look but the eyes beneath them missed nothing. A whisper of a smile playing beneath the neatly trimmed military moustache signalled encouragement or indulgence for some, but was a trap for fools. Old as he was, Mair had learned you had to watch Ven's eyes and mouth. Something of the killer still flickered about them both.

The eyes. Capable of being seductive or mocking or murderous. Without the intensity of all those years ago but unmistakably the eyes of the airman in the photograph.

'I want you to sit down, please, Ven. There's something I have to ask you.'

'But we must have tea!' he cried with mock pain. 'You look as though you are about to impart serious news.'

'All right,' she smiled resignedly. 'Tea first.'

After it was served she said 'I am going to ask your advice on a serious matter. Are you ready?'

'Agog.'

'My father, Aneurin, left me a shade under two million pounds in his will.'

Compton Pacard picked up the bottle of cheap whisky which stood by the kettle and poured a stiff measure into his tea.

'I don't know what to say. Congratulations seems hardly the right word.'

'I found out today from Elwyn Creed who is handling Dad's estate. There were a few other things including a diary and some photographs ... '

She let the word hang in the air but was instantly aware that to expect a response was foolish.

'I didn't know your father well but it seems a great deal for a former police sergeant to accumulate. I shall of course,

68

shamelessly play upon your sympathies and attempt to persuade you not to trot off to a villa in Spain thereby leaving me bereft of company.'

The absence of words that followed was not a silence. A growing wind was snatching at the chimney stack sending small puffs of smoke out from the hearth and in the wainscotting a mouse scuttled as had its forebears for two hundred years.

'I don't suppose I'll even move from my house. Two million pounds isn't that much when you think it might have to last me forty years. What would you do with the money, if it were you?'

'Not a great deal. All that I have ever wanted is in the past. I miss Freddy dreadfully, you know, as I'm sure you miss your father. Death is such a bloody awful business.'

'Should I chuck in my job, for instance?'

The old man reached forward to throw another log on the fire.

'Without thinking twice about it. It's not as though you get a scrap of satisfaction from it any more so why carry on doing something you've come to loathe?'

With the magnetic power it seemed to possess the picture of the girl soldier that hung over the fireplace drew her eyes. Of the several paintings in the house, most of them landscapes, this was the most bewitching.

'I didn't hate it for years. I joined the police I suppose out of idealism but they want to use me as some sort of uniformed social worker doing trendy and impeccably politically-correct things. It's because I'm gay of course.'

'Well, then. You appear to have answered your own question,' Ven sipped thoughtfully at his tea. 'One can take public-spiritness too far. You could travel but neither you nor I are the sort who need a lot in the way of material things. Besides I think you're a home bird. Travel by all means but come back to Blaendiffaith. You wouldn't be really happy anywhere else.'

Before fully realising what she was doing Mair slid the photographs from their packet and handed them to a still-smiling Ven.

'These came in a package together with a diary and a scarf after I'd been to see Creed,' she said, the words tumbling out. Straightaway she saw her move had been clumsy and

69

premature but there was now no way for it to be undone.

'The RAF chap in one of the pictures looks like a younger version of you. He's got the same lovely thick hair you still have but it's the expression on his face and the eyes.'

Damn it. She cursed herself. It sounded like an interrogation, an emotional plundering of an old man's past. What did her curiosity matter? And yet the profound urge to know the past and somehow bind them into her own life thus sending them into some unguessed-at future could not be resisted.

She must know the truth. Her hand was on his arm.

'I'll get us a proper drink. Perhaps now isn't a good time,' she said softly.

The good Islay malt whisky was kept on the sideboard. She poured two fingers for each of them. In the mirror over the sideboard she could see back into the room where the firelight was falling on Compton Picard's face as he shuffled through the pictures several times - but always returning to the one she had picked out.

As he sat with it in his lap Mair could see the glint of his tears.

SEVEN

BRUX? 'Jesus. It sounds like a damned breakfast cereal,' somebody quipped at the briefing and Elmeyer had smiled.

Three hours after that the sky around him was dense with Flying Fortresses and their shielding fighter planes tearing open the sky on the way to the Czechoslovakian oil refineries, a sinew of war buried deep within the bruised and torn body of Europe and only forty miles from Prague.

Luck Be A Lady had climbed at four hundred feet per minute and slotted in with the squadron which had in its turn fitted in with the group and the group with larger formations so that the mass of aeroplanes were like an immense run of salmon speeding and thrashing through a narrow gap on some blind, mad migration.

The old girl had been shot up pretty bad after the last trip Elmeyer mused but the crew chief and his boys had coaxed, conjured, cannibalised and cursed her back into wholeness. Sometimes he amused himself with the idea of one day getting together the few thousand dollars that would be required and buying the old crate after the war. They could grow old together flying air shows and stuff like that. Frenchie would come in with him. That little son of a gun had thousands stashed away. Elmeyer thought of Frenchie squeezed into his gun turret rotating it from time to time so the oil stayed warm and thin.

That was for the future, maybe. Brux was for now.

'Here come the Abbeville Boys right on cue!' Attercop bawled from his waist gun.

The feared yellow-spinnered Messerschmitts fell on the bombers like wolves on a wounded buffalo making Elmeyer break out from his musings with a start. There wouldn't be a future unless he shaped up. Maybe he was battle fatigued. Pull yourself together and heed your own advice, darn it. Keep your wits about you and get through this a day at a time. Keep formation and let the gunners get on with their work. Amelia needs you.

The battle hit like a storm of noise and fire and falling objects, man and pieces of machine tumbling into limpid oblivion.

'Get on the cheek guns, somebody!' Elmeyer shouted and

seconds later he felt a tiny movement in the airframe as a figure scrambled forward. The hatch cover from a disintegrating Fort flew past and Elmeyer instinctively ducked.

'All that stuff falling from the sky like you see in old pictures of Hell. It's weird all right.' Simpson's strained voice was cut off on its rising note by that of Attercop, the other waist gunner.

'What are you tryin' to do, Simpson? Talk the fuckin' Germans to death?'

Simpson and Attercop were the finest waist gunners in the Eighth Army Air Force precisely because they rode one another. 'They're so pissed at having to fly almost touching one another back-to-back that any Jerry that comes near doesn't stand a chance,' Hosbach the navigator had once observed.

Frenchie was even more succinct when he observed that Simpson and Attercop were like a man and a wife who loathed each other snowed into a log cabin for the winter. 'They somehow can't get round to shooting one another so they raise Hell with the wolves. Whoever put those two together was a genius.'

The familiar, bloody, ballet was at a crescendo. Chunks of aluminium skin ripped away by machine-gun fire floated autumnally down. Something torn from a plane in the flight above came tumbling straight for Lady's cockpit. Elmeyer had a couple of seconds in which to see the scorched and blackened form with shreds of a parachute still attached to it before it was snatched away behind them. Now there came a diabolic torment of shouts and screams and oaths and the staccato hammering of beating of Lady's guns as Messerschmitts flew into her zone of fire. A neighbouring Fort, Thin Lizzie, was raked with machine gun fire before the Messerschmitt attacking her was torn into by a hail of lead directed by Attercop.

'You got him! You got him!' Joe Gianotta howled from his turret. The German plane was out of control and tumbling through the sky, fire whipping back from its cockpit. Belly-up it fell through the thin blue air like a dead fish dropping to the bottom of a pond.

And then, as sudden as the attack had commenced, it broke off.

Reduced only to the beat of the engines, the whine of power turret servo motors and hushed and tired words on the intercom the quiet assumed an almost domestic quality. Where a Fort had been shot from the sky another had moved up to plug its gap in the defensive shield. A line of holes had been stitched down her wing but that seemed to be the extent of Luck Be A Lady's damage. The odds of there being ripped hydraulic piping or wiring and the resulting failure of a system were high, but all that concerned Elmeyer was that she was still flying. The fuel tanks weren't ruptured and the Wright Cyclones still churned.

'Those Germans seemed peeved, though.'

Gianotta's husky New York voice was answered by Frenchie in the tail. 'You'd be peeved if some guys were dropping bombs on Schenectady or somewhere. Or somewhere .... or somewhere,' Gianotta mocked Frenchie's high-pitched voice. 'Will you listen to this guy? New York State isn't just somewhere. It's everywhere. Did nobody ever tell you country boys that nowhere else in the entire Union matters a damn?'

'That's crap, Gionotta,' Hosbach, generally thought of as the crew's intellectual, cut in. 'California's economy ... '

'Cut it you guys,' Elmeyer barked into his throat mike. They'd had their nervous release. None of the gunners would have stopped looking out while the banter went back and forth but a sense of deliverance could so easily slip into carelessness. The rules said intercom talk should be kept to a minimum and the rules were usually there for good reasons. Anyway, he didn't want to take risks.

A few days before he had noticed his hands trembling and there had been anxious dreams. In one, Amelia's face had appeared in front of The Lady's divided windshield hovering before him as maniacal war raged about. Before her features faded with a faint mocking smile. Before the mission he'd done some of the pre-flights checks in the wrong order. Not in itself dangerous but it signalled a lack of concentration and concentration was what kept Luck Be A Lady and her crew alive. Right away after that he'd made a pledge to himself not to think about Amelia while he was flying a mission. He'd just touch the green scarf she'd given him and not think about her again until the mission was over. Green, the colour of jealousy.

Jealous thoughts were creeping in now like a poison mist. What if she were with someone now? Come on, Elmeyer, take a hold of yourself. He touched the scarf once more and looked outside.

The bomber fleet above, below and around Luck Be A Lady had been mauled badly. Two ships were trailing smoke and one with a feathered prop would probably have to drop out of the formation and run for home. Like an old and wounded caribou harried by wolves, the Fort would give a good account of itself but the odds were stacked heavily against her no matter what the newsreels liked to show. All he could do was to think about his own ship and crew. Good old lady, Luck Be A Lady. If it got no worse than this they'd be fine.

Elmeyer's hands and feet knew instinctively what to do about keeping Luck Be A Lady in formation but the little tight ball of anxiety was turning to near-panic. Maybe it wasn't Amelia. Maybe his senses had picked upon something with the aircraft. Maybe deadly anoxia, the lack of oxygen, was making him lose his wits. He checked the dial on the A-9A oxygen regulator against the altimeter but it was fine. His hands and feet still more or less obeying the brain's orders were keeping Luck Be A Lady in tight with the formation but the nerves connecting them were close to snapping. He was losing the will to fight, the fight once fired by political faith.

A German fighter zooming from right to left signalled that battle had been rejoined. Just let's get this over and then I can settle down with Amelia and have kids and let the international working class pretty much take care of itself. Self-pity was mixing in with the cocktail of jealousy and fear that was making his hands shake on the controls. Nothing was safe and nothing was sane, Darn it. Just like the aviation gasoline in The Lady's tanks was burning off and would be almost gone by the time they reached England, so his faith in humanity was ebbing. How much of that was due to Amelia? She was wild all right and wouldn't be crammed into any political mould whether designed for the general improvement of mankind or not. Was he really changing his beliefs because of his infatuation with a woman? Infatuation, did he say? It was much more than that. Only love could change him that much. Perhaps the change had been coming anyhow, doubts hollowing out his communist beliefs until all that was left was the hard exterior. Raw physical survival, the most primitive instinct of all was what mattered.

The resumption of the German's attack hadn't completely broken through his wall of self-absorption.

That was bad.

He felt the prickle of sweat between his shoulder blades.

'How far to target, Hosbach?'

There was a croak in his voice.

'A little over three hundred miles, Sir.' The formality was typical. Elmeyer and Hosbach were not close. The relationship between them was purely professional. The navigator's professionalism was consummate. That was the thing about Luck Be A Lady and her crew. He didn't warm to Hosbach and Attercop couldn't stand the sight of Simpson. Frenchie had sensed how his pilot felt about Hosbach and was cool towards the navigator too. In the matter of the rivalry between the waist gunners Frenchie tended to favour Attercop. The plane was a flying bitch factory but somehow it all worked.

'Okay. Thanks.'

An hour and a quarter.

Puffs of black smoke had started hundreds of feet below but the anti-aircraft fire would get thicker and more accurate. A shrinking Reich meant all the enemy's flak could be deployed over a smaller area. Given his distracted state he was relieved that Luck Be A Lady was not flying lead ship. All Mike Wiggins the bombardier had to do was open the bomb doors and press the release button at the same time as the bombs from the lead Fortress fell away. Then they would be able to get the Hell out of it.

Sweat began to trickle from underneath his leather helmet which felt gritty and cold. Now he was thankful for the body and groin armour he had so often cursed for its weight and awkwardness. All he had to do was to keep Luck Be A Lady in position and get the bombs away and then get her home. The words were running through his head like a mantra. Maybe the damage to the wing is all we're pencilled in for today.

The flak was heavy around the target but Elmeyer's body and mind had passed into a state that was beyond fear. They would have to drop their bombs which would mean flying level through the storm of fire. Maybe they would get hit and maybe not but either way there wasn't one Hell of a lot he could do about it. Wiggins was now effectively flying the plane through the computer in the Norden bomb sight.

'Bombs gone!'

Freed from her burden Lady shot up in the air. Elmeyer's stomach had just caught up with her when a heavy thud like she'd been hit by a giant baseball bat came from somewhere aft.

Now she was yawing off towards the battered aluminium flank of the neighbouring plane. Acting on reflex his strength and responses fired by adrenalin, Elmeyer put on power and hauled the controls to the right. Thin Lizzie's co-pilot recoiled as the Lady swerved to within thirty feet of his wingtip and an oath exploded from Hodgson on the top gun as Luck Be A Lady settled back into the formation.

Even above the pounding noise Elmeyer could hear the screams.

'Who's hurt back there?' he snapped.

'Attercop, Sir. It's real bad.' The voice was Simpson's.

'Do what you can. What about his gun?'

'Busted. The sight and the feed mechanism are hit but it's Attercop, Sir. Dear Christ. We gotta do something. He's screaming and his guts are bubbled all out ... '

'Understood. You have to deal with it.'

Simpson would have to take morphine ampoules from the first aid kit near his position and shoot Attercop full of dope. That should quieten him, floating away the pain on a chemical magic carpet, away from the murderous reality of war and dying four miles up in the sky.

Elmeyer's mind ran through the briefing.

The meteorology boys had said the winds would be from one-ninety degrees and moderate. With that headwind component it should be about four hours, three-and-a-half if they were lucky, before they crossed the Channel and were safe over England. Nothing to do now except hold course and wait for the hours and minutes to tick away and hope no more German fighters came.

Elmeyer watched the Fortress above him, the streaks of oil blown back from each of the motors and the contrails streaming out behind her and the blue sky darkening away into space. The seeming infinity of the heavens made him think about Attercop who had stopped screaming.

Somewhere out to the left was a tangle of contrails where American or British fighter planes which had come out to escort the formation were mixing it with Germans attacking another part of the bomber stream.

'How's Attercop taking it? Tell him to hang on. I can see England.'

'Attercop can't see anything, Sir. Not now.' Simpson's voice was shaking.

'You did what you could.'

'Yes, Sir.'

Dozens of ships' wakes were scoring the grey-green of the English Channel as the Fortresses descended, the crews taking the oxygen masks from their faces as they dropped below ten thousand feet.

Half an hour later the undercarriage clunked down and locked, confirmation of this coming from Gianotta's ball turret. Now Luck Be A Lady was into the circuit and he was going through the pre-landing checks. The B-17 touched down gently as if out of respect for poor, dead Attercop who, minutes later, was being carried out from the waist gun position by the medics who'd brought their ambulance up close to the ship's scarred flank.

Wearily, stiffly, the crew dropped through the hatch onto the hardstanding.

Simpson was slumped against the starboard main tyre clutching the small teddy bear that had been Attercop's mascot.

As the ambulance's gears engaged Simpson threw himself at the driver's window.

'Make sure this stays with him. You hear that you guys? Bury it with him.' He was thrusting the bear at the driver who was trying to push him away. Now Simpson had hold of the man's collar and was screaming at him, flecks of spittle flying in the man's face.

'All right. All right. Jesus. I'll see to it personally.'

The medic was pale with fright. Simpson relaxed his hold and allowed the man to pull away, cursing him.

'These flying boys think they're the only fucking ones in the war,' the driver's shouted voice was quaking as he accelerated away. Simpson glared after the vehicle and spat before going over to where the rest of the crew were smoking and drinking coffee. He did not see the teddy bear being hurled from the ambulance.

But Elmeyer did.

Without drawing attention to his movements he slowly ambled towards it and picked up the toy. Someone would get even with the medic. Elmeyer's fists balled. Maybe he'd do it himself. Hitting an enlisted man was the sort of thing that would get an officer busted - but to Hell with that. The driver might be too scared of his rank to put up a fight but he'd take his jacket with its Captain's bars off before giving the man a shellacking. He would say nothing to Simpson who hated Attercop but trusted him with his life, a bond as enduring as love. The teddy bear would be sent to Attercop's wife. Funny. All the missions they'd flown together and he hadn't talked to the gunner about his family. He'd have to write to Attercop's wife. Maybe his love for her was as great as his for Amelia. He tried to imagine her face and her tears as a tear streaked through the grime on his own cheek.

A cycle was slowly approaching, the rider's head turning from side to side. At first Elmeyer thought the man was looking at the scenery or the airfield's bustle but the bicycle and its rider were inexplicably detached from all that surrounded them as if moving inside their own dark column of chill air.

He never saw the Solitary Cyclist dismount nor was he aware of him being close by, but in an instant during which time had been suspended the teddy bear was snatched from his grasp as the cyclist, loosely holding the toy, rode away from where Luck Be A Lady's crew stood.

Elmeyer turned to where Frenchie was comforting Simpson and the rest were standing around waiting for the truck to take them to de-briefing.

'Did anyone see that?' he called.

'See what, boss?' Gionotta replied. 'What was it we were supposed to be looking at?'

'Nothing. Forget it.'

A zephyr of wind blew up making the men curse when their cigarette lighters flared; whipping up dirt and grass, a wind so bitter that Elmeyer thought it must come from Hell, a place of eternal cold and silence even more chilling than battle in the sky.

EIGHT

FRENCHIE cared for Elmeyer more than any other man he knew but he found it easy and profitable to get along with most other people. A smiling face he had learned was good for business. So, sometimes, was losing at cards. Frenchie laughed and shook his head.

'I'll be damned. Money sticks to you like shit to a hick's boot.'

He chuckled the way slightly simple country boys are supposed to, pushing the stack of half-crown coins over to Staff Sergeant Jim Thorpe, crew chief on one of the other B-17s in Luck Be A Lady's squadron.

Crew chiefs were important for two main reasons which taken together gave them a prestige as great as any single member of the aircrew excepting the pilot. They made sure that when a Fortress went to war it was in as fine a fettle as could be achieved. They were tough old non-commissioned officers who knew the dodges and scams. Just about the dumbest thing any aircrew could do was to upset their crew chief.

'You're a darned sight better shootin' down Jerries than you are at cards, that's for sure. Do yourself a favour, Frenchie. Don't even think of becoming a professional gambler.'

Thorpe rammed his winnings into the pocket of coveralls which had once been olive green but were now grimed a shade darker than their wearer's cropped hair.

A good player would have been looking at Thorpe's face or working out the play of the cards but Frenchie was glancing past Jim Thorpe's shoulders to the door through which he could see the lighted hangar and a Fortress's tail.

Truth was, cards bored him stiff.

Mechanics were busy riveting patches over the ship's holes. Next the airframe boys would fit new plexiglass to the Fort's shattered nose where there would still be smears of the bombardier's blood.

'Yesterday's was a tough trip,' Frenchie observed. 'Made a lot of work for you maintenance boys.'

It was important to keep just the right tone in his voice. Say it the wrong way and Jim Thorpe might get the idea he was being gently mocked for being a groundpounder who didn't have to fly and fight.

'We're not getting the battle damage of a year ago,' Thorpe said, standing and shrugging himself into a shearling wool zipper jacket. 'What you boys do to the planes is as bad as anything the Germans can dream up. Jesus, the tyres that get the treads scraped right off through shitty landings. We keep hearing about the merchant sailors who get drowned getting all this stuff across here. They should give your damned pilots the same talk.'

Frenchie smiled his smile which outwardly conspired against the officer pilots but which inwardly said 'What do you know about flying a Fortress five miles up in the sky at forty below zero with some German trying to fry you alive or rip you to shreds you fat, greedy, lazy bastard?'

'They think they're God's gift all right,' was what he actually said as he moved towards his purpose like a hunter stalking prey.

'Let me ask you something about the good job your guys do, fixing the planes and even having to hose out the blood and guts and all.'

'They must get pretty dirty. Cold, too.'

'Cold and dirty as Hell.'

Frenchie watched Thorpe's eyes.

The crew chief had a woman in Cambridge he liked servicing a whole lot more than any damned aeroplane. And the only way a fat and charmless man like him could keep a girl was to have a roll of money in his pocket.

'So what would you say to doing a little business? Hell. You guys deserve a bit more in your pockets.'

Suspicion and avarice narrowed Thorpe's eyes.

'What sort of business?'

'I'm proposing a little financial excursion into the clothing trade.' Frenchie touched the sleeve of Thorpe's sheepskin jacket. 'You write off coats like this when they're too dirty or damaged for use, right?'

'Not me personally. A supply guy does it.'

'Sure. But you tell him when clothing has to be replaced?'

Thorpe looked down at his zip slide. If he closed the zip Frenchie judged, it would signal and end to the conversation.

It stayed open.

'I've heard things about you.' Thorpe scanned Frenchie's face. 'I don't know. It's taking a big risk.'

Hammering, shouts and the hiss and snap of riveting guns

broke through the silence.

'Everyone in this war takes risks,' Frenchie said.

'What sort of things do you want?'

Thorpe was hooked but the trick was to stay the same good ol' boy he'd been during the card game, the same cheerful loser.

'D-1 jackets like the one you've got on. Caps and overalls. Even gloves and socks. Tins of grease, tools; anything that can be sold to the Limeys.'

'Engineering stuff is easy. Nuts and bolts, wrenches and screwdrivers, feeler gauges and tool bags and all that stuff I can write off.'

Frenchie had shown his hand and now the crew chief was feeding from it.

He kept his friendly voice despite a growing loathing for the other man.

'Some tools will be okay but the Limeys use different threads for nuts and bolts so maybe the wrenches won't be a hot number. I'll make some enquiries and let you know.'

'How soon?'

Oh, you son of a bitch. The hook is well and truly fixed in your upper lip.

'Soon. Before tonight. I want the clothing though.'

He was not flying so he would go into town and strike a deal. A couple of garage owners he dealt with would welcome the tools. Most of the British who had cars had taken them off the road but garages were taking in farm machinery and doing local contract work for Americans and British.

'Come again Frenchie. I like playing cards with you.' Thorpe finally zipped his jacket.

'And I like losing to you, Jim. You're a real gentleman.'

Frenchie flashed his smile which said 'We're in business'. When the time came he'd squeeze Thorpe and leave him hung out to dry. Within a month the crew chief would be waking up in the middle of the night from nightmares about the Military Police coming for him.

At which point Frenchie would tell him that the MPs were in his pocket and could be persuaded not to make enquiries, but at a price that price being a steady flow of black market goods. Thorpe was a pig of a man. Pity was he was such a good crew chief. Maybe if he hadn't said that thing about pilots Frenchie would have been more kindly disposed towards him.

Most pilots were all right, but Elmeyer was the best. Off base Elmeyer didn't act like an officer but like a friend. Frenchie never had any doubts that one day he would be able to help Elmeyer out on account of the poor guy having lots of brains about politics and stuff but nothing worth a damn in dollars. At the end of it all Thorpe could end up in the military stockade, or in front of a firing squad for all he cared.

When Thorpe had gone Frenchie began to think about Laura who he'd married when she was seventeen and their little daughter Mary Jo who was coming up two years and sometimes flew into wild rages so that she would have to be tied down in her cot. Almost every night Frenchie would hold the image of Laura and Mary Jo in his imagination before going to sleep. He almost never spoke about them to anybody other than Elmeyer. Now he thought about her long brown hair and figure that looked good even in farm clothes and her round, honest face.

Mostly, Frenchie didn't mind the army. Basic training had been a pain and 1943 had been a real tough year which he had been lucky to survive. In fact he doubted he'd have survived had it not been for Elmeyer. He wouldn't care if, after the war, he never saw any of the crew ever again except Elmeyer. One day, when he'd made a pile he'd find a way of giving his pilot a lot of dough in some way that didn't hurt his feelings and then maybe Cap would settle down with a good woman like his own Laura and stop filling his head with all that politics that could only get him into trouble. The English woman, Amelia, seemed okay but it was difficult to tell with English women. If she made Elmeyer happy though, maybe he'd slip some money to her. She would have to dump the Limey RAF flyer, though. He would think about that some more. In the meantime there was business to get done before chow time. The base's clothing store was a big Quonsett hut the size of a small aircraft hangar. Inside, the overpowering smell of mothballs. A very young Private First Class was about to scuttle off and get Lieutenant Norowicz the lieutenant in charge when Frenchie stopped him.

'It's okay, son. Just take me to him.' The boy could only have been a year younger than him but had the freshness of face Frenchie had lost twenty missions ago somewhere over Germany.

'It's a restricted area, Sergeant.' The boy eyed the caller

with a mixture of suspicion and admiration. The story that Frenchie was someone to reckon with had got around.

'Look on me as a tourist.' Frenchie looked past the boy's shoulder to where stacks of greatcoats and army blankets, socks and boots and silk flying underwear and woollen shirts and ties and khaki pants rose toward the corrugated tin roof.

'Quite an operation you have here.'

The boy looked pleased.

'You guys in stores are the backbone of things, did you realise that?'

Now he looked as though he'd just got a citation for the Congressional Medal of Honor.

'I guess it is kind of a nerve centre,' the PFC said carefully.

'A nerve centre! That's exactly what it is. How would guys like me get into the air if we didn't have all this stuff?' Hell, let me tell you, when I shoot down a Kraut I bless the Lord my Maker that guys like you are on my side.'

'Gee. Really?' The PFC gave a puppyish grin.

'It can't be as important as flying the planes. Or being a gunner.'

Two Women's Army Corps girls were leaning against one of the large racks and laughing and drinking coffee, one of whom looked towards Frenchie, covering her mouth with her hand and whispering to her friend.

An easy lay if he thought that way. Perhaps if it wasn't for Laura and God ...

'Listen, son,' he said, turning back to the PFC. 'Every one of the bullets I fire has to be requisitioned on a form. No form, no bullets. One day soon the shooting will stop but there'll always be forms. And people to fill them in and shuffle them around. That is what the Army is really about. Remember that.'

'I can see Lieutenant Norowicz now.' He patted the boy's shoulder.

The clacking of a typewriter from behind a plywood wall sounded flat, deadened by tons of stacked clothing all militarily in order on labelled lines of shelves containing everything from long drawers to steel helmets.

A primly efficient assistant with a clipboard pursed his lips as a handful of new aircrew arrivals who were joshing and laughing bustled in for their issue of cold weather clothing they would need even on the ground a few weeks from now when the morning dews turned to frost and the wind howled over the fens in icy indignation.

Frenchie moved aside to let two airmen pulling a trolley heaped with flight clothing pass. On top of the trembling pile a pair of A-3 fleece pants was bloodied and torn at the crutch.

Lieutenant Stanley Norowicz was a fat, pale figure with too many chins.

'Have you got anything for me?'

Frenchie neither greeted Norowicz nor saluted.

'Not that stuff over there. Not with the blood.'

The tip of Norowicz's cigar shook as he took a deep drag. Too much whiskey. Frenchie could smell it from where he stood.

'I'm worried. Military police have been snooping around.' Norowicz ignored Frenchie's question.

'It's nothing to do with you and me. Just routine. Believe me, I've got friends in the MPs.'

'Routine my ass.' Norowicz's voice held a tremulous edge of fear. 'One was an officer I've never seen before. They're bringing in people from outside to investigate. I don't like it.' Norowicz's pale eyes slid about in their sockets in a way which reminded Frenchie of fried eggs cooked over-easy.

'Don't get spooked. The MPs run checks on things just to keep themselves occupied. I heard that a guy who drives an ambulance got beaten so bad he'll be in hospital for the next month. Maybe they're after whoever whipped him.'

In reality Frenchie had been behind it. The guy who threw Attercop's teddy bear out the ambulance window had got what was coming after the right words had been whispered in the right ear and a favour called in.

'No. It's more than that. They smell a rat,' Norowicz shook his head.

'They said they're coming back tomorrow. Jesus Christ, Hayes. If they ever find out what's gone missing from here they'll put us in front of a firing squad.'

Norowicz was almost blubbering. Frenchie felt a sudden urge to punch him in the face. He glanced round to make sure nobody was within earshot. The airmen with the trolley had disappeared and the girls with the coffees were deep into their giggling session.

'Stall 'em, Norowicz. Listen to me. You've had the good times. Now you'll have to stand the heat.' He softened his voice.

'It's probably some British bobby who's found a local with

some of our stuff and fancies he might get another stripe if he pokes around and asks a few questions.'

Normally, he might have enjoyed Norowicz's discomfort. Norowicz and that prick Thorpe were birds of a feather but the news about the strange officer was worrying. Maybe Norowicz's fears were well founded. Maybe he should lay low and look around and make plans. Norowicz was spooked and would have to be put on ice. What he had to offer was good stuff but there were other deals which would keep Laura in nice clothes and Mary Jo in the school for kids whose minds had gone funny.

Tyres and fuel was where the action was Frenchie mused and the British end of the market was looking up. There was the RAF fighter jock Dainty who had good nerves. It was a pity he was making a play for Amelia. Dainty had the killing instinct and could live with danger. He wouldn't fold like Norowicz. Frenchie wondered how the whole thing between the Cap, Amelia and the RAF guy would turn out. He hoped the Cap got the girl who was real nice but if he didn't he didn't see it mattered all that much because he reckoned Cap could get any girl.

Dealing with people like Norowicz and Thorpe had given Frenchie an unusual view of the Bassington base which was home to the 391st Bomb Group of the Eighth United States Army Air Force. Combat fliers made the assumption that the whole mighty enterprise had been assembled for the sole purpose of getting themselves and their aeroplanes into the sky; that the collection of huts and hangars, the legions of scuttling and rushing clerks, the stores and the motor transport pools and the bicycle repair shops and the cookhouses and the administrative offices were merely a support tail.

Frenchie knew the truth.

The huge effort ostensibly designed to send planes and men to war had an impetus all of its own and would function whether there was actually a war on or not. If not one single B-17G ever took off from Bassington for the duration of the war the storm of filing and telephoning, moving and accounting for things, coding, decoding, policing, cooking, shouting, driving, conferencing and saluting would still go on.

He put the thought to one side. Something on the airfield was wrong.

Men with binoculars were crowding the control tower and

all over the airfield groups of people were sitting astride bikes or leaning on their handlebars or against walls or sandbags or sitting in Jeeps and trucks, but all straining their eyes toward the East. Ambulances and crash trucks had been lined up, their crews tense. One medical corpsman nearby looked no more than sixteen and already about to spew on the grass.

The buzz or rumble was at the furthest limits of his hearing, or pre-hearing, the zone of sixth sense wherein ancient men learned to detect the approach of predators or quarry. If you didn't have this sixth sense the planes could be from any of the American bases scattered around, or perhaps the first of the Limeys taking off on a night raid in their big, black, bat-like Lancaster bombers which seemed more sinister and warlike than the B-17 but Frenchie instinctively knew they were Flying Fortresses of 391st Bomb Group. Prescience, the skipper had once called it and he had learned the word. Foreknowledge.

The sky was clear and it was getting cold in the early evenings. Frenchie turned up his coat collar as he watched the darts of light thrown out by the setting sun on the aluminium skins of the homecoming Forts.

He had positioned himself on the concrete apron which he knew where some of the planes would swing on to and park.

The first Fortress was coming in one wing low and with a stopped prop. He'd seen it several times before and held his breath. A flare fired from the crippled Fortress indicated that the pilot wanted to land straight away without waiting his turn in the circuit. It must be shot up bad for that to happen, Frenchie thought. Badly damaged aeroplanes were usually ordered to land last if they had enough gas so they didn't crash and tear up the runway, forcing those behind to divert.

When the crowd had first caught sight of the damaged plane there had been a jabber of excited talk but as it crabbed its way onto its final approach a hush fell. As well as a stopped motor a large chunk of tail had been shot away making it hard for the pilot to line up on the runway. Crash trucks were already rolling. Frenchie's mind's eye was inside the stricken Fort, his heart pounding at the unnatural position of the horizon and sweating those few seconds from the point the pilot throttled right back to actual contact with the runway. Even then, it wasn't necessarily over. He'd seen planes hit the runway so hard that they ballooned back up into the air again, crashing on the bounce. Sometimes the tail wheel touched the ground first and brought the main wheels down with a sickening slam.

The pilot had cut the throttles and was holding off, letting the plane run out of momentum. A violent lurch to the right was over-corrected making the whole weight come down on the port undercarriage. For a split-second it seemed as though the landing gear might not take the weight but then in a screech of protesting rubber and a cloud of acrid blue smoke the starboard wheel touched and she was running on both main wheels. A couple of seconds later the tail wheel touched. A patter of applause and cheers broke out. The crash trucks that had been following peeled off to await another casualty but an ambulance had stayed with the Fortress as the pilot steered her onto the hardstanding near to where Frenchie stood. As the pilot blipped the throttles on the port engine to bring her round he saw that the ball gunner's turret had been shattered and blood blasted and swirled around the remaining shards of perspex by the slipstream.

The kid on the ambulance crew started to spew for real when they took the ball gunner from the turret top half first. They were still putting the pieces into bags when the Solitary Cyclist rode by.

Angry and shocked bystanders ran after the bicycle and its silent rider one of them shouting he was going to beat the holy shit out of a goddamned Jonah but the bike always seemed to spirit itself ahead of its pursuers. There was no sound, no backward glance from the shrouded face and Frenchie noticed for the first time that the figure and machine cast no shadow.

The bloody spectacle of the ball gunner should have driven Norowicz from Frenchie's thoughts but the events ran together to add to his general sense of foreboding and made him want a drink. At the sergeants' mess Simpson the waist gunner was there already very drunk. Like many gunners Simpson was stockily built. The most prominent thing about his young and unformed face, apart from large grey eyes which seemed always to have an expression of puzzlement, were his long, dark eyelashes giving him an almost girlish appearance. Attercop had teased him about his looks and once the men had come to blows. Whatever it was between them, Attercop was dead and Simpson was grief-stricken and far enough gone on liquor drunk to be spoiling for a fight.

'I'm sorry about Attercop. He was all right.'

Frenchie said, consolation in his voice, all the time watching for the first dangerous stare or movement of a hand on the periphery of his vision. Simpson tried to focus on Frenchie's face before turning back to his drink.

'Maybe .... Maybe he didn't know too much about it,' Frenchie continued keeping his voice soft but recoiling immediately when Simpson spun round to face him. Frenchie felt the blood rush to his face. It had been a stupid, stupid thing to say.

'Didn't know too much about it!' Simpson affected a mincing voice, made even more menacing by his drunken slur. 'Didn't know too much about it! Did you hear the poor bastard screaming?' Spittle flew into Frenchie's face. Now, at any second, the blow would come. 'He was lying there staring at his own entrails. Do you want to know what I did?'

Frenchie kept his own voice calm.

'You got the first-aid kit and put morphine in him just like the skipper said. I'm sure he didn't feel a thing after the first shot.'

If the punch was going to come it would be now but his eyes had changed somehow and the fight was going out of him. Frenchie was glad. Hitting a drunk even in self-defence was only okay if you were drunk yourself.

'If he wasn't screaming in pain he was screaming with fear or at the smell and sight of his guts slipping all over the place but he didn't scream for long. You want to know why? Because I pumped all the morphine I could find into him.'

Simpson's eyes dropped to his whiskey glass which shook as he raised it to his lips.

'When the morphine in the pack near our guns was all used up I broke open another. I killed him, Hayes. I doped Attercop to death. People said I hated the poor bastard and I killed him.' The voice between a snarl and a scream was like that of a tormented animal.

Simpson's voice had risen to a hoarse cry which made others at the bar turn towards him some with sympathy in their looks but others with anger or contempt.

'Shut up.'

Frenchie's own voice was low and hard.

'Just shut the fuck up and listen. Forget how Attercop died. He got hit and that was all.'

Simpson tried to focus on Frenchie's face but his head was

drooping and his eyes fixed somewhere to the side.

'You're a hard little bastard.'

'Maybe you meant that as a compliment and maybe not but listen to me good because you're not going to hear this again.

'There's trouble going around the base. Big trouble. And when trouble starts you never know where it'll end and for people who kill in US uniform they've just built a nice new hanging shed at Shepton Mallet military prison.'

Frenchie knew no court-martial would ever impose more than a light sentence for what Simpson had done but his scare tactic had worked.

'So crawl off to your sack and try and remember in the morning that you got some good advice and listen, Simpson. I would have done what you did. I hope that makes you feel better.'

'I guess it does. Listen. There's something I need to tell you.'

Simpson beckoned him closer.

'You said about there being trouble around here, right? Maybe you haven't heard.'

'What might I not have heard?'

Frenchie felt foreboding like a sliver of ice down his spine. A silly, drunkard's smile was hovering around Simpson's lips.

'About Captain Elmeyer. The MPs took him away today. Real polite they were, saluting and saying 'sir' but from the way they sat him in the Jeep it wasn't no ticket for being drunk or getting in fights or anything like that. Pretty serious I would say.'

'Did you see it?' Suddenly Frenchie felt like grabbing Simpson's collar.

'Nope. Just heard about it. It couldn't be that the skipper's involved in any of your little shenanigans on the black market could it, Frenchie?'

'You wouldn't be trying to piss me off would you?'

'No shit, Frenchie. What is it the Limeys say? It's the true gen.'

It was almost dark. A small communications plane was landing and Frenchie watched it distractedly as he ransacked his mind. Shooting off his mouth about the working people and negroes and all the rest of that stuff would make sure Cap never made Major but shit, they didn't have to arrest him. Frenchie ground his cigarette into the mud shaking his head.

Educated people. Dumb as doughnuts. No way of figuring them.

NINE

A delicious thrill of jealousy ran through Flying Officer Peter Dainty as he lay by Amelia's side straining to make out figures in the paintings in the low light.

'Do you do with him what we do together?' he asked at last when his growing sense of anger was sufficiently primed.

'Exactly what we do, my darling. Everything is a variation upon a theme.' Amelia's voice was a sated purr.

'That's rather a dispassionate answer.'

He blew a stream of smoke toward the ceiling, watching it coil and eddy in the bedside light. They had made love on top of the covers fiercely and roughly, he plunging into her with relentless force. One thing he had come to realise was that for him jealousy was an exhilarating drug.

'Don't you feel ashamed?'

'Of what? The sex? Not in the least. Although I'll be ashamed if you want me to be ashamed, which I suspect you do.'

'I'm not playing games. I hate to think of you doing it with that Yank, what's his bloody name?'

'You know very well his name is James Elmeyer. You're not thinking of challenging him to a duel, are you?'

'I just don't like to think of you in this bed with him. It makes me sick and angry.'

'I think you don't altogether mind being angry. A lot of men draw mental pictures of their women with other men. It makes the woman the whore they want them to be.' Amelia was now fully awake and putting a teasing edge into her voice, probing the limits of this fierce, passionate young man's anger.

'It's also a way of justifying their own queer instincts. You know, intimately touching where another man has been.'

'Poppycock! Psycho-analytical mumbo-jumbo!' he shot back but she was threequarters right, damn her. Her instinct for this sort of thing showed through in the paintings. Her depiction of women in particular, although usually dressed, exuded a sort of lustful compliance.

'The headshrinkers say everyone's a bit queer. Do you believe that? Even touching yourself is a sort of queerness. It must be when you think about it.'

Her voice was honey and the touch of her hand started a slow explosion deep within him and he lay waiting for the surge of primal power to build up and overwhelm them. It was a fierce and cruel thing and the only thing he had ever felt like it was when he flipped up the cover over the fire button on his Spitfire and loosed a deadly stream of fire into his quarry.

At first when she had brought men home Amelia had tried to hang on to mental pictures of her husband. She could recall the first couple of years of happiness but after that the images dissolved into a fuzziness of dark bitterness. At first there had been guilt but that had long since gone much of it evaporated by her work. Now she almost never thought about David fighting his war far away somewhere in the vastness of the Pacific Ocean. In his last letter posted from Australia he had written about the Japanese planes that were smashing themselves into American ships. What should have made her fearful for her husband (she wondered if that had been his intention) in fact made her dwell upon the fanatical courage of the men who piloted the flying bombs.

But what of this one beside her, suddenly tautened like a young, alert animal? If the Devil had taken her soul it had taken his, too. From their first meeting in the Limbo Bar and on every occasion since his eyes had hardly left her. They drank her up, observing her so intently that she had begun to think he might be a little bit mad. If he was though, she was enough of an artist to realise that beneath the boy's talent for war and destruction lay a creativity on the point of ignition. A writer, perhaps, storing up images for the future. Of one thing she was sure, whatever he chose to do he would be as ruthless in achieving success as he was in war.

'So, what would you do if you met James, your brother-in-arms but rival in bed?'

'I have no idea. Not pistols at dawn or swords. That sort of thing is far too posh for me. If I was going to do for Elmeyer or anyone else it would be fists and boots down a dark alleyway. Better still I'd get someone else to do the job.'

Just like a lazy and careless young animal, his mood had now slipped over into a cosy jokiness as though, having gorged, he was licking the blood off his paws.

'Aren't I worth hand-to-hand combat?' she asked with mock coyness.

'Of course you are. It's just that I'm getting rather tired of having to do things myself. My New Year resolution for 1944 was that after the war I'm going to pay other people to do the things I don't want to. Anyway, why do you ask? Are you seeing him soon?'

There was a silence lasting several heartbeats.

'Truthfully, yes.'

Their eyes engaged. Amelia did not blink although Dainty could sense her apprehension. Of course she knew that he was capable of the most extreme violence; wasn't his job to kill people he'd never even met? And yet she had held his gaze. There was a wry smile on his lips as he turned his gaze away.

'I'm glad you're square with me at any rate,' he said at last.

'You've been a perfectly wonderful lover and sensitive in a peculiar sort of way and I'm grateful for the interest you took in my pictures, but one night together doesn't mean that we own one another. You must know that.'

'You sound so damned reasonable and sophisticated!' The mood switched back to anger. 'I said I was grateful for the truth, I'm not particularly grateful for the lecture. There's something ... I don't know ... corrupt about you.' He ripped a cigarette from its pack, thumbing the wheel of the lighter until it lit the third time. 'Why do you want to be a Yank's bit of stuff, anyway, as if I didn't bloody well know.' The words were almost spat out.

He was still a boy. Given a plane with the power of ten racing cars and empowered by the country to deliver instant death but still inside a boy.

'If you think it's anything to do with the Americans having more money you're wrong. Anyway, you seem to have lots. Do you think I went to bed with you because of that? I did it because you excite me. And I need that almost as much I need to paint. I love James. I might as well tell you that.'

'Could you love me?'

'Darling. Come here.' He went to her and she kissed his forehead. 'You're a man in every respect except that you are only just finding out how these things work. The answer to your question is, yes. I think I could. But not yet. Perhaps not ever.'

He had used the word 'corrupt' in the special sense of over voluptuous or sumptuous, ripe to the point of decay or so she assumed. He was probably right. Compared with her, his own simple greed for her body was innocence itself.

Men and their passions were touching in so many ways, like little boys coveting the same toy.

TEN

'ENTER.'

Mair did so, ignoring the nod indicating where she was to sit.

'Please sit down,' Chief Inspector John O'Driscoll said tonelessly.

The unnerving thing about him was that he never seemed to blink. Mair wondered whether his eyes had a reptilian inner lid.

Slowly, she did as she was bidden, folding her hands on her lap as a gesture to exclude intimacy something she knew he would note. He had probably already jotted down 'can be difficult in dealings with her superiors' for inclusion in her annual report. It didn't matter after the talk during which Ven had helped her make up her mind. She was coming round to the idea that two million pounds in the bank could banish career anxieties.

'Thanks for calling in. Have I said I'm sorry about your father?'

'You have, Sir. Thank you.'

'One of the old school from the days when all we had to do was to catch the villains and stand them in front of a magistrate. Nowadays we have to see ourselves as a holistic part of society.' He seemed pleased with the word. 'Less of a force and more of a service with a real relevance and commitment to the community, eh?'

'All that and probably more, Sir. But I don't suppose you invited me in here to talk about the philosophy of modern policing.'

'No indeed. I'll come straight to the point.' O'Driscoll laid his pencil exactly in line with a piece of paper placed face down in the middle of his blotter.

'I wondered if you've ever thought of the benefits of early retirement?'

She had. Quite a lot, but it amused her to watch her superior's face as it worked to assemble the appropriate expression of seriousness and concern.

'Mair - you don't mind me calling you that? - You have been an exemplary officer from just about every point of view. Many years of sterling service to the, ah, community including, I see, a Chief Constable's commendation. I'm surprised that CID never appealed to you, nor promotion.'

Aneurin's fault, really, she thought. Or at least a fault secreted within his genes. Not enough ambition, and by the time she realised she wasn't totally absorbed by policing it was too late. She had proved to be her father's daughter even more than she thought, loving words in books and on the stage, a Welsh Valleys bohemian trapped inside a blue uniform.

'Oh well, Sir. It's a bit late now, I suppose.'

O'Driscoll said nothing, his hands, palms down and parallel, hovered above the single piece of paper in mute concurrence.

'I think you are going to like what you see when I turn over this piece of paper. As I remember local history is one of your interests isn't it? I've often thought I would like to delve into it more myself.'

Making it sound thought Mair like the very last thing he would like to do.

'Of course, you don't have to give me an answer right away.'

'I want to. I accept.'

'You haven't seen what's written down yet.'

'I don't care all that much. I accept. I'll sign now.'

'Before you do, there's something I'd like to say.' O'Driscoll's smile was even more intense than usual.

'What might that be, Sir?'

'May I be frank?'

'Absolutely.'

'Very well. I have always found you to be a supercilious smart-arse who is wedded to some antique view of our work and who evidently holds my attempts to quantify and manage the very many problems we face in barely concealed contempt. You no doubt consider yourself a solid, old-fashioned copper. I consider you bloody-minded in your refusal to adapt to modern policing methods.'

'I shall, of course, say none of those things at your official going-away presentation.'

Mair was aware of the shock searing her face and for the first time she saw that O'Driscoll's blue eyes were laughing along with his mouth. Her own mouth was hanging open in amazement at the unexpected onslaught.

It was several seconds before she could organise a reply.

When it came she felt angry tears searing her eyeballs.

'And you, Sir, are a cynical bastard who only got promotion in the Northern Ireland Police Service because you were Sinn Féin's preferred man. You are all in favour of change not because you think it results in better policing but because it gets the approval of politicians obsessed with notions of political correctness. Your involvement with RACE is nothing more than a cover for your own opportunism. People like you make me sick.'

O'Driscoll was already beaming but now his eyes lit up, dancing like the sunlight on a Connemara stream.

'At last! I've been waiting years for one of a dreary procession of mealy-mouthed sods to say something like that but you're the only one to have the bloody guts. You're well out of it girl, if you ask me. There's far too many ambitious toadies in the job nowadays!'

And the amount totalled on the document O'Driscoll turned over was gratifyingly large.

Even for someone who already had two million pounds in the bank.

ELEVEN

OUT on the tarmac a Fortress's engines were being test run, the sound reaching Elmeyer as if from another world.

The tall man pacing the stuffy room looked ill at ease in his uniform as though being in the Army was something he'd thought of yesterday.

A much shorter man with slicked and thinning hair combed severely back was immaculate. It was half an hour since he had been escorted to the room by the military policemen who would be standing guard outside the door.

They had been talking a lot, firing questions fast to make him trip over his tongue but Elmeyer's subconscious had honed his wits to meet the assault.

'You appreciate the problem we have Captain Elmeyer,' the tall rumpled officer ran his fingers through a wayward mop of hair.

'I appreciate the problem you have created for yourself, Colonel,' Elmeyer cut in. 'The order has gone out to root out communists and ex-communists and I'm the Red under your bed. Except that I no longer concern myself with carrying a political message other than I do genuinely think that fascism is bad for the health of nations.'

'Spoken like a true communist,' the dapper man snarled.

'I apologise, Major. I somehow imagined we were all in this war to fight fascism.'

'Don't get smart, Captain. Otherwise we might conclude your clever-dick attitude to be the well-rehearsed responses of a card-carrying comrade.'

The tall Colonel, Elmeyer judged, would strike casually without any particular rancour. The smaller one was a compressed ball of hate. It was to him Elmeyer spoke.

'You're too well dressed for this war. I can smell your brilliantine from here. If I smelt like that my crew would get to thinking I danced kind of light on my feet.'

It was said slowly and deliberately. Elmeyer watched for the momentary flicker deep within the man's eyes signalling he was about to lash out.

The little man's fingers curled and uncurled but no punch came. He shot a glance at the tall interrogator who wore the trace of a smile. The small man was hissing with rage, purple rolls of fat trembling over the top of his immaculate collar.

'You want to hit me. Go ahead and hit me.' Elmeyer's voice goaded mockingly.

'Prove yourself a man. Go ahead. Hey, I bet you'd do it if I was tied down now wouldn't you?'

His eyes stayed locked on the short man. His peripheral vision did not pick up the movement.

The punch caught him low, doubling him and making him retch. In the next instant the tall man had seized him by the lapels of his jacket and dumped him back in a chair.

'Do you know what happened there?'

The tall Colonel lit a cigarette and exhaled thoughtfully as Elmeyer sank back. 'You made the assumption that no good guy is going to give you a belt in the guts right here on an American base in dear old fair-minded England, isn't that so?'

Elmeyer said nothing. The Colonel continued: 'It never ceases to amaze me how communists who believe in violent revolution look so surprised when somebody hands them a pasting.'

The man's voice was educated and without a hint of threat.

'I know what you thought when you entered this room. You had me picked out as the reasonable guy and my colleague as the one who would do the beating with a hosepipe. Am I right?'

'Something like that.' Elmeyer winced, regarding the man whose face was now a picture of benign charm.

'Supposing I told you that before the war I had a comfortable and peaceful job teaching philosophy at a state university but that like you I decided that violence ultimately has to be met with violence. Would you begin to see my point of view? Perhaps you'd like to think about that over a cup of coffee.'

Elmeyer nodded assent. 'Yes to the coffee. I'll think about the rest.'

'Good. Perhaps the Major here can rustle some up.'

Before the Major left the room Elmeyer smiled at him in a way he hoped would be taken as insolent.

'You didn't seem to hit it off with my colleague,' the Colonel said after the door had closed.

'Perhaps you and I will get on a little better. I expect you have heard of the Committee for Un-American Activities?'

It was the indulgent voice of a teacher, dusty with tobacco

and good Scotch addressing a bright undergraduate.

'It's not something you read much about in *Stars and Stripes*. I've heard of it that's about all,' Elmeyer replied.

'The committee's task is to root out enemies, or potential enemies within our society,' the tall man said. 'Since we're fighting a war against Germany, Nazi sympathisers are clearly of very great concern but so too are communists. You fought on the republican side in Spain and have frequently expressed communistic views so I'm sure you see why you are of interest to us.'

The words were soft and carefully uttered, as if the tall man had put forward an academic proposition which it was now Elmeyer's job as a starred student to take apart.

'I did fight for the republicans in Spain against Franco and his fascists but like many foreign volunteers I was not a member of the communist party.'

'Go on.'

'By fighting to defend an elected government I was defending democracy. That's all there is to it.'

How trite that sounded, Elmeyer thought. The tall man's grave nod signalled that he was digesting what had been said rather than agreeing. But he'd been drawn on the subject and now he felt like a small animal lured into a trap.

'Do you realise at the time that under federal law anyone who fights for a foreign government can have his nationality taken away and be put in jail?' The Colonel examined the tip of his cigarette.

'A reasonable law if consistently applied,' Elmeyer came back.

'But what about the Americans who fought in the RAF's Eagle Squadrons before our country came into the war? I seem to remember the newspapers making a big fuss of them. Not only were they not arrested for violations of federal law but were later absorbed back into our air force where they were even allowed to keep their British decorations and pilots' wings.'

The tall colonel continued to smoke slowly, inhaling deeply, until he had finished the cigarette which he ground out in a cheap tin ashtray. Ash, which he had not bothered to brush away flecked his lapels. His smile was accompanied by a slight rueful pursing of his lips.

'You've got this all figured out, haven't you? Like a

schoolboy who has done his homework but who can't quite see that the world is about more than providing pat answers to largely hypothetical questions.

'Nevertheless you interest me, Elmeyer. You achieved good grades at school, with a healthy interest in football and the social side of college life. You are hewn from the social strata that provides most of our young commissioned aircrew. Sporty and intelligent but not fine-tuned. You tend toward the thoughtful, one might almost say the intellectual.' The tall man leaned forward in his chair fixing Elmeyer with an unwavering look.

'I would very much like to know who or what set you on the perilous path to Spain, for my own satisfaction as much as anything else. And there's one more thing I'd like to understand.

'You've volunteered to fly extra missions. Was that because you have declared a personal war against the Nazis or is there a less cerebral purpose. To forget a woman, perhaps?'

He paused, still watching Elmeyer who made no reply.

'However it can hardly be that now, given your current involvement with Mrs Amelia Kershaw.' He paused again, noting the flicker in Elmeyer's eyes. 'You seem surprised.'

'She's British. You bastards can't bring her into it.' The Colonel's reflective tone of voice had lulled Elmeyer but now his defences snapped back into place.

'Rather naïve but as it happens we're not interested in her. It's you. A communist even a disavowed one who was a war hero would be of considerable propaganda value to the Red cause back home. All the metal bashers, riveters and grease monkeys who make the planes you fly and the ships and the munitions of war for Uncle Sam all being told that having overthrown the Nazis they should go on to throw the capitalists out on their ears. Talk like that is bad for business and America is about business.' The Colonel shook his head.

'What's worse is you look like a goddamned film star which will have the women workers now a big part of the workforce wetting their pants. It wouldn't surprise me if they put you in a film and once you're in with that crowd of Hollywood self-regarding band of fellow-travellers ... but do I have to go on?'

Elmeyer was silent. Out on the servicing area the aeroplane's engine cut off. He imagined himself levitating out of the window and back to the world he knew. Luck Be A

Lady's battered and stained cockpit might not be the freshest place to be but the smell was of men and machinery going to war. The room they were in stank of lies and manipulation. An instinctive bloody-mindedness would not let him tell them the truth which was that even the mention of a grand cause left him feeling empty and stale and exploited. To Hell with them all; America and the air force, these couple of goons, the workers' fight that had been picked up by union bosses and fucked like a cheap tart. To Hell with everything that kept him from Amelia.

'If things are as you say Colonel, I'm a busted flush. All you have to do is send me home and bury me in a flight instructor's job somewhere in the middle of Kansas.'

The tall man lit another Chesterfield. Perhaps his nerves were bad Elmeyer thought. That's what must come of living in a world in which lies and the truth mingled and spiralled madly together like a plane in a fatal spin.

The Colonel resumed his examination of his cigarette-tip seemingly absorbed for a few moments by the coiling smoke.

'You have a point, although that would be a waste of a good combat pilot. Of course I could just ask the MPs who are standing outside this door to step aside and you could go back to your squadron which is precisely what I intend to do.

'Thank you for calling by. You are dismissed, Captain. Good day to you.'

Elmeyer found himself standing and snapping off a salute.

The MP who must have been listening opened the door from the outside.

It was cold now and getting dark. A badly shot-up Fortress with a huge hole punched under the co-pilot's seat was being towed to a repair hangar. Elmeyer had to steady his hand to light a cigarette.

The suddenness of his dismissal had surprised him but to Hell with it all. He wasn't going to give them any problems. One more mission to sit out and take the flak and then everything would be for Amelia.

Damn them and the coffee that never came.

*   *   *

A hundred miles away and twelve thousand feet up Peter Dainty was humming to himself and thinking that there could never be a time in his life when he would feel more alive.

Anvil-headed storm clouds boiled up beautiful and dangerous into the stratosphere and the darkened earth below created a sinister light. He never thought about women or business when flying. To do so was a good prescription for ending up dead but thoughts of Amelia had entered the Typhoon's cockpit like the smell of wild flowers.

Soon he would plunge through the murk and strike at the target assigned to him under the 'cab rank' system when he would be vectored onto a target. A reconnaissance plane had spotted some German armour dug into a wood in the path of advancing Americans. At this height the earth was a brown-grey carpet slashed with the dull silver of rivers and canals. As he descended the uniformity began to reshape into a tapestry of villages, farms and fields.

Dainty knew the killing-ground well.

Below, people would be scurrying in from the impending storm having bought or bargained meagre loafs and shrivelled vegetables or whatever else was obtainable while a war was being fought on their doorsteps, hearing and probably cursing his ground attack aeroplane.

At three hundred feet he could see the flickers of small arms fire pooped off by frightened soldiers who hadn't a hope of hitting his aircraft.

The wood he had been directed onto was no more than a copse with vehicle tracks leading up to it. A gift horse. Like shooting rats in a barrel.

Dainty put the aircraft down almost to hedge height having taken the decision to attack hard and fast and over a rise, coming onto the position before the gunners could fix on him.

Now the one terrible moment for which the aeroplane had been built and he had been trained. He kicked the rudder and moved the stick to the left and then took aim on the wood which was on a slight elevation, the tops of the trees actually higher than the Typhoon. Flecks of fire were haphazardly coming at him as the ground below flashed past at great speed but his whole being remained fixed on the copse.

Hold it. Hoooold ....

Ignore the fire coming up from the copse because you've got excellent armour and anyway, there's a big engine up front which can soak up punishment. Even if you did got shot down you'd almost certainly be able to make it back to where the Allies were pushing forward. Don't worry. Wait until you can almost see their faces …

With a wild exultation he jabbed the fire button, sending cannon-shells boiling into the copse at point-blank range, so short that there was no drop in the shells' trajectories.

In that vivid, violent moment, the carnage which he could have glimpsed for only the tiniest fraction of a second expanded and he could see and hear the German soldiers at close quarters as his shells ripped and pounded metal and flesh. His inner eye saw the blood and carnage, the shredded and shrieking metal and torn bodied as the treetops flashed by only feet below his wings and he was down over the rise and climbing as he turned setting himself up for another deadly pass.

A punching sound and a sudden rush of air made him swear and his leg warm and wet. He knew he hadn't pissed himself. It was blood. He levelled out a prudent distance from the target and surveyed the damage. The needles on the gauges were where they should be but a lucky bullet had found a gap in the cockpit armour and tore into his flesh. He banked sharply and again lined up on the wood.

Somewhere down there a man was moving, the one who had fired the lucky shot, perhaps.

Well, the bastard was for it.

Now!

A hammering crescendo of cannon fire and stench of cordite. Dainty felt the plane lose airspeed from the recoiling cannons sending a murderous hail into the copse.

This time he left it too long and the tops of the trees snatched at the belly of the aeroplane.

You're hurt and letting it get personal. Think. Resist the temptation of another pass which would give the gunners the chance they needed.

Away to left the storm which he would have to out-run was about to break. The bad flying weather was unlikely to persist but it didn't matter. The wound would mean no flying duties for a couple of weeks at least, giving him time and opportunity for the wooing of Amelia.

The pain was coming now but it had worked out well.

Unknowingly, and in his last seconds on earth an unknown young German had dealt him a good hand.

Rain squalls were hitting the windshield like handfuls of gravel.

Dainty remembered how once as a cadet doing a cross-country solo he'd been caught out by a brewing storm and his desperate, terrified attempts to find the airfield.

When he had at last seen the lights which had been put out for him he'd landed haphazardly and afterwards was grateful for the poor visibility that had shrouded his clumsy arrival. All that seemed a long time ago and flying was now instinctive. Within half-an-hour he was entering the circuit and running through the pre-landing checks.

From the air the forward airfield looked less military encampment and more a primitive agricultural undertaking. Now he could see several aircraft at their dispersals. He set the propeller pitch and lowered the undercarriage and flaps. His right leg was stiffening and felt cold and he winced as he kicked the rudder to make the aircraft line up with the runway. He bled off more power until the descent was set up as it should be and waited for the bump and rumble of the wheels to announce his landing. Now he was down and gunning the engine to send the plane nosing towards its parking dispersal like a fat pig at mealtime, noticing the anti-aircraft gunners in their flat British tin hats and the shot-up German planes which only a few weeks before had been based there, their carcasses bulldozed to one side and stripped for souvenirs.

Two minutes later ground crew were lifting him from the cockpit and sitting him on the grass while a medical orderly was sent for. Somebody threw a groundsheet-cape over his shoulders against the now-driving rain. The feeling of intense cold dissipated when a needle was slipped into him just before he was helped into the battered ambulance. Through the parted canvas tilt he could see the ambulance bucking wildly but it seemed to Dainty that he was wafting gently on an angelic breeze. He was slightly disappointed when the vehicle stopped and he was taken out into a tent, the wet smell of which induced a reverie of school days and camp fires and singing and small trout caught in a Westmoreland tarn.

From violent action to sleepy calm within the same hour. There would be no briefing in the morning. His aircraft would be patched and made ready for another pilot. All he need do for the moment was to lie wrapped in the womb-like warmth of the morphine.

For the first time in many months Peter Dainty the warrior craved peace.

TWELVE

'IF you don't mind me saying so Cap, you look kind of worried.' Frenchie flipped the letter across to Elmeyer.

'Maybe this will cheer you up.'

It was Amelia's scent, exquisite and expensive with a light smell of summer flowers and sunshine.

'Aren't you going to read it?'

Elmeyer had hoped to read it later, savouring the words and the smell of the paper and the perfume in which it had been doused and the thought of Amelia's hand hovering over each well-shaped letter. A lot of his intentions had yielded to Frenchie's potent mix of charm and persuasiveness and now was going to be no different.

'Sure. Why not?'

Work was being carried out on Luck Be A Lady's starboard outer motor. Elmeyer used a mechanic's feeler gauge left on a workbench to slit open the letter. Frenchie watched his face intently as he read it and chuckled.

'It's done you some good anyhow. Does it read as good as it smells?'

Elmeyer grinned and shook his head. 'It's very descriptive.'

'What about?'

Frenchie looked even more of a kid when he asked questions.

'Personal things.'

'Gee, is it really that hot? She always seems such a lady to me.' Frenchie flushed slightly. 'Not that she isn't. These English girls have something about them. So cool, even when they bang like shithouse doors. What is it that's so different about them, do you suppose?'

'You have a feel for words, Frenchie.'

Elmeyer's eyes screwed up as if he were seriously pondering the point.

'It's a big question which I'm not all that sure I can answer. Only people who don't speak English think us and the British are alike.'

It was no good. He slid the letter back into its envelope for reading later. Anyway talking to Frenchie would wash away the sour taste his interrogators had left in his mouth.

'Do you remember the little booklet called *Over There* the army gave you when you first came to England?'

'I remember it. I don't read all that much.'

'Well, it's a little masterpiece that will tell you practically all you need to know about the British. By the time you've read it you will be bewildered which is a good starting point for understanding.'

Frenchie looked doubtful.

'It's a strange thing. My name is English which means that my people were English way back. How can I be different from myself?'

'Well let's see. Your forefathers maybe two hundred years ago were English but as the years went by they changed from being in America.'

Elmeyer sniffed the letter once again and slipped it into the pocket of his flying jacket.

'Your great-great-great-granddaddy didn't bring much with him to America except maybe his wife and his religion. Everything had to be learned afresh in a new land. At some point they realised that the knowledge they brought with them wasn't enough and that new ways would have to be found of doing things.

'Without even knowing it they were leaving their old lives behind and becoming something new and different.'

'You know Cap, you should teach college after the war. I can listen to you. You know a lot of things.'

Elmeyer smiled to himself.

'Not many of which have done me any good. Anyway, college professors will be a dime a dozen after the war.

'Guys like you who know how to make money will be pitching pennies at people like me.'

A shout from an armourer distracted Frenchie who excused himself.

Elmeyer pulled the thick creamy paper from the lined envelope and smelt it once more, pleased that Frenchie's nosiness had been deflected. The letter carried an invitation. Amelia wanted him to go with her to Wales and 'share in the delights of a far, high place'.

He let the letter rest in his lap and fixed at a point in the middle distance, all thoughts other than its invitation driven from his mind.

To be alone with Amelia and to escape the squalor, danger

and corruption of London and the war.

If he got in a leave application quickly it could be cleared within a week. Sure. He'd do it. He'd seen Wales on flying charts and knew it to be about two hundred miles away. During the Spanish war he'd met a few men from there; short, dark, tough colliers whose passions could be roused to song, tears and fighting within the same five minutes.

The difficulty for him lay in summoning up the idea of a country that seemed to have a dimension other than the physical. At the geographical level he got the impression of a place something like the Ozarks or Appalachians with their forested and secret valleys. But in such places the ancient ghosts that haunted the land were those of the red man. Wales was populated by the spirits of the Celts whose blood, however thinly, ran through his own veins.

Frenchie returned from a discussion with an armourer about what he said was Luck Be A Lady's rear gun mounting.

'I'm going to Wales, Frenchie. Amelia's invited me to a little place she stayed with some artist friends before the war. Somewhere I can't get my tongue around.'

'Give it here, Cap. I'm good with English place names.'

'Then I shall defer to your superior knowledge.'

Frenchie seized the letter and gave what to Elmeyer seemed a reasonable imitation of some stranded sea creature opening and shutting its mouth as it gasped for air.

'Jesus. It doesn't even look like English. What the heck language is that?'

'Welsh. I once met some Welsh men in Spain. Their language is one of the oldest in the world and was spoken all over Britain long before the English got here.'

'See! There you go again, getting me all confused,' Frenchie said thrusting the letter back.

'If the English didn't come from England to begin with where the heck did they come from?'

Elmeyer thought about his own name and the genes which resided somewhere within the complex chemistry of his own body, Germanic but with a twist of the Celt from a forebear on his mother's side.

'From mainland Europe. The part we regularly bomb the shit out of.'

'The English are, or were, a collection of Germanic tribes who came here about a thousand-and-a-half years ago and

106

gradually drove the original inhabitants westwards. Those people were what we now call the Welsh.'

'So the English are Krauts?' Frenchie shot back.

'Most of them wouldn't thank you for putting it *that* way.

'Look. Remember what I said about people becoming American? It's the same with the English. They've been here so long that their language and way of life has changed into something else.'

Another voice shouted for Frenchie but he waved it away.

'I want to get this straight otherwise I'll go crazy. We're all here because the Germans already here want to stop the Germans who didn't make it getting a slice of the pie. Is that what this war is about?'

'Frenchie.' Elmeyer gave a sigh of mock-resignation.

'I wouldn't worry about it too much. It was all a long time ago. Our government and England are at war with Germany and we're caught up in it. Don't send yourself nuts trying to work out why.'

'Okay, Cap. Anyway, they want me to look over something in the plane.'

With Frenchie gone Elmeyer's mind strayed back to the tall rumpled and urbane Colonel and the slightly crazy little Major.

His own rejection of communism had come about after exhausting himself fighting for a cause and seeing the enormous blood-ransom that sooner or later all political creeds demanded.

But Karl Marx had been right about one thing. Which Frenchie in a small way had demonstrated. Those expected to do the working and fighting would be asking many more questions from now on. The Frenchies of this world saw the absurdity in war. They lived for the day and for their families and let more foolish men get on with the theorizing and political posturing.

Love was all that mattered. The exquisite sensation which drove the race forward to some destination which he could not imagine but was not yet ready to believe was God. Love was everything. For if there were no purpose in love could there be meaning to life itself?

THIRTEEN

AMELIA.

Like honey on a Welsh love spoon but Amelia who?

A woman would have written down the full name of her lover dwelling lovingly and longingly over the shape of the word, mouthing it as she wrote but the word stood alone.

Neither was there an address nor telephone number in the back of the diary although the name appeared several times from the midsummer of 1944 onwards. Perhaps Mair was wrong, reading into the shape of the letters something that wasn't there. Perhaps it had been with Amelia and the diary's owner as with thousands of couples caught up and tossed around by war; lives interlocking for a fleeting moment before being blown apart. People jumping into bed with one another whenever the chance arose and yet with the conventions of a more reserved age still observed. Discolated and with little possibility of a successful outcome. A bit like playing a high-speed computer game with the instructions in Aramaic script.

Mair was in her own house with a rather larger than usual whisky by her side. Having put down the diary and having allowed her thoughts to stray she once more picked it up, feeling the slight curvature which, even after almost seventy years indicated that it had once been carried in a man's hip pocket.

Amelia. The one who ameliorates, or makes better. What comfort had she brought to the diary's owner?

It was while searching inside the back cover where an address for Amelia might have been jotted down that she found the secret pocket.

Had it have been well-used there would have been a smudge or stretching and curling of the edge caused by poking fingers but there was nothing to betray its presence.

And there was something in the pocket.

Afraid of mauling or marking the piece of folded paper she retrieved tweezers from a boxful of oddments in the kitchen and coaxed out the coarse white paper.

It unfolded stiffly revealing words unread in a Biblical life-span.

She spread it out with a vague trepidation as though a spell was being broken.

'The Colliers' Arms, Blaendiffaith, Monmouthshire,' was printed at the top of the receipt.

'Received from Capt Elmeyer three pounds eight shillings and sixpence for bed and breakfast,' and a date: 'August 24, 1944' together with a telephone number NEW 551.

A jolt like a mild electrical shock surged from eyes to fingertips. Words began to form but left her body only as an exhalation.

The receipt had been slipped inside the diary's pocket as a record of the Colliers' address and location but also as a memento of a treasured moment.

Wild thoughts raced through her mind before breaking up into a kaleidoscope of confusing patterns.

The diary had been left to her father. For no reason which was obvious he had planned for her to inherit it at the same time as a very large sum of money. Why should this be?

Mair sipped her drink and let the fumes mingle with tangled images drawn from a fusion of memory and imagination.

Her very first recollections of the village came from the very early 1960s and were of coal fires and the sun heating the bracken to a drowsy warmth and boiled white cotton sheets pegged out to dry and puffed up like a galleon's sails with trilling skylarks piping praise to their Maker.

The last of the mines had gone almost 30 years before and with them many of the young people, driven down the valley like yearling salmon making for the vast and unknown ocean of the outside world. Even in her own lifetime the lines of drab, neat cottages had seen laughing brides carried across their threshholds and corpses feet-first in the opposite direction. Those same doors were now painted in bright colours with cars jostling to park outside them but still something of the past remained like a mysterious echo in an empty room speaking of a lost past of community spirit and togetherness in both tragedy and triumph.

She set the receipt to one side taking up each of the wartime photographs in turn not only to look at them but to feel them, rubbing them between her thumb and forefinger as if some hidden meaning might be coaxed from the heavy paper.

In the black-and-white 1940s the taking of a picture was an event for which men and women put on their Sunday best. Hats were thrust jauntily to the backs of heads and cigarettes flourished. Both men in the photographs were handsome but there was a shyness about the one in American uniform she found appealing and the thought crossed her mind that any man she slept with would have to be something like him.

There had been men in her life. At one time in her childhood boys had seemed the most mystifying of creatures, strangely attractive despite their repellence. She and the other girls had teased and laughed at them but each had treasured the shy glances meant only for them, cast at a time when the boys were growing and thickening, their voices dropping and the smell and the power of them working joyous mayhem with the female heart.

And what of the RAF man? The eyes which looked cold and capable of killing at another level would absorb love just as a boy racked with guilt and exultant cruelty at the killing of a small animal might seek comfort in his mother's arms. She had noted that in Ven's face, not many times, but each time she had seen it she had remembered. Was it possible through the veil of years and the imperfections of an ancient photograph to see the face of Compton Picard, her dear old Ven?

She took another sip of the whisky. So many questions and after such a long time no hard facts from which to quarry an answer. History she reflected was the most teasing and infuriating of all human endeavours because when the time came to ask the most important questions those capable of answering them had passed beyond reach.

And yet.

The woman's name and piece of paper folded into the diary made a link between the man in the picture who must be this Captain Elmeyer and Amelia almost certain and not only that. Compton Picard, who every instinct in her body told her was the RAF man in the picture was living in Blaendiffaith which in 1944 had obvious significance for the American and Amelia.

The whisky which was supposed to have eased her mind had instead made it fretful and when she got out of bed in the early hours of the morning heavy rain was drumming on the slate roof. As dawn broke she fell into an uneasy slumber dreaming of three people - the American in the picture, herself and Compton Picard - reaching out towards each other but just failing to link hands as lightning flickered and the downpouring of a storm rose to engulf them.

*   *   *

The next day was one of signing forms and talking to people on the telephone about impending retirement and of Aneurin's funeral.

Not all that long before the two things were distant events regarded much as inhabitants of remote islands might hear reports of great storms which they hoped would never make landfall.

Now they hit like a tidal wave driven on by the force of a gale.

It was not until towards the end of a busy day during which she had typed out her resignation and spoken to the undertaker who was both brisk and cheerful that Talfan's name came into her head.

Talfan was the father of Tomos, the Colliers' present landlord and still alive, as old as Methuselah. His incumbency must have stretched at least as far back as the War.

After work she went home to change and then to the Colliers' where she sat in a patch of sunlight picking at the *Daily Telegraph* crossword and watching specks of dust spiral in the shaft of light coming through the window and waiting for Talfan's son to emerge from the cellar where she could hear him stacking beer crates.

Unaware of her presence Tomos Evans lowered the heavy cellar trap door behind him and humming tunelessly crossed to the sink to rinse his hands. He looked up when she gave a cough and gave a smile in return.

'It's a few years since you were last in here with me.' The words held no reproof. In her tomboy childhood they had been close playmates.

'Duw, you bring back memories,' Tomos said softly.

'My Dad and yours sitting where you're sat now talking about plays and books and religion and politics upon the last two subjects there being much disagreement. The Pontypool Thespians was safe topic though, the shenanigans as well as the productions. Loved the stage your Dad did but a big lump of a fellow. Couldn't see him in anything by Noel Coward.'

Despite herself, she began to cry. The day's duties had demanded she keep emotions in check but safe in the warmth of an old friendship she could let the mask slip.

'I feel as though he hasn't gone very far away. Do you suppose he will haunt this place? Him and Talfan cronies for ever?' Mair was aware of the rising inflection in her voice. The grief at her father's death was catching up with her and making her hysterical. She allowed herself to be led to a chair.

'I hope so. Now, have a drink with me. We have an excellent ale despite its being brewed in England. Then we shall sit and talk. It is possible to grieve and to be content at the same time.'

The beer was hoppy and strong and came in a pint glass, no other being permissible in the Colliers'.

'Is that better?' Tomos asked after they had sat in silence for some minutes just listening to the ticking of the ancient clock.

'Now you've had a drink with me I don't feel so uncomfortable asking you whether this is a personal or professional call. Naturally I would prefer the former.'

Tomos, although nearing sixty and never married, had a reputation with the ladies. A *'cavaliere servente'* Aneurin, who loved the sound of words even if he did not know what they meant, had called him.

'Nothing to do with officialdom and anyway I'm leaving the police. I was hoping you would put on some food after Dad's funeral.'

'With pleasure.'

'And there's something else. Something to do with him and my dad going right back to the war has been niggling at me.'

Tomos cocked an eyebrow.

'Something private and personal if such concepts exist in Blaendiffaith.'

Tomos's upheld hand conveyed a magnanimous patience.

Half-an-hour later Mair was driving eastwards on the country road towards the nursing home the location of which Tomos had marked on her map. Even with the aid of the Ordnance Survey and satellite navigation she took two wrong turnings before arriving in front of a two-storey building of weathered brick facing south towards the Blorenge mountain blue in the distance.

She was unprepared for the figure that greeted her once she had signed in at reception and been shown to the room. Talfan Evans was clearly determined to stem the tide of years with the dual weapons of physical presence and high spirits.

'Tomos called me shortly after you left to say you were coming. Come and drink some of this. Guaranteed to keep senility at bay. I take a couple of bottles a week at present but I suppose I shall have to increase the dose as time passes.'

Eccentrically splendid in a yellow silk dressing gown with a tumble of silk handkerchief from the breast pocket and with a mass of groomed white hair Talfan held out a glass towards her.

'I shouldn't really.'

'Bugger that, girl. This stuff is ambrosia, the drinking allows you to view the world through a benevolent golden haze.'

They clinked glasses.

'Tomos also told me you wanted some information bearing upon your father. I suppose I should be grieving for him except that at our age there is a feeling that one is on the next bus, so to speak. In some ways I hope the Christians are right. I should like to think I shall shortly be seeing the old devil.' Talfan sniffed his wine.

'It's the younger ones like you who are left behind feel it the most but perhaps I should not be so bloody cheerful in your presence.'

'It's all right. Honestly.' Mair tried to check a tear with a smile.

'It's an odd thing but I still smell his pipe.'

'Oh, there's my girl.' Talfan eased himself from his seat and placed his hand on Mair's arm.

'Let the tears come. These are the worst days. After the funeral and time to feel sorry for yourself there will be only pleasant memories.' The old man took out his handkerchief and gave it to Mair. It smelled pleasantly of lavender.

'I'm sorry. I feel a fool.'

'Sorry for your feelings? But come now and tell me your news. Still with the sworn enemies of the working class, are you? I never approved of your being a policewoman I told your father straight. I can see him now sitting there stuffing that smelly old pipe of his. 'Talfan,' he would say with not a little pompousness, 'It is only parliamentary democracy that allows you to preach your Godless bolshevism. Do you imagine Comrade Stalin would put up with your nonsense for so long?'

'To which I would reply 'Aneurin. If your precious parliamentary democracy could change things at more than a snail's pace they'd make it illegal. Anyway,' I would add telling him something I don't think he ever quite grasped, 'Leon Trotsky is more to my taste. Pure international socialism with no borders anywhere in the world, except of course the one between Wales and England.'

Talfan sat back and poured his second glass of wine.

'To the dictatorship of the proletariat!'

Mair allowed her glass to be refilled and raised it a couple of inches, the biggest concession she felt a servant of the Crown should make.

'However. I don't suppose you came here to talk about my memories although I must tell you. I have decided to adopt a more open mind on the question of the Hereafter in the hope of seeing Aneurin the reactionary old bugger sometime very soon.'

'It's wise to keep your options open,' Mair smiled. 'But I did come in the hope of ransacking your memories.'

She passed him the photographs.

'These were with Dad's things. There's a strong possibility the man in American uniform was in Blaendiffaith during the war, possibly with a woman. It's a long time ago, I know.'

Mair watched Talfan shuffle the pictures, his eyes flickering from one figure to the next.

She was holding her breath, a habit with her since childhood.

'I can't recall the man in the RAF uniform. As you said it's long time ago,' handing the pictures back.

Mair had built up a picture of Ven as the RAF man into a near-certainty. Talfan must have caught her look of disappointment.

'I am sorry.'

But there was a teasing quality in the words which sent her eyes back to scrutinising his face across which flickered an impish smile.

'I'm surprised though you didn't ask me about the Yank and his girlfriend. I remember them as if it were only last week.'

For several seconds Mair was speechless and then said as if challenging the words to escape. 'You knew them? You spoke to them?'

'Indeed so.

'The Yank was of a similar political persuasion to myself

although perhaps not quite so avid for the immediate imposition of working class rule under a South Wales soviet.

'I thought she was generally on the right side but a bit flighty in her politics. She was an artist and therefore to be excused the rigours of dialectical materialism on Bohemian grounds.

'She came back after the war and took the Old Rectory where your friend Mr Picard now lives. How's that for recall?'

'She came to live in Blaendiffaith, in the Old Rectory?' Mair said, excitement pulsing through her.

'Close your mouth, girl, you might catch a fly. That is what I said.'

'Do you remember her name?'

'I believe I do.' Talfan sipped his drink and glanced at her, enjoying the theatricality of the moment. It was several seconds before he spoke.

'Amelia. I can't remember her last name but definitely Amelia. She bunked up with the Yank at the Colliers' some time towards the end of the war. I met him a few times before he was killed on the mountain. Damned strange thing that was. Some thought it a bit fishy. He had a funny foreign-sounding name. Let me think, now.'

Mair ached to help the old man to form the name written on the receipt. A pulse tickled in her temple as she waited breathlessly for his word.

'A bit Germanic. Ah, yes. I remember. 'Elmeyer' E-L-M-E-Y-E-R. James Elmeyer. I'm sure that was it. The girl was a bit of all right with a nice swing to the hips and a throaty laugh that could cause a fluttering in the dovecotes. Both of them were well educated or long in the head as we say around here and it sticks in my mind that she might have been married although not to the Yank. If she wore a wedding ring nobody paid it any heed. In those days we could forgive a lot in the name of love. We are in love with love, us Welsh.'

A playful beam of light illuminated Talfan's face in profile, lessening the shadows of his eye sockets and making a lighted veneer which covered the wrinkles of his great age. He was once handsome and was still beautiful, Mair thought.

'Do you want to know why I remember her name? It was the same as the great American flier, Amelia Earhart who came to Wales in 1927, the first woman to cross the Atlantic by air. I remember as a boy reading about it in the *Western Mail*.'

A cloud passed over the sun darkening the room and she could see in the low light that Talfan was very tired.

'Do you know why they came to Blaendiffaith, Amelia and her American?' Mair asked softly.

'If I could only find out her surname. There's a reasonable chance of her still being alive.'

Talfan turned towards her to meet the question, collecting the skeins of far memory.

'They came here for the same reason as any two attractive people might want to bunk off together. I don't know why those chose Blaendiffaith but it's as good as anywhere and better than most. Your father, being a nosey policeman, would have made it his business to know her name but we never think to ask the questions that matter while the person who can answer them is alive.'

Talfan reached out to touch Mair's arm once more. Mair sensed the interview was moving towards its end.

'I'm not sure I ever knew but listen girl, I am sorry about your father. The bloody infuriating man was my friend for over eighty years.'

'You have asked me questions so I am going to ask you one back. Have you a lover as we speak?'

The question was not unwelcome. It was the privilege of the old to ask such things.

'Not for two years. The loss hurt very much until very recently but now it's been overshadowed by Dad and I've got a bee in my bonnet about Amelia and James Elmeyer and Blaendiffaith. Perhaps I'm getting obsessed: an ageing spinster grasping for things long in the past.'

'Surely the money must put a different light on things?'

No point asking Talfan how he knew about her inheritance. He might have known for years. Anyway, news in Blaendiffaith travels fast sometime arriving even before it happens.

'You know the old saying about money not buying happiness. James Elmeyer never had the chance to see where love took him for better or for worse. Get another lover is my advice.'

The glint in the old man's eyes was as if fading embers had been blown back into a hot and mischievous life.

'Anyone will do for a kick-off even if it ends up not liking them very much at all. You've got to keep the emotions and the tear ducts exercised, see? It wouldn't be Welsh not to and remember this. A lonely retirement lasts a long and bloody lonely time. Did Aneurin leave you much, if you don't mind my asking?'

'Yes. A lot. Much more than I was expecting.'

Talfan nodded and smiled and it crossed her mind that he knew more than he was telling.

'Well, remember. A shroud has no pockets.'

Talfan had drained his drink and his fingers were kneading his knees as though doubting their mortal presence. He began to doze. Gently, she once more held out the picture of the RAF man. Talfan slowly shook his head.

'I can't ever remember seeing him. Handsome bugger though, isn't he?' he said with a curious little chuckle. 'But look I'm getting tired so I'll let you go. I suspect a surfeit of wine. Wonderful stuff for encouraging the reveries but with a tendency to send you nodding off.'

His eyes closed and a soft breath whistled out from between gently pursed lips. Mair stood, bending down to kiss him firmly.

'God, girl. I could have done something about that thirty years ago.' And then a long and suspenseful pause.

'Why does the name Kershaw stick in my mind?'

It was said in a whisper so faint that Mair had to stoop to hear.

Her mouth began to shape a question, but Talfan already was lost somewhere in his enviable dream.

*   *   *

The Valley, stingy with its rations of sunshine even in late summer had this year relented and sent a large part of Blaendiffaith's people to the seaside or to barbecues in their back gardens. They would all tumble in later, sun-pinked and jolly, but now the Colliers' was warming its slate and lolling in the sun like an old dog with its tongue hanging out, empty apart from Mair and Tomos.

'It's an afternoon for the relishing of a strong dry cider with a sharpness to set the teeth on edge.'

Tomos shepherded Mair to an outside table overlooking the village and fussily pushed her chair in behind her as she sat.

'Local stuff from under the counter. Mumbling juice they

call it but with a good profit margin.'

Mair took a few more sips and gazed over a Blaendiffaith dazed into a near-silence by the unaccustomed heat.

'Not bad at all. Talfan would approve of your purely local arrangement.'

She looked over the rim of his glass and tried to give him an official look which was countered by a grin. It must have been forty years since she mused that as a little girl the Blaendiffaith Players had given her a walk-on part in Gilbert and Sullivan's *Patience* at the Miners' Institute while he had been wreathed in laurels for his rendition of Reginald Bunthorpe. He knew her in those days and their mutual understanding had survived the years.

'I remember our dads sitting here on fine days and when it got colder and wetter retreating to the fireside in the snug. Theatre, books, philosophy and occasionally religion although neither of them were particularly adept at polishing chapel pews with their backsides.'

Tomos smiled into his glass but his eyes were far away in the past.

Mair had gone to the grammar school long after dreamy Tomos with his wide brown eyes had gone to the secondary modern and after that joined the army. She could remember him coming home on leave in his coarse woollen uniform with creases so sharp you could have cut your fingers. After that he'd worked on the buses before coming to help his father at the Colliers'. An air of theatricality had always clung to him and sometimes she had wondered why he hadn't sought a career on the stage rather than coming back to Blaendiffaith which, for all its cosiness, was where ambition was born to die. About Mrs Evans his mother she could remember almost nothing. Probably she was of that Valleys breed of women that served their husbands dutifully and cosseted their sons into a wistful and gentle inertia.

'Aye. On winter nights when the wind is whistling around this place I shall see the old boys by the fireside. But you didn't come to exchange nostalgic ramblings is my guess.'

'You should have been a detective,' Mair said lightly.

'Psychologist more like. Every publican should automatically qualify for a degree in the subject.'

She produced the diary and photographs.

'These were sent on to me after my father died. I wonder what if anything you make of them.'

Tomos took the diary and as she had done held it to his nose, smelling the old paper. He glanced at the pictures of the two men with the woman before singling out the snapshot of the group posing by the nose of their aircraft.

'Luck Be A Lady. Good name for a plane. A B-17G Flying Fortress, instantly recognisable to all small boys who were given model aeroplane kits for Christmas. This version of the bomber was introduced towards the war's end and since the crew appear to be wearing only light clothing and the trees in the far background are in leaf, a reasonable assumption was that this photograph was taken in the summer of 1944, around the time I was born in fact.'

'Where do you think it was taken? Not around here, surely?'

'A long way from here. Most of the American bases were in the East of England, Essex, Suffolk, Cambridgeshire and Bedfordshire although the Yanks regularly flew over Wales on training exercises. During the war a plane like this crashed up near the Tump. They used to say it was a German on a special mission but you know how folk like to dress things up. Some of the wreckage is still up there. It's an eerie spot.'

Mair remembered the place from a golden day when holding hands they had climbed through the fields of bracken bounded by tumbledown stone walls to picnic near half-buried wreckage, the twisted aluminium remains whitened with corrosion making her think of the bones of a giant prehistoric creature. They had drunk wine and laughed and had embraced and afterwards frightened each other with stories.

'I'll get us another drink,' Tomos volunteered. 'The day is too good to waste.'

He disappeared into the pub's cool darkness the clacking of the lifted latch unlocking a little cell of memory when forty years before she would call at the Colliers' for lemonade. She wondered how many thumbs had pressed the latch since then and whether tiny imprints of their owners' passing had been absorbed into the old pub's stones. Perhaps that's what ghosts were; traces of someone's vital life-force locked into wood, stone, brick and plaster.

The latch clicked again and Tomos emerged carrying two glasses of cider and a small and scuffed attaché case hooked around one finger.

'Something I've dug out might interest you. My poor old dad's memory must be going. I'm surprised he didn't tell you about his little archive.'

The case's stitching had rotted away and its cheap metal hasps rusted. A pen-knife and much pressure from Tomos's thumb were needed before the locks yielded. Mingled with the smell of old leather, paper, decaying glue and cloth lining arose the faintest aroma of lavender. Tomos pulled out the contents and spread them on the table.

'Let's see. Diaries going back to Lord knows when and photographs.' Tomos held up some tiny snapshots which were little better than smudges of grey.

'One of me as a nipper but what's this?'

Beneath the first stratum of papers lay a picture sketched in charcoal on heavy drawing paper which Tomos extracted and blew upon to disperse the dust.

'Let me have a look at the Yank again.'

Mair produced Elmeyer's photograph and Tomos held it next to the charcoal drawing, eyes flicking from one surface to the other.

'Now what do you make of that?'

As her eyes fixed on the signature pointed to by Tomos her heartbeat quickened.

'It's the same man and the signature on the drawing is Amelia Kershaw.'

The name was written in a sloping hand and in full and with the name of the village and dated September 24, 1944.

*　　*　　*

The sky was of a darkening blue and a coolness had crept into the air. Soon the sun would be below the ridge of the mountain putting Blaendiffaith into a premature darkness. Two days from now the sun would rise on the day of Aneurin's funeral.

While her father lay in the chapel of rest she had come to think of him as not dead but resting. Soon it would be time to commit his body to the soil of the village he loved. Grief, she knew, would hit her in waves. Her inheritance and its elusive connection with the crashed wartime bomber had insulated her from the sharp edge of sorrow but now it began to cut keenly.

There had been another child David, the brother in the RAF who had been killed early in the war. Mair found her thoughts turning towards him aching for something to give her image of him some reality. Blood of her blood, bone of her bone and now eternally a citizen of the mysterious republic that was the past together with Ursula, Aneurin's second wife and Mair's mother.

One day Mair herself, last of the line, would lie in the little graveyard and the moss would grow over her grave and there would be nobody left in the village to speak of her.

After more riflings punctuated by occasional chuckles Tomos pulled out *Argus* and *Western Mail* cuttings in which her father was mentioned his performances rated as 'masterly', 'convincing' and 'played with verve and brio'. That, in the end, was what it all came to; a few mentions in a newspaper, the memories of an old friend and the tears of a daughter.

In that's night fitful sleep Mair's brain had taken the black-and-white photographic images from the diary and turned them into grotesque parodies cavorting and laughing in sinister silence.

The morning of her father's funeral broke as grey and solemn as a dirge. Compton Picard was the first to arrive at Mair's house. The two made polite talk and drank sherry. Villagers began arriving and relatives ate cake and drank tea and spoke in hushed tones while discreetly investigating Mair's living arrangements.

When at last the two big black cars came Ven and Tomos were invited into the one reserved for principal mourners. As was still the custom in the Valley a top-hatted undertaker walked in front of the hearse for a hundred yards before climbing into the front passenger seat for the half-mile to Bethesda Chapel. There, the flower-covered coffin was placed in front of the covered baptismal bath.

Mair met the quick smiles and oblique glances reserved for funerals. Chief Inspector O'Driscoll, half-a-head taller than the rest caught her eye and gave a solemn nod.

Mair took her place directly in front of her father's coffin which seemed too small to contain the remains of such a big man. Ven in the pew leaned forward to squeeze her elbow, Ven who had let her into his rich imaginative world and for who for the sake of her quest she would have to hurt.

There were hymns and the minister austere in dark suit and collar and tie spoke of Aneurin as though he had known him well which he had not.

The superb excavatory skills of Blaendiffaith rabbits who must have had mining in the blood had cratered Bethesda's graveyard and such markers as still stood jostled and leaned like a rugby crowd craning to watch a thrilling passage of play as the coffin was carried out.

The displaced soil from Aneurin's grave had been heaped neatly and covered with artificial grass, a chemically-lurid green clashing with the wispy, pale fronds of cemetery grass waving in a light breeze. Aneurin's ghost had a fine blue sky to patrol and make sure that everything was proceeding in peace and with dignity. His last connection with the world would be severed when they gently lowered his coffin into the grave in sure and certain knowledge of the Resurrection.

How many times in his watch over Blaendiffaith she wondered had her father passed Bethesda and the very spot where he was to be buried?

Perhaps on dark nights he had stood by the graves of his wives and son and spoken tender words of remembrance. As a child one never thought of adults grieving but now the knowledge of his pain at the death of handsome and doomed David and his wives one of whom was her mother made her want to cry out.

Mair prayed to God as Aneurin was lowered into Blaendiffaith's good earth.

FOURTEEN

THE storm snatched away their laughter and scattered it in the Jeep's wake, battering at the canvas tilt as the little car bounced westwards.

'Do you think we'll get to Wales before dark?' Amelia shouted excitedly over the noise of the engine and the storm.

'Who cares if we have to spend another night on the trail? It's an adventure!' Elmeyer bawled back.

'I just wish they'd fitted electric windshield wipers to these things. This way is tough on the arms.'

'I'll do it.' Amelia took the handle at the top of the windscreen that operated the manual wipers and gave it a crank but to little effect. 'Even a tempest can't dampen my spirits!' she shouted back and kissed him on the cheek just as he swerved to miss a looming pothole.

'A whole week away from London and on a real-life adventure. I've never been to Wales before. What do you suppose it's like? Perhaps the locals won't like us.'

'Why shouldn't they? We're just two young people in love. Everybody likes young people in love. It says so in all the magazines.'

'You're younger than me. Only a little, but still younger. Does that worry you?'

Elmeyer laughed but knew the question warranted his engaging her eyes for a split second.

'Does it look as though it's been preying on my mind?'

'You never know. You're a foreigner and you might not always show your emotions.'

'That's rich coming from an Englishwoman.' Elmeyer waited for a straight stretch before risking a snatched kiss.

'Barring a blow out .... '

'Puncture?'

'Puncture, or being arrested as spies we should make Chepstow by evening. After that it's another twenty-five, maybe thirty miles. Anyhow, what's the rush? Have you got shares in whatever this place is called?'

'Blaendiffaith. They told me how to pronounce it when I telephoned. You'd better learn to say it. People are impressed if you speak a bit of their language. 'Blaen' means the 'head of' something, like the head of a valley.'

'Okay. So what does the rest of it mean, smarty-pants?'

'Don't be tiresome. I'm just giving you a taste of the language. Isn't this absolutely marvellous away from the war and dear, dreary old London?'

After a few miles the wind dropped and the rain relented giving them a view of fields bounded by dry stone walls. Villages in dips between low, tree-crowned hills, each with its church spire slender as a thorn.

'Where are we?' Elmeyer asked.

She frowned at the dog-eared AA handbook of 1920s vintage.

'Miles yet. We're not even at the Gloucestershire border. I can't understand why they don't save a lot of botheration and put the road signs back up. It was a good idea to try and bamboozle invading Germans but they're hardly likely to invade now.'

The last part of the sentence was drowned out as a bomber plane roared overhead at no more than two hundred feet.

'A Halifax. The RAF boys are busy today.'

Amelia had intended to show off her increasing knowledge of flying but bit her tongue, sensing rather than seeing Elmeyer's darkening brow.

'Busy is something I've come to associate with the RAF of late,' he said wryly, immediately cursing himself for an utter damned jealous, lovesick dope.

'I'm not altogether sure what you meant by that.'

'Nothing. It's just my big mouth.'

Behind them another Halifax bomber clawed its way into the lightening sky. Elmeyer pulled the Jeep into the side of the road. Another aircraft was landing and he watched it so that she should not see his eyes.

'I'm not angry, Amelia. I haven't the right to be. We haven't made any promises between us. I just want to know what I'm up against. I will fight for you, you know.'

Amelia shot a malevolent glance in the direction of the RAF planes as if blaming them for the destruction of a charmed moment.

'I suppose it was Frenchie told you about Peter Dainty. I don't blame him. He worships you. Perhaps the scarf was some sort of a warning. Green *is* for jealousy.'

A bomber about to land sank from their line of sight as another turned onto its final approach.

'Flying Officer Peter Dainty. Dashing sort of a fellow don't you know, or so I'm told.' The mock-British accent was mincing with a bitter edge.

Amelia looked straight ahead her lips compressed, gripping the AA handbook squarely as might an apprehensive student about to face a test.

'American innocence which can be so charming can also be bloody irritating.'

Each word flew like a chip from a block of ice.

'Yes, I know Peter Dainty and yes, I've spent time with him and he intrigues me. I'm sorry but you don't own me, James.'

She lifted the AA book up and lowered it slowly and precisely back onto her lap.

'People are much crueller in wars. Not just us. Everyone.'

'What about your husband fighting for King and Country? Does he accept this new code of moral behaviour?' Elmeyer shot back, hearing the aggrieved note in his voice and hating it.

'Oh, for Christ's sake, James! I don't imagine that when his ship docks in Australia or Hawaii or wherever else he signs up for Bible reading classes while the rest of the crew screws everything with a pulse.

'I suppose you're going to ask me whether I've slept with Dainty. Yes, I have.'

Tears began to well but her expression was fixed and gripped the book hard.

'None of us can afford to invest too heavily in somebody else surely you must see that. The Germans are pounding London with rockets again and you might be shot out of the sky at any time and that goes for Peter Dainty and thousands of other mothers' sons. What if the war against Japan goes on for years? Am I supposed to stay at home like Ulysses' Penelope weaving a shroud to flummox potential suitors while she waits for her husband to come home from the wars? The rules have changed, James. We all have to take what we can when we can.'

That's what it came down to in the end, Elmeyer thought. Everyone trying to make their own way in the face of inscrutable and powerful forces. Amelia trying to find love; Frenchie trying to make money for his young wife and sick child; himself, losing his political faith and now just trying to get through the next couple of missions.

And Dainty ... what of Dainty? A crook and an adventurer and the thief of other men's girls. Oh, for God's sake, man, he chided himself. Do you realise how pathetic that sounds? You quit the cause that other men have died for without too many regrets and you're actually in the process of stealing another man's wife at this moment. Drop the damned hypocrisy.

'I've hurt your feelings, James, and I'm sorry.'

Amelia took the guide book from her lap and lay it behind the seat. He took her in his arms, kissing her fiercely pressing her breasts from outside her clothing and listening as her breathing became sharper and harder. Her face was cold with the wind and rain but her lips warm and, as he prised them with his tongue, tasting of something sweet, sweeter than the finest confection.

She had opened his fly and now it was his turn to gasp as her cold hand began its rythmic work. He found the hem of her skirt, enjoying the feel of the satin lining and the comparative roughness of the wool as he thrust it back from her knees to her hips.

'Oh, my God. You're so sweet,' she whispered, first probing his ear with her tongue and then biting it quite hard, a wicked little act which in turn made him drive his finger further into her.

'God may or may not have much to do with it, and I'm not that sweet. Hurry. I want you.'

Clutching his trousers and almost doubled Elmeyer sprang from the driver's seat and around to Amelia's side where he knelt on the sodden grass, his lips and tongue finding the spot his fingers had been so ardently exploring his previous anger charged with jealousy now transformed into another, urgent passion.

His tongue having done its work in that place he pulled away his lips and put them to her mouth at the same moment thrusting into her with bruising force.

'Is it better now that you're fucking me? Not so jealous now?'

She was gripping him fiercely.

Elmeyer gave a deep moan as his body tautened into a last spasm, one the fringes of his consciousness sensing a rumbling which he thought must be upheavals within his own body.

So utterly had they been absorbed in the violence of their coming together that they'd failed to hear approaching vehicles.

With a roar of engines and blasts of exhaust smoke the first of a convoy of British Army trucks drew level with the Jeep and a chorus of bawdy cheers went up. Elmeyer hoisted his trousers and tugged Amelia's skirt into an approximation of where it should be. He buried his face into her neck as if to kiss it but could sense that she was looking beyond him. Now she was smiling and waving.

'Come on darling, wave to them!' she cried.

'Acknowledge a salute from one gallant ally to another!'

*   *   *

With the passing of the storm they made good progress.

'That bout of passionate lovemaking was really quite naughty of you. You're well on your way to becoming an uninhibited Bohemian,' Amelia ribbed him. 'I can see you in sandals and a sloppy old sweater agonising about things.'

The late summer sun emerged from behind the retreating storm clouds touching them with pink and gold and releasing the sharp smell of rain water on limestone walls as they sped westward.

'It's so incredibly beautiful, especially in this light. No wonder the people who lived here thought they were God's anointed'.

The words were spoken softly and to herself.

Elmeyer had unsnapped the Jeep's canvas and cellophane side windows. Amelia took in lungfuls of rain-freshened air as they drove westward, her city-accustomed eyes taking in the rolling fields and darkening blue of the sky.

'This was England's Texas, did you realise that?'

After the fierceness of their lovemaking an intimacy had come back into her voice.

'All the lovely houses and churches were built on the wool trade. Quite literally on the backs of sheep.'

'Sheep and men and women who had to do all the work and got screwed with poor wages and short lives. Every time I see beauty I wonder how much suffering went into making it.'

'Now you're talking like a dreary communist. For goodness sake relax darling. God's actually quite forgiving of people who create beautiful things.'

'Are you sure? As a painter you might have an interest in saying that.'

'I tell you what. There's a church spire a couple of miles ahead. Why don't we stop and ask the Almighty?'

Elmeyer pulled the Jeep in close to a stone wall into which was set a lych gate and they walked hand-in-hand towards the ancient grey oaken door of a church which seemed too imposing for the village in which it was set. The clunk of the latch being raised echoed around the greenish, submarine interior in which there lingered a faint smell of incense mixed with that of dust, ancient wood, polish and flowers.

'I should feel oppressed by this but I'm not,' Elmeyer whispered but if Amelia heard him she did not reply. 'It's ... tribal. British people look like Americans and talk the same language but the guts of it come from a different place. How old is this place do you suppose?'

The green scarf which Amelia had used in the Jeep to fend off the drips and draughts now covered her head. The small act of humility surprised him.

'The oldest bits might go right back to the Saxons over a thousand years ago but most of it is Norman with the Victorians putting in their pennyworth. Of course the Celts might have had their incantations and ceremonies on this site long, long before all of that.'

'It sounds spooky the way you say it. Did they sacrifice people do you suppose?'

'Certainly. Burned them in wicker cages or draped sacred oaks with their entrails.'

A burnished brass plaque with its ornate lettering picked out in red seemed to suck in and reflect the church's sepulchral light.

'Look here. A memorial to the human sacrifices of our age. Americans used to find it hard to understand what the loss of so many men in the Great War meant,' he said. 'I guess we're beginning to get a handle on it now.' His finger hovered over one name.

'Here's a guy who was in the RAF. Your air force was only formed in the Spring of 1918 which means he must have got the chop in the last months or even weeks or days of the war. Just a little longer and he would have been home and safe. The Almighty must have been dealing off the bottom of the pack.'

Perhaps this would be the way he would be remembered. A church with a record of his baptism would claim him as one of their own despite his lack of faith and put his name on a plaque. That and maybe a government-issue headstone the only memento of James Elmeyer's passing.

'The names are so English,' he said after a while. 'Do you suppose their relatives still live round about?'

'Very likely. Not all that much will have changed here in the last twenty-five years.'

'The RAF man must have been a flier, like me.'

'Fighting a longer war, too,' Amelia said with the finest sliver of reproof which Elmeyer detected and understood.

It was easy to get exasperated with the British, Elmeyer thought, but they'd fought the Battle of Britain and lived through the the Blitz while America was sitting with its thumb up its ass.

For some reason - superstition, perhaps, or the feeling of one aviator for another - his finger hovered over the British airman's name.

'They're all in order of rank with the officers at the top and down to the enlisted men. That's so class-conscious. So British.'

'It is rather. Still. I expect all that will be changed when we lose the war.'

Elmeyer looked at her quizzically.

'The chances of your country being on the losing side are as we speak about zero. I don't get you.'

Amelia gave a teasing smile at his earnestness. 'Oh, not to the Germans, darling. To you Yanks.'

They came down from the Cotswolds into Cheltenham, old, threadbare and snug as a pair of slippers and, skirting Gloucester to the North commenced their journey to the Severn shore. After lunching on beer and gristly pork pies they pressed on until the road dipped in obeisance to the River Wye and the stern Norman flanks of Chepstow castle.

'Is that the border with Wales? They must have wanted to keep you English out pretty badly,' Elmeyer got in with his own wisecrack which was met with a cool school-marmish voice.

'Actually, the Normans built it to control the Welsh,' before adding with more warmth, 'Anyway it's rather lovely in the clear light that can follow a storm. We should make a promise.

Once across the border neither of us is to speak about the war or anything to do with it. Agreed?'

'Scout's honour!' He reached across and kissed her. 'Except for just one teensy weensy thing. Frenchie, whose genius for relieving the US Government of all its property passes all understanding has fixed it up for us to top up on gas at a US facility in Newport which is the nearest big town to the border.'

'With an excellent art college I might point out. Honestly, James. Do you think I've never heard of the place?'

Within an hour they were at Newport and had been directed to a former British Army camp occupied by an American engineer regiment.

Elmeyer dropped Amelia at a public house with a quiet saloon bar before driving to the guard post where an MP threw up a salute and sent him to a hut behind the raw red brick main building.

Three large fuel tankers were parked by the hut inside which a Technical Sergeant and two Corporals were playing cards. They came sluggishly to attention as he entered. Elmeyer mentally crossed his fingers and pushed Frenchie's piece of paper at the senior of the trio. The Technical Sergeant gave it barely a glance.

'We don't see so many air force people around here, Sir'. The Sergeant swung around to one of the corporals, a short young man who had been regarding Elmeyer with ill-concealed curiosity.

'See to the Captain, Sam.'

'If you'd like to follow me, Sir.'

The corporal led Elmeyer towards the fuel truck turning to face him once they were out of earshot of the others.

'I'd give anything to be in the air force, Captain,' he said with an earnest intensity. 'What the Hell good am I doing here? When the war's over and the kids ask me I'll have to tell them I sat on my ass in Wales doling out gas. Jesus.'

Elmeyer's smiled and remembered his own determination.

'I can give you advice son but it's not going to be what you want to hear. Stay here and pump gas and play cards with your buddies.'

The name tag on the soldier's fatigues was illegible under a layer of grease but the Sergeant had called him Sam. The boy looked Italian and had a thick New York accent.

'Five years from now nobody's going to care what you did in the war and fliers are a dime a dozen. They'll be melting aviators' badges for scrap.'

Even to him the words sounded hollow. To the boy they must be the purist, most pungent bullshit.

'I don't suppose there'll be ticker-tape parades for storemen either. Square with me, Sir. If the Army said we could swap jobs would you do it?'

The boy had him over a barrel. Elmeyer knew he would loathe the kid's job. He knew full well that being aircrew, even a sergeant gunner, gave status. He had no right to direct the boy's path.

'I can see your mind is pretty well made up. Speak to your commanding officer about training as a gunner. You're short, which is a big advantage if you're dumb enough to want to do it. Do you get claustrophobic?'

'Sir?'

'Do you mind being cooped up in little places?'

'Hell, no. I've been in Britain for two years.'

'That's good. It's cramped in the ball turret of a B-17 and once the hatchway is swivelled out of alignment with the opening in the fuselage you're dangling in a ball of perspex with nothing but miles of empty space underneath. Take some time to think about it before putting your application for transfer in.' The boy's face brightened. It couldn't have been three years since the kid was making model aeroplanes and hanging them from his bedroom ceiling, Elmeyer thought.

'I won't change my mind and thank you, Sir. Maybe we'll meet again.'

'I hope I last that long. Meanwhile you're still a corporal in the supply branch and I'd like my gas.'

Frenchie's arrangements had been efficiently made. By the time he got back from the urinal the Jeep's petrol tank was brimming and two full Jerry cans had been loaded in the back. Elmeyer returned to the pub to find Amelia happily chatting with a young woman.

'This is Patricia. She works here,' Amelia said. 'Patricia's been telling me how to get to Blaendiffaith. Did everything go all right?'

Elmeyer placed his cap on the table and smiled a greeting at Patricia. A Scotch had already been bought for him.

'Oh, sure. Courts-martial and firing squads entered into my thoughts a couple of times but everything went without a hitch.'

A quarter-of-an-hour later they were spinning northwards with the sides of the Jeep's tilt clipped back, he with his cap off and the wind tumbling their hair. Farm labourers looked up and some waved including a gaggle of Land Army girls sharing tea from a flask.

Near Pontypool a policeman confirmed Patricia's directions and shortly afterwards they were following the road which led through a dark tunnel of beeches up onto a high moor and a little after that a village which Amelia confidently announced to be Blaendiffaith.

FIFTEEN

THE Colliers' Arms was primly whitewashed and stood apart from the rest of the village like a haughty if somewhat compromised bride.

It's younger rival for the attention of Blaendiffaith's men was the Workingmen's Institute, a large brick building tricked out with architectural fripperies defiant under their coating of grime. Both establishments were frowned upon from the other side of the common by grey, slab-sided Bethesda Chapel. A traveller coming from the South could take in a clutch of dignified detached houses known as The Posh and the uniform ranks of colliers' cottages in a glance. The single road to the village bisected a common where sheep and retired pit ponies grazed between the clumps of bracken.

Miners with faces as black as minstrel entertainers were coming off shift. Women daily and religiously scrubbed the steps to their cottages and swept tiny back yards all of which displayed ramshackle sheds with zinc baths hung against the wall while pristine sheets blew and billowed under a blue, windy sky. Over it all like some pagan prayer-wheel offering benediction the pit wheel spun out the time by which Blaendiffaith lived its life.

Mr Talfan Evans met Elmeyer and Amelia with a smile that managed to suggest that he personally had laid on the bright day as a special greeting.

'I am pleased to welcome a brother-in-arms in the fight against the scourge of fascism,' the rotund figure announced.

'The silver band would have been here to welcome you were it not for most of the boys being on shift and the tuba player detained last night in Abergavenny by the uniformed agents of international capital following a slight altercation. My name is Talfan Evans, innkeeper and very nearly a graduate of Aberystwyth University. Do please enter.'

The summer sun entered as if on tip-toe to briefly warm the worn stone floor until eventually surrendering the job of bringing light to a small fire crackling in the hearth. The smells were of coal, polish, beer and tobacco. Amelia squeezed Elmeyer's hand. Elmeyer knew about English country pubs where horse brasses seemed almost compulsory. Here the brasses were of little figures of miners, pit-heads, drams and ponies, pin-bright and placed on virtually every flat surface not already inhabited by a piece of pottery or polished miners' lamps. Over all a fox's head looked down with glassy eyes and a grandfather's clock imperiously ticked.

The couple were taken through the bar and a door with a clacking latch and ushered into a room the windows of which had been thrown open to the village.

'It's perfect, isn't it James?' and turning her most vivacious smile on their host, 'Thank you Mr Evans.'

With a little bow Talfan left them alone with the old-fashioned washstand, basin and jug, a wardrobe and sideboard; two chairs and bed with a white coverlet all plumped up and as soft as a newly-baked loaf.

'Well?' Her eyes shone as she drew him down for a kiss.

'As you say. Perfection.' He let the words serve for the Colliers' Arms and for the kiss which followed.

'Comrade Talfan seems effusively friendly. I was worried that people might not be all keen on Yanks throwing money around,' he said before remembering their bargain.

Shut up about anything to do with the war and live in the glowing moment as he had promised Amelia.

'How did you ever find out about this place?' he asked with a change of tone.

'Oh, you know how it is with artists. We're always looking for new Edens. Actually, a friend who had a lecturing job at the art college in Newport told me about it.'

'This artist friend. Male or female?' Elmeyer said, mock-suspiciously, gently shoving her towards the bed.

'Female, actually.'

'Really?' He tried to pull her down to him but she wriggled playfully away.

'You Yanks are insatiable. Hanky-panky can wait. I suspect we're required downstairs for inspection by the locals. This is a little inn stitched deeply into the life of a Welsh village not some anonymous place in America where people go to fornicate. What are they called?'

'Motor lodges or universities. Either one.'

'Ha ha. I don't think we have motor lodges here but it's marvellous we have the Jeep, isn't it? Frenchie is awfully good to us. You like him a lot, don't you?'

'His optimism and belief in the future helps me to keep going. He's funny but tough and relentlessly American.'

'To see America is to see into the future, they say,' Amelia said. 'It's usually Americans who think that, though.' The teasing earned her a playful poke in the ribs.

'Us Americans are brought up to believe that theirs is the only way of life worth fighting for although I suspect our new friend Talfan will be pleased to debate the point. Shall we go?'

Downstairs a reception committee was warming to its task.

'No, Mun! Capitalism is already in its dying throes!' Talfan Evans was alight with a fervour kindled by his eighth pint of what the British, mistakenly to Elmeyer's mind, called beer.

'What happened in Spain was a reversal that I will grant you. But it is in Russia that Marshal Zhukov and his boys gave the Jerries a pasting!'

'Aye! And shot half their bloody officers as counter-revolutionaries too, Talfan Mun!' piped a voice.

'You would say that, Dai Reaction,' Talfan growled. 'Anyhow. The young lady and gentleman haven't come to Blaendiffaith to listen to your eccentric political views.'

Having walked into a debate in full spate Elmeyer had a jug of beer thrust into his hand for which he tried to pay but was fended off by Talfan's raised palm.

'The wings on your tunic amply demonstrate that you're doing your bit for democracy alongside our own increasingly class-conscious boys and their Soviet allies. Anyway ... Talfan let his speech tail off. 'This public house is particularly fortunate in the matter of acquiring beer freely and at quite reasonable cost although I would not care to say very much more in front of my friend Police Sergeant Aneurin Hughes when he comes in.' To general laughter Talfan gave the couple a huge conspiratorial wink.

Arguments swirled and lulled and swirled again around the tap room and Elmeyer was reflecting on the virtues of living in a little village which seemed to have negotiated its own way around wartime beer shortages when a police sergeant entered the tap room and pointedly took stock of the newcomers before proceeding with great dignity to the bar.

Having washed their tonsils the reception committee was now tuning them up. Flicking ale from his moustache the large police sergeant who they assumed to be Sergeant Aneurin Hughes turned inwards to the drinkers. And with a fruity baritone expressed with a great working of the mouth and heaving of the chest joined in, the whole room now vibrating to the rich mahogany notes of a Welsh hymn that neither Elmeyer nor Amelia knew but which swelled and boomed around the bar setting glasses shaking and the brass knick-knacks ringing in consonance.

'We are working very nicely in the baritone but a little more is needed in the bass section,' Talfan, who had taken upon himself the role of conductor shouted at Elmeyer and Amelia, owners of the only lips not formed around the rolling sibilants of the old hymn.

'Ah, but relief is at hand!' Talfan exclaimed as a big man fresh scrubbed from his shift at the pit, carbolicked and with a bright white boiled shirt and hair still wet from the bath, eased his way through the throng.

'Big Colin for the bass! And now for choral perfection in praise of a God in which I do not of course believe!' Talfan shouted and in the ten seconds it took the spotless new arrival to down a pint of beer and join in the singing the sound had deepened, coming as though through black seams of coal funnelling and booming through shafts and levels, up through the village's very foundations and soaring up to the moon and stars.

The music ended abruptly on a rising note but somewhere in Elmeyer's inner being it still echoed and he was surprised to find that a tear had formed. As he surreptitiously wiped it away his eyes fixed on the new arrival.

'Colin?'

The Colliers' snug comfort seemed to shiver and reshape into a poor Spanish tavern with chickens pecking on the floor, the smell of unwashed bodies as sour as the wine and sacking nailed over the windows in an attempt to keep out the killing cold of Teruel.

The big man had not been in the *escuadrilla* in which Elmeyer had flown as a teniente for long but he'd noticed him for his laughing round face with its topping of dark hair which in the strong Spanish sunlight was tinged with red, blue eyes and nose broken at the pit face or in a fight.

'Lieutenant?'

Elmeyer was caught in a crushing embrace and the big man ruffled his hair as if the American were a ten-year-old.

'What the hell brings you here, Jame?' pronounced in the

136

guttural way of the Spanish.

'Teruel was where we were last together. I heard you had to make a run for it across the mountains to France barely a kilometre ahead of the fascists. It was a different place to this we last drank together, eh, comrade?'

A cheer and general hullabaloo broke out as the men gripped hands once more.

'Bloody Hell, Yank. You didn't let on you were in Spain,' bawled one known as Little Colin over the din. 'That makes you a bloody hero in this Valley! Get these boys a drink somebody and let's hear their stories!'

Yet another mug of beer for which Elmeyer was acquiring the taste was plonked down in front of him even before its predecessor was drained.

'This looks like men's work. Perhaps I should excuse myself,' Amelia called over the din, just managing to catch Elmeyer's eye before being pressed back into her seat by a coal-scored arm.

'You sit there, my lovely, and listen to something you'll be able to pass on to your grandchildren.'

The words uttered by an old miner called Gerwyn whose other arm had been crushed in a roof fall in 1917 made her glance at the wedding ring she still wore.

Elmeyer led Big Colin towards their table. Amelia smiled a welcome.

Her circle of London friends contained several who had been to Spain more she suspected for the benefit of their literary careers than the international working class. Big Colin was not such a man. Know him and another piece of the complex picture that was James Elmeyer would be painted in.

'It's been five, almost six years since we last spoke.'

The remark was addressed to both Amelia and Colin. Elmeyer looked at them in turn anxious that they should be friends.

'Good years for you, by the look of it.' Elmeyer patted Big Colin's stomach now making greater demands on his belt than he had remembered. The face had filled out too and a shiny scalp showed through hair now flecked with grey. Big Colin was about five years older than the American.

'I've a good woman to look after me and there's plenty of work for miners with this war on.' But the satisfaction in his voice was tinged with something else.

'But you can damn me for a fool 'cos I'd rather be fighting the fascists just like we were with those little Polikarpov planes. I'm in a reserved occupation see and there's no shortage of younger men. All they'll let me into is the Home Guard and a fat chance there is of them being needed now.'

Elmeyer clapped Big Colin on the arm. 'You've done your share, old buddy, twenty times as much than half the staff officers with their natty uniforms and medals just for polishing chair seats with their fat asses.'

'You're billing and cooing at each other like a couple of lovers!' Talfan cried.

'Tell us a story about Spain; fighting for the cause at the crossing of the Ebro and handing a thrashing to the bloody fascists!'

'Aye. And the heat and the senoritas and the dark, bloody and sensual ritual of the bullfight and all the stuff that bloke Hemingway writes about,' Gerwyn with the crooked arm chipped in but Elmeyer spread his hands.

'What can I say that hasn't been said already? We thought that if the republic lost to Franco a much bigger war would follow and we were right. The backing of Britain and France would have let the Germans and Italians who supported the fascists know that sooner or later their ambitions to expand would be opposed ... '

'Aye, bloody disgraceful, begging the lady's pardon!' a man who had sang with the tenors piped up. 'Non-bloody-intervention, Duw! Like walkin' the other side of the road and pretendin' to see nothin' while a gang of bloody larrikins beat an old man with sticks! I would've given the buggers non-intervention that I would!'

'Then why did you tell the Army you had flat feet, Dai Bloody?' a teasing voice came from the throng.

'I would loved to have been there, too,' said the one called Dai Bloody, sixty-five if he was a day but keeping up with the young ones in the matter of sinking draughts of ale. 'Only I'm a martyr to my feet. I would have gone if it hadn't been for bloody fallen arches.'

'The way I heard it you were too busy seeing to Bob Potter's missus to have much time left over for the international proletariat!' Iolo Gittins shouted.

'The role of women in society is an important issue in our bloody day and age. I was advancin' Madge Potter's political consciousness if you must know,' Dai Bloody countered in an aggrieved voice.

'There's a new name for rampant fornication!' another voice jeered as Dai buried his face in his pint pot, shooting baleful glances at his tormentors.

'Come on then, let's have some stories about Spain,' Talfan pressed to a chorus of 'ayes'. Amelia squeezed Elmeyer's hand and smiled as Big Colin shot him an uncertain look.

'I'll lead off, then,' said Big Colin. 'For an incident involving James here comes readily to mind.'

He spoke as though each snippet of recall was a semi-precious stone not lightly to be given away.

'It was a night attack, and my *centuria* which in that army was what they called a company of about a hundred men and James' centuria had been picked to capture a hill defended by a machine gun post holding up our advance.

'Our air force had been broken and we were fighting as ground soldiers. It was just my luck that day to be stuck with the noisiest little bugger in the company who what with his clanking mess tin and loud whispering was making more of a racket than a one-man band as we crept forward hoping to kill the fascists with our grenades. All was going as planned when what does this daft sod do? He drops a spare rifle magazine which clatters on the stony ground and straight away brings a storm of bullets about our ears. Now I am a big man and it was a very small dip in the ground into which I threw myself. The machine-gunners flayed us and the little man paid for his carelessness with a burst that cut him almost in two. I was pretty sure I was done for. Just then a dusty figure comes dashing towards the foxhole I am by this time convinced will also serve as my grave and I see the *teniente*, the man you see before you, who must have spotted the grenade in the dead man's hand. Anyway he lands next to me with hell of a thump, snatches the grenade from the corpse and hurls it at the machine-gunners. There's an almighty explosion and screaming which went on so long we began to pity the gunners fascists though they were. When the screams had become wimpers and then stopped altogether we moved forward cautious as cats. One man was barely alive. He must have been the one who was screaming. We all looked away as our officer did what he had to do.'

'A brave thing, indeed,' said the Police Sergeant standing at the bar, from whom up until that point they had heard little.

'Braver even than I have described it,' Big Colin came back.

'Because the noisy little fellow had got as far as pulling the grenade's pin. James judged his impetuous and dusty arrival to within half a second. The blink of an eye longer and I would not be here to tell you this story.'

It was gone half-past eleven and still creamy pints of porter and slopping glasses of beer were being pulled by Talfan's arms working like pistons. The latch on the door leading to the Colliers' tin-roofed urinal was clacking like castanets as the good ale took its predictable effect with laughs and coughs and snatches of song coming from every corner of the pub.

'I was under the obviously mistaken impression that you guys had something called rationing.' Elmeyer touched glasses with Amelia who was being monopolised by Dai Bloody. The rich, bitter ale smelling of hops was a thousand times better than the stuff sold in cans to GIs, he had by this time benevolently decided.

'Difficult circumstances can be made tolerable if one puts one's mind to it,' Talfan replied steadily.

'Living for so long next to the English has taught us that.'

The weather front which had brought the storm had rolled on to the Brecon Beacons and would probably reach Cambridgeshire the next day Elmeyer thought as the steam from his gratifying copious urination rose from the zinc outhouse trough. That would mean flying would be cancelled and those marked for death would have a day's reprieve.

An owl hooted nearby and a whisper of a breeze rustled the ivy which all but covered the urinal. Inside the Colliers' Sergeant Hughes drained his glass and with some emphasis placed it on the bar and pulled out his Full Hunter watch by its chain.

'It's been a long but rewarding day,' he announced, which was the signal for caps to be clamped on heads and coats to be shrugged into and farewells to be called and hands to be shaken and the company to depart under a full moon.

That night they made love gently but with relish and when it was over Amelia climbed down from the tall bed with its plumped-up pillows and opened the tiny double windows which looked out onto Blaendiffaith and turned down the old paraffin lamp watching the crescent of hot wick glow dimmer and break up into segments of dying fire. When she got back into the bed she reached for Elmeyer's arm and placed it about her smelling the manliness of him and stroking the sweat-glossed curve of his shoulder.

'It's been a marvellous day. We've been magically transported to another country. Don't you feel that?'

Elmeyer kissed her. 'It's a strange place in the nicest sort of way. You get the feeling that there are still fairies here, and trolls and giants. Can you hear the stream? Everywhere else streams gurgle. Here they talk.'

Fast cold streams frisking and bustling down the mountain chattered to the hunting owls and foxes and in the bracken of the mountainside small creatures moved.

'There must have been a lot of rain some way upstream,' Amelia murmured. 'But we're safe and dry and snug here. Everything awful seems so far away. The fighting ... '

She felt him tense and make a slightly fretful sound.

'I'm sorry. But perhaps one day we'll come here again. After the war, I mean, and be happy.'

'That's a beautiful thought to go to sleep with.' He kissed her and within a few minutes they were fast asleep, oblivious to the dull rumbling of thunder far away, over the Brecon Beacons.

SIXTEEN

RAIN returned that night drumming so hard that it awoke Amelia who lay listening to the distant thunder and to the water washing in sheets over slates just a few feet above their heads.

At first the storm had been a commotion in the distance sending her back under the covers with reveries of childhood. Her imagination alerted she tried to conjure pictures of the storms disturbing the sleep of travellers across the great North American plains; wild, battering things borne on black columns sweeping across the vast openness and running down the backs of lowing bison and sending gophers skittering for their burrows.

Eventually and secure in her snugness she fell asleep to be gently eased from her slumber by Talfan tip-toeing in with a big jug of hot water. She washed carefully and slowly before an open window feeling the freshness of the morning after the storm on her skin. After she had finished she pressed her warm facecloth against Elmeyer's forehead awakening him to a kiss. From downstairs came the smell of frying bacon and brewing tea. Elmeyer uncoiled and gave a pantherine stretch and she saw that in physical terms he was still a youth. Yet so old. She imagined eight or nine like him packed into an aluminium tube and sent on their way to bomb and burn and in their turn be burned and maimed and killed. Dear God. How she wished the war would end and they could be by themselves in Blaendiffaith, far from the war. And yet she knew that another mood would, after a time, settle upon her, starting as the merest flickering of feeling which could not at that stage be described as a thought, yet as the days went on growing into a yearning for a life which contained an edge of tension and even danger. That was the forbidden world of which Peter Dainty was a part.

'Come on, Sleepyhead! I can smell breakfast and I'm starving!' Yet even as she roused him she was aware of a slight anxiety or sadness betrayed by the strained sound of her own voice as she wondered how many other women had woken him in this manner. Still, what right had she to think such thoughts? Elmeyer shook his head and scratched and slopped water over his face like a young animal at its riverside ablutions saving enough of the hot water for a shave.

Breakfast was served on a bar table over which a clean but frayed tablecloth had been thrown.

'Days like this must be rare,' Elmeyer remarked through a mouthful of toast. 'Your eccentric climate was a big problem when we came here almost three years back after training in Texas and Georgia and Florida where six out of seven are flying days. Over here it's a miracle anyone manages to get off the ground.'

'Other countries have climate. We have weather,' Amelia chipped in. I suppose it's why British cadets go to America and Canada to learn to fly?' she asked not really wanting to talk about the war. Peter Dainty had been one such cadet, she remembered.

Elmeyer nodded, munching happily.

'I guess so. That and the fact that in America they are a long way from any Kraut who fancies a shot at an easy target. The mountains around here are notorious for killing pilots who suddenly find themselves caught in the clouds with hard centres. Cumulus granitus is our ghoulish name for it.'

Breakfast over they walked out into the bright day to the sound of glasses from the night before being cleared and a cheerful shout from Talfan.

At first the Jeep wouldn't start and Elmeyer had to push it from its sheltering barn and roll it downhill with the ignition on before throwing it into gear.

'It's the barn taking it's revenge,' Amelia said as the Jeep backed up to where she was standing. 'It doesn't like having cars in it. Lovely old barns like this have bats and mice and swallows not noisy modern contrivances.'

'The plugs were damp,' a panting Elmeyer said. 'It's as simple and as unromantic as that.' He smiled as the engine note settled down into a regular beat.

'See?'

They climbed steadily through tiny fields past a broken gate onto a wandering track stopping atop a rise with a view of blue mountains and a distant boomerang-shaped lake. With an airman's eye Elmeyer noted that in the wilderness of mountains all of which seemed to be about the

143

same height the lake would make an excellent navigational way-point. Hundreds of planes must come this way on training exercises, pilots and navigators flying on dead-reckoning allowing themselves a brief moment of satisfaction as the stretch of water marked out on their charts came into view.

Even as he watched a twin-engined aircraft coming from the South turned several degrees to the left having found the lake and continued on the next leg of its flight. Intruding thoughts of flying and war only fled when the plane had disappeared over the hills and its engine could no longer be heard. Amelia passed him a thick slab of bread on to which real butter yellow and tangy with salt had been thickly spread.

'Talfan's done us proud.' She lay back on Elmeyer's raincoat testing the springiness of the wet heather underneath. 'Don't you feel like me that you could stay in Blaendiffaith for ever? It's like a magical little kingdom lost in the mountains obeying only its own rules. Shangri-Lla as I expect the Welsh say.'

'I don't know so much,' Elmeyer said, the witticism having passed him by.

'The police sergeant seems to keep a close eye on things.'

He thoughtfully examined the marks his teeth had made in the butter.

'He's an interesting guy. I got the impression he's artistic. You and he have something in common. Maybe you'll be pals.'

'He's rather handsome, too isn't he?' Amelia teased. 'For an older man, I mean. With an air of natural authority. Are you like that when you fly your plane? Don't shake your head. I'm sure you are really.'

'When I'm on the ground I'm annoyed with the routine and the way in which everything that once seemed worthwhile and even glamorous is actually sordid. In the air I'm shit-scared at least half the time. That's as near as I've got to analysing my feelings.'

She had snapped off a sprig of heather and was twisting it as if testing to breaking point the emotions within her.

Elmeyer was sweet and fine and kind and damaged and the love within her yearned to heal the wounds. It should be enough for any woman but there was something else

144

stirring in the depths of her soul more wicked and more exciting.

Peter Dainty's appeal was dangerous even to acknowledge but she knew that a part of her wanted to answer his wild call. With James Elmeyer she would find love and comfort but Dainty had the killing instinct. For the American, Spain and the air war had happened through some sort of political conviction not from a lust for adventure.

They munched at their picnic each with every sign of outward contentment but Amelia's thoughts fluttered like a moth inexorably drawn to the lethal flame that was Peter Dainty.

SEVENTEEN

LUCK Be A Lady bucked in the propwash of the Fortress in front, her four roaring motors adding to the din caused by two hundred Wright Cyclones throttled back for taxi-ing and Elmeyer extracting what comfort he could from knowing he was an insignificant part of a very large war machine who might just be overlooked when death was dealt out.

To his right past Henry Gadgett's pre-occupied features he could see the steeple of Bassington's parish church within which efferies of knights and ladies lay in cool darkness, the antithesis of the thrashing maelstrom of alloy and steel that was the world outside.

Elmeyer and Gadgett who had been assigned to replace Steiner went through the power checks together but he knew exactly what Luck Be A Lady's other crewmen should be doing. Luck didn't just happen. It was made and made in part by seeing to the small things.

Frenchie had fussed over his guns with obsessive care and on the way to their target he would test fire them. Frenchie was the best gunner in the group, maybe even in the whole of the Eighth Air Force. He and Frenchie looked out for one another. The air force didn't like officers hanging out with Sergeants but the air force could go to Hell. It was good to know Frenchie was back there. Elmeyer trusted nobody like he trusted Frenchie.

The target was marshalling yards at Munich.

It was late September and soon another year of war would be coming to an end. Maybe the war wouldn't go on for another twelve months but what remained of it would be tough. The Germans were fanatical bastards. The best of their aircrews had been killed but some of the fighter pilots who had come up for a fight had been suicidally brave. Literally so. He hadn't seen it himself, but stories of German pilots ramming American planes were doing the rounds.

Elmeyer touched his lucky green scarf and eased the throttles forward as the Fort in front of him began to roll.

Many of the other planes were in their natural aluminium finish it having been deemed that with increasing air superiority camouflage was no longer needed. Luck Be A Lady still had her olive-green camouflage paint with sky-blue lower surfaces but bare aluminium patches and replacement panels gave her an increasingly piebald look. She was already the oldest ship and a lucky charm to the rest of the Group. Other ships wanted to be in close with her so that some of the luck might rub off. When other pilots joshed him about his luck Elmeyer always laughed and said it was no luck, just the awesome defensive firepower of the B-17G, the huge P-47 Thunderbolts and the slick, fast little P-51 Mustangs fitted with long-range Tokyo tanks that nowadays could provide long-range escorts and a healthy sense of self-preservation. He knew though, that you could have all these things but still one German fighter pilot who was luckier or cleverer could kill you. Still, Luck Be A Lady was a good old crate and it paid to show her respect.

The Fort in front was airborne. Luck Be A Lady would need every ounce of power the Cyclones could offer to heave herself free of the runway. She surged forward, a living thing compounded of man and machine, a million bits of metal and muscle, wire and sinew, valves and pistons, servos, toes and fingers and levers and switches, a million connections and interrelated parts both mechanical and human, all brought to a climactic point as she lifted off the ground and became something which was neither mechanical nor human but something else, a deadly new life form released into its killing element.

With a whine and a soft thump the Fort's wheels retracted into their bays. Gadgett checked the temperatures and pressures and cowl settings leaving Elmeyer to fly Luck Be A Lady into her place in the formation.

Officially it was still summer. It had not been described as such in meteorological briefings or noted in any diary but Elmeyer knew that no matter what the calendar said there was always a day which humans and animals, in their bones, recognised as autumn's outrider. Something somewhere in the polar regions had stirred, an imperceptible movement of air two or three thousand miles away, sniffed and detected by the most ancient part of the brain and triggering an indefinable feeling of sadness, loss and change.

Intermittent stratocumulus with increasing mare's-tail cirrus marking the advance of a warm front had been forecast, which Elmeyer had interpreted as a good omen. The formation would still get its share of attention from the

Luftwaffe's fighters who once through the cloud themselves would be able to see the contrails but at least the anti-aircraft gunners' job would be harder.

One more mission to go after this.

Elmeyer looked out along the wing where already the bright aluminium patches were proliferating. It was his habit to hover around the mechanics while they worked on Luck Be A Lady, a habit which mightily irritated engineering officers and senior non-coms. That was too bad.

The more a captain knew about his aircraft and the men given the job of mending and flying it the better his luck seemed to be.

There was something else, though. The crew chief was a surly bastard and he suspected involved in the stealing of Government stores.

He'd warned Frenchie not to get involved with Thorpe but there was some kind of business going between them. So long as it didn't affect the rest of the crew or the efficiency of the ship he could push it to the back of his mind but it was there and it worried him.

They were in formation. Elmeyer settled down, taking in as he had dozens of times before the smell of the greasy and battered seat which must have absorbed gallons of his own sweat, the oil, the electrics and the hydraulic fluid, all of which added up to the distinctive B-17 whiff. His glance took in the scored and worn consoles with their rows of switches and dials and the Boeing badge set proudly in the middle of the control column as if sending men to get killed in the finest damned machines America could make was something to proudly advertise in a sales brochure.

Puffs of blue smoke were being trailed by other Forts as their guns fired.

'Okay. Test your guns.'

One by one the gunners hammered off a few rounds and reported their guns in order. They would leave them cocked and on 'fire' from now.

The Suffolk coast at Orford Ness was sliding away eighteen thousand feet under their bellies.

Squadrons and groups had formed up into larger formations making a swarm of Flying Fortresses to the right and left; above and below, as far as the eye could see, a glittering armada climbing into the strange and silent place where no bird flies and no mountain reaches, which is unchanged and unchanging, the faces of the men covered by oxygen masks so that even the sound of death is silent.

The time had been when Elmeyer had actually wished for an attack early in the mission to break the unnatural peace and the crawling passage of the hours. But not now.

'Here they come. Four o'clock!'

They had been flying for just under an hour and a half.

With Frenchie's shout came the familiar, liquid feeling that spelled the end of false hopes.

Only a few fighters had come up to meet the bomber stream and seemed to be occupying themselves elsewhere.

'Our luck's running true to form. They're keeping away from us,' Gianotta, the stocky little ball gunner curled foetally over his weapons said.

'Shut up about our luck, Gianotta,' Hosbach the navigator growled.

'All of you pipe down,' Elmeyer snapped into the mike. This near the end of the tour skittishness was creeping in that could be lethal. They were a tough and experienced crew who knew what to do when trouble came but they were right at the end of their tour and getting what the RAF called 'demob happy'.

Elmeyer glanced at Gadgett who remained absorbed in his tasks, eyes ranging over the instruments and occasionally flicking switches or jotting notes on a kneeboard. If it had been Steiner the jottings would be turned into some kind of report meant to undermine him. A vast shapeless fear smothered his senses like a fog. He was sweating and his hands trembled on the controls. His racing mind seized upon the contrail which happened when the heat generated by the furnaces of another Fort's cylinders finally surrendered to the mortuary-cold air. The Wedgwood-blue of the sky like the ceiling of the church he distantly remembered … angels and God always appearing from the sky … funny the connection between the sky and things holy … did what they were doing have the stamp of holiness or the mark of the Devil?

'I'll take control.'

From Gadgett. Not a request but a command.

He felt a push on the control yoke as the co-pilot made a correction.

'Affirmative.' His tongue stumbled on the word.

'Give me half an hour and I'll feel fine.'

Gadgett was a pro who did what was asked of him in the air and was amiable on the ground. Elmeyer yielded the controls to him and checked his oxygen flow. Insufficient supply brought on anoxia which would account for his flushed confusion but the flow was normal. His mind was the thing that was faltering. Elmeyer closed his eyes and thought hard about his aeroplane and its crew, forcing his brain to accept reality. Presently the sweats subsided and he felt well enough to resume control. Gadgett handed over without any sign that he had noticed anything amiss. Fighters attacking the edges of the formation had for the moment peeled off for their bases where they would refuel and re-arm. British Spitfires were providing the escort for the first part of the trip out. Early in the fighting the Americans had relied on the British a lot. Now, not so much.

A British plane dropped down and flew alongside Luck Be A Lady like a lean collie shepherding its flock. Elmeyer returned its pilot's wave. He knew and trusted the fighters. About the RAF bomber men in their blue-grey uniforms, even though he saw them when he was on leave in London or in Cambridge, he knew almost nothing. They inhabited a parallel world flying mostly by night their aircraft painted black like giant bats. The RAF had been in the war longer and made damned sure the Americans knew about it. All this stuff about the British and the Americans being brothers-in-arms was a crock of shit. After the war the Americans would move in and gobble up the world the British thought they owned. The American and the ex-communist in him understood it well.

'Ten minutes to target, Boss,' Hosbach intoned after what seemed an age had passed.

Puffballs of anti-aircraft fire flak burst nearby but no Forts had been hit so far as he could tell. A flare was fired by the leader of the combat box indicating that the IP - the initial point signifying the beginning of the bomb run - had been reached.

Elmeyer saw the box leader's bomb doors swing open. Now came the moments which stretched into an infinity, each man feeling his heart pounding within him as the Fort held steady, waiting for the moment when the bombardier operated the toggle which in a hellish whelping let drop the five thousand pounds of mixed high explosive and general purpose bombs, sending them tumbling towards the target where a combination of blast, vacuum and shock would smash and rip and destroy; atomise murder and maim.

Luck Be A Lady leapt signifying that the bombs had dropped.

'Bombs gone! Let's go home!' Mike Wiggins the bombardier shouted.

'Let's get this lucky lady's ass out of here!' was something Elmeyer always said and which had become almost a joke except this time he could not altogether hide the quaver in his voice.

There was little talk and thoughts were of home. Every man was settling back to his task, Hosbach hunching over his charts and wind drift calculator and the gunners each quartering the sky as fragments of a shell punched into the plane above Elmeyer's and Gadgett's positions.

The hurricane of thin, freezing air blasting through Luck Be A Lady could not altogether disperse the stink of cordite and burned wiring.

'All stations. Report if your heated suits don't work.'

Each crew member checked their suits as working leaving Elmeyer to wonder. If so much wiring could be destroyed without any apparent effect on the electrics what the hell was it all for?

'Okay. Keep your gloves on and don't touch any metal. That particularly applies to gunners. I don't want the medics to have to chop your frostbitten hands off at the wrists. Do you copy?'

A chorus of 'sures' and 'fines' and 'okays'. The only thing now was to keep in formation and set Luck Be A Lady down on Bassington's runway. Nothing else mattered. Elmeyer pulled his goggles down over his eyes. Getting the plane back with a gale screaming through the ripped fuselage would be a torment but thoughts of Amelia would carry him through. His instinct was to ask Hosbach for the estimated time to their airfield but he resisted. Maybe he would do it later when some of the distance had been gobbled up. The hole torn by the shell fragment would enormously increase drag on the airframe which in turn would increase fuel consumption. Also, there was a danger of the slipstream tearing away even more of the aluminium skin. Now they were slow and vulnerable and would be using up too much gas. Hold onto the controls and keep formation. Do not fail. Do not fall into the soft, seductive embrace of hypothermia. Do not let the body satisfy its craving for an end to all cold and all pain. Endure. Pray for the gas to hold out. Another trip and it would be over and perhaps the next trip would be a milk run. Then he would apply for a staff job at Eighth Army Air Force headquarters at High Wycombe less than thirty miles from London. He'd seen the country around there and it was fine, fields and low hills each with a little copse at its crown and little pubs tucked away among the beech trees. Amelia could easily find a cottage and set up her studio and together they'd sit the rest of the war out. He could see himself with Amelia walking down a little path shaded from the heat of the sun by overhanging beeches, a little pub with its warm beer and cheese and pickle sandwiches beckoning to them from the depths of its Chilterns dell. He'd go through the motions and pretend the war had something to do with them and wait for Blaendiffaith's beckoning call. They would sit by the fire in winter time; feeling the warmth permeate their bodies, the soft, lulling warmth of a fire ... he jerked up in his seat, shaking away the reverie which would soothe him to his death.

'Pull yourself together. Keep this ship in formation'. He said it out loud. Now he could ask Hosbach for an ETA at Bassington. Then he'd add on a certain number of hours for the next mission - a generous number in case it was a long one - and he'd have worked out more or less the remaining time he had to spend going to war in a Flying Fortress.

The extra drag caused by the rent in the fuselage was making the engines work harder but he was keeping up with the formation and each mile that slipped away beneath them diminished the chances of attack. Like a single fish that had suddenly decided to swim in a different direction to the shoal a British Spitfire caught his attention and he could see the pilot inspecting the damage to Luck Be A Lady. The British pilot gave an encouraging thumbs up. Elmeyer regarded the face largely hidden by helmet and oxygen mask. The gunners were accustomed to seeing American escort fighters and might easily mistake the Spitfire for a Kraut. What were the chances of a gunner opening fire and shooting the British plane down? And what were the chances of that particular pilot being Dainty? Jesus, he was losing his mind thinking like that. He shook his head in an attempt to banish the tiredness and the unsettling thought that had now set its barbs into his imagination. Crazy to wish for but it would solve everything. A burst of fire smashing into the cockpit and all the fears for Amelia and himself would be ended.

He knew it was a crazy thought yet there would have to be some sort of a reckoning with Dainty. No time now though to think about that.

He raised a thumb in response to the Spitfire pilot's gesture and with the peeling away of the British plane vanished the dark thought.

Four miles below Europe was sliding almost imperceptibly past. The escorting fighters were on the job but if the Messerschmitts did come please God let them hit another Fort. Luck Be A Lady was just a poor old girl making her way home.

As if in conscious rebuttal of this the German fighters came screaming in.

Simpson hammered away on his guns but Frenchie the more experienced air gunner shouted to him that the black-crossed fighters were not yet in range and to save his ammunition. Way over to the left a Fort was cartwheeling earthwards. Elmeyer counted only four parachutes.

No more attacks came after that. An hour later they were in the landing pattern and Luck Be A Lady's wheels were down with Bassington's runway coming up to meet them but from too great a height and too quickly. Elmeyer put on full flaps and raised the nose and chopped the power. The landing knocked the breath from him but Lady was down. He taxied to the dispersal and went through the closedown checks. One by one they dropped down onto the hardstanding and threw themselves onto the grass and lit cigarettes. A medical orderly jumped from an ambulance and threw Elmeyer a lazy salute which he didn't trouble to return.

The intelligence officer debriefing them wore a neatly-pressed uniform and wire rimmed spectacles and was persistent about whether the Luftwaffe's new jet powered Messerschmitt 262 fighters had joined the onslaught.

'No.'

Elmeyer's reply was curt and hostile but despite it the IO's voice remained low and calm and courteous.

'And anti-aircraft fire? More concentrated in any one place?'

The man's pencil hovered over his clipboard. A snarl came from Elmeyer.

'That's not such a stupid question as it sounds. Quite a bit of it was concentrated on us.'

Other pilots were jostling around, eager to give their reports. Like the others Elmeyer wanted to get away, to be left alone.

'Are you through with me now or are there more ways you can come up with of wasting my time?' Elmeyer spat.

The expression on the intelligence officer's face was hard to read but it was not angry.

'Knock it off, Elmeyer. You're holding up the line,' somebody shouted from the middle of the press.

'Leave the guy alone. Can't you see what he's wearing on his chest?' another, angrier voice shouted.

'He's a pilot the same as you for Christ's sake.'

'I'm sorry. I shouldn't have said that.' In his welter of anger and fear and bitterness Elmeyer had glared only at the man's face. Now his eyes dropped to the silver-winged badge of a combat flyer.

'Yeah. Kiss and make up and let's get the fuck out of here,' the angry voice came again.

'Don't give it a second's thought Captain.' The intelligence officer spoke with a soft Southern burr. 'You took a beating but it will soon all be over. I know how much you want that. We all want it.'

Elmeyer shook his head. There was nothing to say.

Bassington's officer's club was a Nissen hut which in shape resembled a Swiss roll cut longways where steak, fried egg and good coffee were served to returning aircrews. The gunners who were sergeants had their separate arrangements. Elmeyer smiled wryly at the recollection of what he had said to Amelia about the British class system. Men who had flown a lot of operations usually ate slowly barely acknowledging others. New and untested crews chattered too much or else were pale and silent.

These days, the days since he had met Amelia, he tended to eat alone even though he knew the other officers in the crew were getting sore about it. He acknowledged the arrival of Mike Wiggins Lady's bombardier with a grunt.

'It was pretty bad today. Cold. Jesus I've never been so cold. After Steiner and Attercop I kind of wonder whether we've been fingered. By fate, I mean.'

Just twenty-one. Wiggins was already rounding out and his sandy hair thinning.

Elmeyer looked up from the plate upon which a fried egg had been precisely cut into strips.

'I've lived through worse. Attercop was okay but Steiner was nuts.'

'He was like a slide rule calculating everything. Steiner wouldn't have been sorry for you. Just pissed that a good pilot wasn't there any more to look after his precious ass. The guy gave me the willies to tell you the truth'.

'Speaking of which did I ever tell you he showed me his foreskin?'

'Why would he do that? You mean Steiner was queer?'

'Superstitious, maybe. Which means that deep down he was just like the rest of us. He had it in a little glass jar which he took up with him I guess as a good luck charm.'

'Who was the guy who said you might as well believe in God because if it turned out He didn't exist you hadn't lost anything?'

'It might have been Pascal. You surprise me. I never had you down for a philosopher.'

'Heck no,' Wiggins blushed. 'Nothing like that. But it seems to me that charms are like that. By the time you find out they don't work you're already dead. Speaking of which Hosbach's intent on going into Cambridge tonight and raising Hell. What do you say to a party?'

'I say I'm pooped. But have fun.'

Half an hour later Elmeyer stripped to his underwear and flicked his cigarette butt into the upturned GI helmet doing service as an ashtray and fell asleep. The dream was disconnected and puzzling.

He was awoken by a banging on the thin plywood door.

EIGHTEEN

SHE awoke letting the feeling of guilt that was not entirely unpleasant steal over her. Dainty stirred.

'A penny for them,' he said thickly, touching her thigh in a way that annoyed her faintly. With Elmeyer there was no need of pet words or little games and rituals to conceal true feeling. Dainty was like a cruel child. One day her need for him would fall away and only Elmeyer would remain in her heart and in her bed. Dainty's energy was destructive, a boy smashing toys and oblivious to the needs of others, grabbing greedily at love.

But for now the physical force of his lust was good and her guilt a necessary part of what was to come. The greater her contrition the more complete would be her devotion to Elmeyer.

'I was thinking about Wales and about how nice it would be to work there.'

She turned to face him and surprised herself by having almost to force a smile. 'I'm so bored with London. It smells of war. I just want to get away from the greyness and the smell of boiled vegetables and bloody uniforms.'

Dainty swung his legs off the bed and gave her the sort of knowing grin she found irritating in one so young. At five feet eight inches he was not a large man - a good three inches shorter than Elmeyer. He was naked. She wanted to talk about Wales but he was touching her which at first made her even more peevish until a new feeling began to take over. Now he was probing the moistness of her, hurting and exciting her.

'We could go to Wales together.'

He nibbled her ear making a shiver go through her. She shifted slightly to feel his hardness. 'The war will be over within a year and the air force will push me out. We could get married and settle down there and you could paint. I bet there are a million things to paint in Wales.'

'You sound a little doubtful. Are you sure you wouldn't be bored?'

'Me? Not likely. I've got too many irons in the fire. Talking of irons in the fire ... '

His fingers were hurting her and there was a hardness about the set of his mouth. He was frightening and strong and her body was crying out for his. Dainty pushed her back roughly on the bed.

'Do you still sleep with the Yank?' The words were spat out as he lunged at her.

'Do you want me to say I do? Will it excite you?' She was laughing, her eyes wild.

'You're bloody wicked. There's something ... corrupt ... about you.'

'Come here. You're delicious. Don't tell me you don't get a kick out of screwing somebody else's woman because you do. Go on. Admit it. Go on.' Dainty thrust at her with a savage urgency and in the moments that followed nothing else mattered to her; not painting nor the war, nor even, for a few blinding, heaving seconds at the end, Elmeyer himself.

'Are you sleeping with him, really?' Dainty pressed as they lay side by side blowing smoke at the ceiling.

'Darling. That is not an appropriate thing to ask somebody in the middle of a war when everybody is doing it with everybody else,' she replied nonchalantly but now thinking of Elmeyer.

'That means you are. I don't want you to. I could kill him.'

'I shouldn't like you to do that.'

'All the same. I have an idea about Wales. I happen to have quite a lot of money, which might surprise you.'

'Frenchie told me you might have.'

'He's your Yank friend's gunner, isn't he? We've had some dealings. Perhaps he'll introduce me to Elmeyer. It makes a change for a man in my job actually seeing the person you are going to kill.'

'You have no intention of killing Elmeyer. You're sleeping with his girl. If there's any killing to be done I would have thought it would be by him. For Christ's sake can we talk about something else? Tell me about yourself and what you're going to do after the war.'

'I've thought about that quite a bit and I'm pretty sure I'd like to write. No. Not newspapers nor any of that rot. Books. About the war, perhaps.'

'What if you're no good?'

He smiled. 'I can afford to fail. In fact you'd be surprised what I can afford. One of your pictures for instance.' Dainty pointed his cigarette toward the picture of the bathing ATS girls.

'That one.'

Amelia had painted it two years before as part of a commission for the War Records Office. Two weeks ago the office had written offering an exhibition in Birmingham and she had sent off her acceptance by return of post.

'Most men like that. It appeals to the voyeur in them.'

And yet, she noted, he was looking at the painting with an absorbed expression as though it were a marvel to be adored for the first time.

'It's lovely. Tell me how you came to paint it,' he said quietly, still not taking his eyes from the work.

'There's not all that much to tell. I spent a week on the Sussex coast with women on an anti-aircraft battery. The picture came of observing some of the most unselfconscious people I'm ever likely to meet.'

'Is it worth a lot of money?' Dainty said suddenly.

'Not at the moment but putting false modesty to one side I expect it will be. Eventually.'

A review in one of the broadsheet papers appearing the previous summer had described her work as *'marching apace with the turbulent world in which we find ourselves yet at the same time as re-assuring and refreshing with its use of natural themes'*. She had taken this to mean that she painted modern subjects such as the girl gunners using backgrounds that people instinctively responded to.

'Modesty be blowed. After the war some people will have money to burn.'

'One of them being you?'

'Yes.'

Dainty got up and began to dress. Amelia lay naked watching him move in the enjoyment of his own masculine power. He was struggling with a front collar stud when he threw himself back on the bed beside her.

'Let me give you lunch. We can talk about me buying your picture. I've had a brainwave.'

'I do so love marvellous ideas. Thrill me with it.' She took his face in her hands and kissed it, enjoying his boyish blushes.

'I could buy your picture. Then you could go to Wales and look at places for us to live.'

His beseeching look reminded her of a thoroughbred puppy.

'Of course I've got to go back to my flying station but you could take my car to Wales and have a dekko at the place, perhaps find a remote cottage sort of thing. Roses around the door and all that.'

'Oh, Peter. I don't know.'

She had been tracing a finger from his chest down to his navel and back. Now she stopped. Dainty sat up, the glint of combat in his eyes.

'It's the Yank, isn't it? Christ, I could kill him.'

In an instant sentimentality which was almost childish had changed into compressed anger.

'Like the rest of his bastard breed he'll go home when his tour of duty is up and that's the last you'll see of him. They treat our women like streetwalkers.'

The harshness of the words could not disguise entirely an underlying petulance which she detected and at her core despised.

'For goodness' sake, Peter. You picked me up in a bar and we're having a good time but I had a life before I met you and that life goes on. Anyway, I might not want to sell you the painting. In fact I'm thinking of exhibiting it.'

She drew him into a kiss so as to hide her confusion. James had seen and admired the picture as well. What would he say when he saw that it had gone? Her face glowed hotly as she took her lips away.

'Selling it to me makes perfect sense for us both, don't you see? And anyway my jalopy is straining at its leash and I can wangle the petrol and I'm on sick leave anyway. We'll have a delicious little holiday during which time I'll talk you into a sale. Tell you what. Why don't we take the car for a spin? My car isn't far.'

It was parked in a mews garage ten minutes away. Dainty fished in his pocket and produced a key.

'The flat belongs to a chap on the squadron who lets me use the garage for a consideration of course. He drew back the doors. There she is. My pride and joy.'

The poor light entering the garage gave a depth to the blue of the machine's paintwork which she appraised with an artist's eye.

Layer upon layer of paint, each one applied thinner and finer than the last, had created a lustre that seemed to glow from within. Burnished chrome gave off a dull sheen. The smell was a complex one; petrol and oil, but with a bottom note of old wood and leather.

'It's absolutely divine. The most beautiful car I've seen in my life. More than just a car. It's a sculpture.'

Dainty flicked on a light to reveal the car in its gleaming magnificence. Huge round chromed headlights had been fitted with black-out hoods giving it something of the appearance of a sleepy, dangerous animal. The blue could now see was light, the blue of a summer's sky in Tuscany. The badge above the oval radiator said 'Bugatti' which meant nothing to her except that it fitted the car perfectly. No other name, strong on the first syllable and with a surging urgency to the second, would have done for such a beautiful machine.

'Oh, please let me sit in her!' Her voice which she found herself having to check was that of an excited schoolgirl.

'Get behind the wheel. I never had you down as the mechanical type I must say.'

'I'm not, but something like this could convert me. It's powerful and masculine and ... ' She allowed the sentence to change course ... 'Utterly beautiful'.

Her fingers stroked the rich chrome around the instruments and the silky graininess of the wooden dashboard, taking a delight in the way the controls fell to hand and when she sniffed the polished leather she fancied that she caught a scent of the Bugatti's owner.

'Shift over. We'll go for a ride.'

Wriggling first backside then legs onto the passenger seat she yielded her place to Dainty. The Bugatti started immediately its engine note settling down to a deep lusty gurgle. Dainty let out the clutch and moved the car far enough forward so that the garage doors could be shut behind them. Minutes later they were turning into Shaftesbury Avenue narrowly missing an Auxiliary Fire Service canteen wagon driven by a blonde woman who sent choice expletives winging after them. At Piccadilly Circus scores of American GIs were lounging and smoking and chatting with heavily made-up women and a shout of cheerful encouragement went up as the Bugatti chortled by.

'This is marvellous!' she shouted over the sound of the engine and the rushing air. Now they were driving along the Embankment heading West. At Cromwell Road Dainty pulled in and ordered her into the driver's seat.

'Don't worry if you make a hash of it at first. Come on. Give her a try. You can drive, can't you?'

'I have a licence. But this is a beast!' She let out the clutch too quickly and stalled the engine. Dainty's laugh was good-natured as he took her through a restart. Uncertainly but with mounting exhilaration she began a slow progress, unsure at first but gradually synchronizing mind and muscle with the power of the car.

'If you can handle her in town you shouldn't have any trouble once we're out on the open road,' Dainty bawled. 'Another half-an-hour of this and you'll feel like you've been behind the wheel of a Bugatti all your life.'

'No such luck!' she shouted back. Most of the traffic was military both British and American with fire service and Women's Voluntary Service vans, mobile canteens, horse-drawn brewers' drays and delivery carts following less regimented routes, weaving between the gaunt and tall brick-built buildings and further out, the newer detached and semi-detached houses.

'Gosh, this is sublime! I'm going to let her rip!'

The buffeting slipstream roared in her ears and made her eyes water. Dainty saw the police car to which she remained oblivious to.

'Bandits at three o'clock. Drive down this turning and stop,' Dainty shouted, a laugh in his voice.

Amelia was thrown back into the passenger seat as Dainty threw the Bugatti into gear.

The police car had at first shot past their turning but reversed as the constable on the passenger side spotted them.

Dainty's eyes and hands moved in deft co-ordination pushing the Bugatti forward as if propelled by a supernatural wind. At first the police car, which now had its bell clanging, was able to keep up with them but as he worked the gears, expertly judging speeds and distances for overtaking, constantly glancing in the mirror, the gap between them widened. Inside twenty minutes the pursuer was no more than a dot.

Outside Slough they passed a huge army convoy, the line of trucks and guns towed behind squat, crab-like tractors seeming to go on forever. Dainty pulled into the roadside and they swapped seats once more. She had seen the smooth professionalism of his driving and marvelled at it.

'You're doing marvellously,' he said after a quarter-of-an-hour's speedy progress. 'It's a bit like flying. You have to feel that you're controlling her from some point low down near your bum. That's why we call it flying by the seat of one's pants,' Dainty shouted and Amelia tossed him a laugh.

'Okay. Change down here and turn off to the left.'

Briskly she double de-clutched sensing his approval and sending the car nosing down a narrow lane. Cow parsley beat at the car's flanks its juice smearing the wing mirror as after another five minutes Dainty ordered her to slow right down and turn into a gravelled car park in front of a large country inn.

A green sports car with its top down, a big Wolseley saloon and three Jeeps, one with American markings and two British were the car park's only other occupants.

'A born driver. And one who has very definitely earned her drink!' Dainty sprang from his seat and went to Amelia's side opening the small door.

Most of the other customers apart from those in uniform she put down as doctors or lawyers or the more important sort of ministry workers. Two American women, one an officer and the other a sergeant sat under a vine tree near enough for Amelia to be able to catch odd words of their conversation. The officer was the younger and prettier. A fleeting touching of hands told their story.

Dainty returned to the table carrying her gin and tonic and a large whisky-and-soda for himself.

'Gosh, it's marvellous to get away from the smell of people, smoke and bad drains. I had almost forgotten what fresh air was like.' Amelia shook her head and ran her fingers through her hair. The drive had brought a fresh tinge of colour to her face and her eyes were still sparkling with the excitement of the drive.

Further conversation was drowned out as a large aeroplane flew overhead. Dainty shaded his eyes to watch it.

She thought of Elmeyer watching the British planes at Brize Norton and the subsequent row and violent, reconciliatory lovemaking.

'A Yank Flying Fortress.' It was almost as a growl.

'It's almost as if we're in one huge air force now although I can't say I get on with the Yanks terribly well at a personal level.'

Amelia shot a glance towards the women in American uniforms but they were totally engrossed in each other.

'Brave lads, all the same,' he added although whether a genuine observation or an attempt to rectify his earlier outburst she could not say.

She stared into her glass, inwardly cursing the plane which had made James Elmeyer an unseen presence at their table.

'Don't let's spoil a wonderful day by talking about Americans, Peter.' She could hear the strained note in her voice and despised herself for it. She knew that sometime soon she would have to tell this man that for all his powerful and contained aggression, his cocksure good looks and his persuasive charm - perhaps *because* of those things the issue between him and James Elmeyer had been decided in the American's favour.

And yet Dainty was like a powerful drug at once soothing and stimulating but leaving her loathing the very addiction that her body craved.

'All right. But I shall make a fight of it, though. Not with fists or pistols or anything like that, but I want you and I intend to win.' Expressions played across Dainty's young open features like wind soughing across a field of waving grass or corn. Now she saw it set hard. Such moods perversely attracted her. It was as though she needed him to be angry with her.

'I feel so wretched. I suppose somebody has to get terribly hurt. And yet ... '

'What?'

'Nothing. I was going to say ... no, nothing.' A flicker of shame and anger moved within her. On the surface she was feeling guilt but if she could peel away the layers of thought, action and words concealing which lay at her very centre, what should she find there? For Dainty she had a physical obsession that had danger and excitement at its very core. Elmeyer she loved already with a deep, secret union of their minds and souls. Peter Dainty, she knew, loved her with the fecklessness of a young man and would make plans to win her. James Elmeyer met her duplicity with a grave acceptance yet that, too, threatened her. Caught between the two men her heart had been reduced to the passive status of an arena in which their egos were paraded and she was obliged to watch half horrified, half fascinated, as they jousted for her affection, body and soul.

'Anyway we were talking about Wales.' Dainty's abrupt

switch of tactic dispersed Amelia's inner thoughts.

'I wasn't shooting a line about buying a place. In fact now is the prefect time. My gut feeling is that within a couple of years the more out-of-the-way places will be full of people trying to forget the war by writing their bloody memoirs. Buy now before the prices of picturesque and tumbledown cottages start to go up, I say.'

The warm sun and the slight headiness brought on by drink was beginning to work on her mood. How easy it would be simply to say that one brief word, Yes. She had a little money of her own which came with the growing critical appreciation of her work. The painting Peter Dainty so much admired would indeed be worth a tidy sum when as it was sure to do the art market picked up after the war's end.

'Let me buy you a drink,' Amelia smiled, taking Dainty's glass before he could object. She went to the bar and ordered and returning to their table set the drinks down firmly.

'I have a business proposition to make.'

'Go on.' Dainty's beaming smile as if directed at a child who had done something clever she found mildly irritating.

'Don't be so damned patronising. This is it. You advance the price of a house in Wales and I'll pay you back within a year. How does that sound?'

She could hear the blood thundering in her temples. It was a gamble. For it to come off the art market would have to pick up with the end of the war and her Birmingham exhibition would have to be a success.

'You can have the picture of the ATS girl as security against the first year's loan or a deposit if the sale of my work is slower than I expect it to be.'

It was the world of bargains and deals that Dainty understood. His eyes danced like sunlight sparkling along the ridge of an iceberg.

'I say we have a deal. Or would you prefer to sleep on it?'

They clinked glasses but the taste in her mouth was bitter-sweet; sweet with the anticipation of renewed seduction and a house far away in Wales but with the wormwood of betrayal.

She allowed Dainty to draw back her seat and place her cardigan over her shoulders. As he did so the American woman sergeant older of the two American servicewomen eyed her appraisingly. She shot a smile back to a fellow conspirator in a tangled emotional plot.

NINETEEN

SWIFTS dipped and looped over the broad squat cottage clinging to the mountainside above Blaendiffaith. Sheep had left copious evidence of having sheltered in the large south-facing room Amelia had already picked as her studio.

On clear summer nights she would sit outside looking at the village a mile or so away down a bracken-flanked track. In the mornings she would rise to view it still wreathed in mist.

'It's wonderful, Mr Creed. Just perfect.' The words came out despite her having resolved to maintain an off-hand air.

'Of course it needs a lot of work doing to it. Clearing the sheep shit out for a start.'

'Creative lady, are we?' Creed winced at the word 'shit'. Since from the cut of her clothes and her accent she obviously wasn't a factory girl he would assume bohemianism to be the cause of her licence. That, or being English.

She ran her eyes around the room for the umpteenth time. The original windows had been replaced by larger metal framed ones which admitted the light but had not made such a good job of repelling the sodden south-westerlies blustering up the valley. Several slates were missing but most were held in place by sumptuous layers of moss and lichen. Outside, a patch of springy turf a quarter the size of a football pitch and enclosed by a low and ancient stone wall she supposed had been enthusiastically burrowed by rabbits and badgers. The patch - 'garden' would be a wholly inappropriate term - was approached by means of a kitchen with a stone sink fitted with taps of industrial dimensions, flaking distempered walls and a cooking range which, beneath a patina of rust, looked as though it just might be usable. In her mind's eye she had already cleared the kitchen range of its charred contents, fired it up to a cosy glow and was sitting by it, cup of tea in hand, sitting and looking out over her Welsh haven, her very own oasis of peace and contentment.

'I'm an artist.'

'An artist. Very nice. Very cultured.' Said by Creed in such a way as to not quite shroud his distaste.

'Oh, but a very restrained artist. I shan't be throwing parties with cocaine-fuelled women tearing their clothes off and slim-hipped young men trying it on with muscular young miners or anything of that sort.'

Jehoidah Creed blanched as she fixed him with her chilliest smile. She'd taken a dislike to the man since the instant she'd walked into Bishop, Evans and Creed Solicitors and shook his flabby hand. Now she wanted him out of what she already thought of as her future house.

'You can go if you like Mr Creed. I'll let you know by Friday morning.' Which was two days hence.

'There is another prospective buyer,' Creed wheedled. Which, having already made enquiries in the Colliers', she knew there was most certainly not. Aneurin Hughes, the police sergeant, whose job it was to know everything had been very forthcoming in this respect. 'Be careful how you deal with that mendacious snatchpenny Creed,' the policeman had warned. 'He's as slippery as an eel with about the same human warmth.'

'If you would let me know as soon as you have decided.' Creed's voice was almost a whimper. 'Mrs Creed is expecting, you see, and I would like not to have to stray far from her bedside during her time of trial.'

'Go to her now, then. I'll let you know on Friday.' Amelia said, at the same time wondering what sort of woman would marry the man she had decided to nickname Creepy.

'Yes indeed. I shall be away and let you be alone with the cottage. A house is a very personal thing. It has to speak to you.'

'I hope all goes well for Mrs Creed.' Amelia sounded more charitable than she felt. 'What are you going to call the baby?'

A moist look replaced the greedy light in Creed's eyes and his lips began to move as if in recitation of prayer.

'At first we thought Myfanwy, if God blesses us with a girl, although it's a bit common now. Abigail, perhaps.'

'And if it's a boy?'

Creed's eyes brightened once more.

'Oh, we are in complete agreement. He shall be called Elwyn.'

166

TWENTY

FORCE yourself to imagine how people thought seventy years ago before the world was saturated with images, before the picture became the word ...

Mair had pored over the same photographs for more than an hour, searching the backgrounds and the faces for clues which might unlock the story of figures captured in one instant of time. It was a mistake. Photographs weren't like paintings by Old Masters with intricate layers of encoded meaning. Even people who hated each other appeared side by side smiling broadly when somebody pointed a camera at them especially in those days when film was scarce and the taking of even one picture quite an event.

The diary had to be the key.

With the photographs still fanned out in front of her Mair picked up the little green book feeling its stiffness and the powdery texture of the old varnished-cloth cover and smelling the sharp mustiness of its yellowing pages.

Whatever else he may have been Captain James Elmeyer had not been a literary man. Entries were matter-of-fact and reduced in many instances to code. The meaning of 'Red Cross Party' on the night of December 31, 1943, was clear enough but what did the 'Fr' written just before 'five pounds' on the Thursday in the first week of January mean? France? From? Father? 'Calais' appeared one day early in the year and scattered throughout the first three or four months several other French locations intermixed with German place names, and others that might be Dutch or Belgian. Perhaps 'Fr' did mean 'France' after all (although if that were so, what did the 'five pounds' presumably English money, indicate?).

After the diary had come to her Mair had spent some time reading up on the Allied air campaigns in Europe during the Second World War. Virtue and the evil constantly intertwining, the ingenuity, courage, folly, bravery, cruelty, comradeship and the machinations of power at the very highest level were matters she found both complex and utterly compelling. As her knowledge grew so little pieces of the jigsaw represented by diary entries fell into place. Thus June 6, 1944, had 'three missions' entered. A flurry of short-range missions across the Channel had obviously been in support of the D-Day landings.

After such frenzied activity flying operations tailed off somewhat in the following weeks.

And then, on a summer's Sunday, a little group of words which struck with near-physical force:

'With A. to Bl. Wales.'

There it was in blunt, thick pencil strokes. An irrefutable connection between the people in the photographs and her native village, shoring up the evidence of the receipt tucked away in the diary's pocket. An unruly rabble of thoughts raced and rioted through her mind. It was a racing certainty that 'A' was the Amelia to which Talfan had referred and almost certainly the woman in the photograph. 'Bl' could only be Blaendiffaith. Nowhere else. How much nearer though did all this take her to forging a connection between her father and the people in the photographs and her yet unexplained and sudden fortune? Twenty years before when she had been a young constable there must have been a score of people in the village who could have trotted out the story chapter and verse with only a little embellishment for good luck. Now the story of Elmeyer and Amelia and their wartime visit to Blaendiffaith was beyond recall, as remote in time as the enigmatic King Arthur and his knights of the Round Table.

Except for Talfan.

And Compton Picard, the Venerable One and her friend, who even seen through the veil of seven decades looked very much like the young RAF pilot who stared out of the picture with a confident, almost cocky smile. Two slender paths back to the past, their ways so poorly defined that they might easily peter out into the flat, unmarked terrain of forgotten time.

But Talfan first. Only then would she approach Ven.

Before setting off she stopped at the newsagent next to the workingmen's institute to buy the *Morning Star*. She arrived to see Talfan sitting unshaved by his window. His pyjama coat was clean but she noticed done up on the wrong buttons.

'Don't get old, Mary.' The voice was weary. 'I do not feel so well today.'

He had called her by her mother's name. A skein of mortality brushed her face.

'It's Mair. Mary and Aneurin's girl.'

'Aye. Of course it is.' And a thin hand reached out to pat

hers. 'How are you my lovely? What news from the outside world?'

'I've brought you the *Morning Star*. They still have it in the shop.' She tried to insert jokiness into her voice. 'There must be another incorrigible Red in our midst.'

'I hope so. We'll form a united workers' front, just the two of us. I miss all of that from years ago. There were causes in those days and some bloody passion about the place. Oh, you should have seen and heard it, Mair, the arguments in the Colliers' and the Workingmen's about Spain and about which side should be supported. I don't mean Franco or the government, I mean which of the parties and militias on the republican side. The communists had the most support in our valley but the Trotskyites and anarchists had their supporters and by God there were black eyes and bloody noses in with the dialectical materialism. Duw, the names of the people and the parties from those days are picked out in gold thread on my soul even to this bloody awful and dying day.'

'I envy you in lots of ways. I don't expect you believe that.'

'Not my old age, surely?'

'That most of all. Even though you've barely been out the county you've seen a world which was beyond my reach. The past, with my father, and you and Amelia and Elmeyer is a place from which I'm locked out and yet I so want to understand it.'

Talfan sighed. 'I don't think there's all that much to understand. Men and women were pretty much the same then as now. A bit happier perhaps. Strange how people always seem more content when there's a war on.'

'There were a lot of shortages though, surely?' Mair put in. Talfan's thin shoulders shrugged.

'They say so but Blaendiffaith didn't do so badly. There was full employment in the pits for a start. The Colliers' was always pretty well awash with ale and there was usually butter for your potatoes so long as you knew which counter to look under. Nothing terribly illegal mind you else your father would have something to say and he'd probably choose a very long word to say it. Blaendiffaith in those days decided that since misery usually seeks you out there is absolutely no point asking it in through the front door. There was plenty of coal of course and miners are buggers for their gardens and allotments so there was fresh produce. And whoever heard of a Welsh valley that went short of mutton and lamb? But most precious of all was the human warmth which even the very best steam coal cannot provide.' Talfan turned slowly towards her. 'The sort of warmth if I am not mistaken which attracts you to its fire?'

Mair nodded. 'I still can't get the story of a woman called Amelia and an American named James Elmeyer out of my mind. We talked about it before, do you remember?'

She looked into Talfan's eyes but they were looking beyond her own as if to some high and distant place. He nodded weakly.

'I have a gut feeling that my father was in some way involved with them in a way I do not as yet understand,' she persisted. 'At first what happened here in 1944 was of passing interest only. The sort of thing that would make a nice little article for the history society magazine or be material for a talk at the library. But something has reached across the years and touched me personally. It's like seeing a ghost. You might be frightened of what it means but still you have an irrestible urge to communicate with it. Will you help me?'

Talfan had been listening quietly with a finger to his lips as if in mute concealment. Now he took the finger away and softly spoke.

'Sometimes I think that expecting to find a prelude for one's own life smacks of vanity. Are you sure it is not better just to let things be?'

A wistfulness had come into the old man's voice and Mair knew that his own life harboured much disappointment. As a young man he had been fired with conviction at the outbreak of the Spanish Civil War and yet had not gone to fight. 'Ah, a great man for the theoretical socialism. I wish the rifle I carried in Spain knew half as much,' known as Big Colin had said good-naturedly of Talfan.

Burdened with diappointment of his own why should Talfan go to any lengths to dispel hers?

The silence of evening was invading the room. Miles away Blaendiffaith's hills were crowned with mist perhaps as they had been almost seventy years before when the American aeroplane had dashed itself against their flank. As if a thread from the tapestry which is the past had come loose she saw the crash with a terrible immediacy; the explosive sound of metal dashed against rock and screams of terrified men, the acrid smell of burning plastic and rubber; peat ploughed and ripped and rock scored by the skidding and smashing of the big plane's body.

What if one or more of the crew had survived the impact, only to have their life ebb away on the high and bleak moor? For an instant, as if through a loophole in time, she had seen the last few seconds of the aeroplane and its crew but now the spell was lifting.

She slumped in her chair, suddenly quite tired.

'Did you know Aneurin left me a lot of money?' she prompted.

Talfan shook his head. 'His pay would have been good for the time and your mother ran the house well. Apart from a mildly dandified taste in clothes and tobacco for his pipe and of course the odd pint of beer Aneurin's needs were not great.' His words were laboured, as if the weight of years were pressing down on him.

'When I say a lot I mean a couple of million pounds.'

Thoughts of her father, as yet unburied, were bringing her to the brink of tearfulness.

'For a sum to have gathered that much interest it must have started off in the tens of thousands which was a phenomenal amount during the war. How did my father come by it? You must know. You were his best friend.'

The light outside was fading fast and a chill had crept into the room despite the subtropical efforts of the central heating system.

'Friends. That's a good word.' Talfan smiled faintly and began to cough.

'Did you know that Amelia and Compton Picard were friends? Very close friends indeed. He was something to do with her coming to live in Blaendiffaith, that I know.'

At first she was not sure she had caught what Talfan had said. The tired speech of an old man close to death, perhaps.

But although softly spoken the diction had been precise.

'Amelia came to actually live in the village?'

'That's what I said.'

Mair allowed some seconds for her pulse to return to normal and for her brain to prepare itself for what might follow.

'When was she here?'

'In Blaendiffaith? Not long after she first visited with the Yank.'

'She spent a lot of time on the mountain where the plane crashed. She was a painter, they say. People liked her well enough at first but she took to moping around the mountain and it was generally agreed that she had dropped sixpence on the way to being a shilling short of the pound. She was in the village for a couple of winters after the crash and left never to be seen or heard of again.'

The words were no more a whisper, their last syllable spent as the last light left the hills.

It was several minutes before Mair Huws realised that Talfan Evans had passed away.

TWENTY-ONE

IT was the forty-seven pence that made her smile.

One million, nine hundred and twenty-three thousand, six hundred and twenty-four pounds and forty-seven pence. Precisely. An enviable circumstance at almost fifty years of age.

Yet, as the money in the bank grew so would her uncertainties. How could such an amount have been amassed without her having the slightest inkling of it? One fear dominated all else, one which like a vile and putrescent creature had slunk into the darkest corner of her soul. Suppose her father had been corrupt? She shook her head as if to physically shake off the thought. It was probable, indeed likely, that Aneurin had turned a blind eye to small-scale black marketeering. Such things would have been within the discretion of a policeman in those days. Such discretion though would never have been for sale.

She would think only of the present.

Tomos and her were now united in their mourning and their fathers who had been good friends in life were now companions in death.

The Colliers' was open. Looking through from the lounge she could see Tomos's back as he pulled pints in the public bar.

Perched upon the old and shabby bar stool Tomos had claimed as his own territory was a woman, a folded newspaper on the bar top in front of her. Brown eyes set in a round face had flicked up to meet her own. The woman was about forty-five years old and not more than five feet one or two. The smile had been friendly, wrinkling the corner of her eyes and dispelling a momentary impression of severity.

Mair gave the plunger of the bar-top bell a hefty clout which brought Tomos to her. The required solemn courtesies were exchanged. As the landlord pulled Mair's half-pint of ale the woman slipped from her seat allowing her to observe the blue lambswool sweater and well-cut slacks, flat suede shoes and pale blue socks matching the jumper. She wore no rings. Her medium brown hair was bobbed and cut into a neat fringe. If the woman was curious about Mair it didn't show.

Mair sensed that a game was about to be played.

'What crossword is that?'

'Saturday's *Daily Telegraph*.'

The voice was guarded although Mair noticed that the stranger had put down her pen.

'Isn't that a tricky one? I can usually do the quick crossword in *The Guardian* but cryptic puzzles go a bit above my head.'

The eyes now appraising her had depths into which she found herself being drawn. There was challenge there but also humour in her reply.

'Stretch yourself then. You can help me with this one.' 'GSEG'. Six and four letters.

'Oh dear. I'll put my mind to it. Actually I popped in to see Tomos.'

'Then don't let me hold you up. He hasn't been all that well since his father died. I'm here to help out for a bit. Jane Staunton by the way. And its broken eggs.'

The handshake was firm and quick. Mair introduced herself. Jane Staunton's eyes flickered giving the impression she was waiting for something. A verdict or a sign perhaps.

'Are you staying in the village?'

The proffered hand had been slender. The taking of it consented to the next level of acquaintance.

'I'm a distant relative summoned to help out with the funeral catering and serving drinks and the cleaning up. I think Tomos wants me to stay on for a while,' adding after a short pause, 'It's not as though my life is desperately busy.' An implicit invitation to more talk.

'Well then. I wouldn't mind learning how to do the cryptic puzzles.'

'I suspect you are quite adept at picking up clues.'

Jane Staunton's eyes engaged with Mair's for just an extra fraction of a second, a tiny sliver of time in which nothing is said but much understood.

'Tomos is taking his father's death rather badly,' Jane said and lifted the wooden flap giving them access to the public bar where Tomos had returned. The newcomer was shorter than Mair and tending towards plumpness. A heavy bosom and good hips. Neat, narrow ankles and a lithe movement which might have been employed upon a stage.

Tomos had seated himself in front of the coal fire reading the *Morning Star* and looked up at Jane's approach.

'Honest labour is a good thing but has to be leavened with food for the mind.'

'Of course. Which is why you are studying the racing tips.'

There was an easy familiarity between the two. Mair wondered why Tomos had not mentioned Jane before.

'If you two want a natter I'll take over behind the bar,' Jane offered turning towards the bar but then stopping and turning to face Mair.

'I'm sorry I didn't connect when I first saw you. Tomos told me about your father. I'm sorry.'

Mair smiled her appreciation and watched Jane serve two saloon bar customers with a brisk cheerfulness.

She stooped to kiss Tomos's cheek.

'Talfan was a part of the village's social cement as was my father. I'm afraid that things will begin to fall apart now that they've gone.' Mair put a hand lightly on his shoulder and he raised his face to regard hers.

'It's for our generation to hold it together now, isn't it?' Tomos said. 'We're the ancient worthies now. My father built his life around this pub. He's part of the stonework perhaps literally. Old places like this speak to people. I swear I heard him only a moment ago.'

Tomos's shirt was open at the neck to reveal greying hairs and skin that had largely surrendered the elasticity of youth for the parchment of middle age.

'I'm half afraid to go into the other bar for fear I'll see his ghost sitting on the old stool near the till.'

In her mind's eye Mair saw the bar stool but with Jane Staunton replacing the late landlord. How quickly the woman had joined the cast of characters in her life.

'I'm very, very sad about not being with the old fellow when he died,' Tomos continued, his eyes moistening. 'I'm glad that you're here though,' taking Mair's hand and gave it a squeeze.

'Your father was looking out of the window towards this valley,' she sad gently. 'He died just as the light failed. The very old at the point of death are already somewhere that gives them a glimpse of their final destination. I hope that doesn't sound trite.'

'Did he say anything at all? Any last words? Liked a touch of the drama, did Dad.'

Tomos was still holding her hand.

'He said he loved you, and that he was happy.'

A white lie but surely deserving forgiveness.

'We had been talking about the war and the crash on the mountain. Did you know my own father left me quite a bit of money?'

Tomos nodded.

'I did hear. Not much gets past Blaendiffaith.'

'Well there's a connection between my inheritance and a couple who came here during the war. Your father mentioned a woman called Amelia and James Elmeyer an American pilot who was her lover. He also said something about my friend Compton Picard. Then he quietly died.'

Tomos made a little noise somewhere between a chuckle and a sigh.

'And you want to know more about what happened back then?'

'Yes.'

'My advice is to take the dosh and don't ask too many questions which often lead to uncomfortable answers. Ask no questions and be told no lies has always been Blaendiffaith's motto.'

'I've taken the first step and there's no going back. Curiosity has a frightening power.'

Tomos made no immediate response but said after a while 'You're perturbed because you don't know how your father came by the money. Am I right?'

'You've heard how much it is?'

'My information isn't one hundred percent. I can't remember what came after the decimal point,' Tomos smiled. 'All I'm saying is does it really matter? Leave things as they are and let your imagination fill in the blanks. If you ask me the truth is overrated anyway.'

Mair produced two photographs each showing the same woman but one with an RAF man and the other an American at her side and handed them to Tomos who studied them intently before getting up to rummage for a magnifying glass kept under the bar.

'It's surprising how little some faces change with age.' Having scrutinized the photos for some time he tapped one with the lens. 'Combat aged men a lot. I'm always surprised, looking at pictures of wartime fliers how men of barely twenty could look twice their age.' He handed the picture back.

'I would be prepared to swear that the RAF man is your friend Compton Picard. I would have thought that even if you hadn't just mentioned his name. Do you know who the others are?'

'The American officer is almost certainly a Captain Elmeyer and I'm prepared to swear that the woman is his sweetheart Amelia.'

Tomos squinted at the pictures again. 'Against my own advice this matter is beginning to intrigue me.'

Typical. An Evans would climb out of his very grave to nose about in other people's affairs, Mair thought with affection.

'Will you excuse me while I make myself presentable?' Tomos laid the glass down and rose slowly but already there was a glint in his eye. Come upstairs with me and I'll show you something that might take your investigation forward quite some way.'

The Colliers' old pipes groaned and vibrated as in the bathroom in Tomos's living quarters he turned on the shower. Mair diverted herself by examining the spines of his books occasionally taking one down and flipping it open. Many of them had clearly been Talfan's; cheap Russian reprints of Marx and Lenin and pre-war volumes published by the Left Book Club. Politics had never interested her much and she passed over these quickly. Another section, separated from the rest, was fairly obviously Tomos's domain. In almost every instance the titles were something to do with aviation; 'Boeing' and 'fighters', 'Army Air Force', 'aircrew', 'aircraft', 'high', 'Liberator', 'USAAF', 'RAF' and 'Mighty Eighth' were words that re-occurred. What communism had been to the father, Mair mused, so aviation was to the son.

It seemed an age before Tomos re-entered the room preceded by a powerful whiff of cologne and pulled out a large book that Mair had not not long before put back in its place having seemed quite dull.

'What was the Yank's name again?' a fragrant Tomos asked.

She told him. Tomos began flicking through the pages until finding one at which he ran his fingers down a column.

'Captain James Elmeyer, aged twenty-seven, from

Winnetka, Illinois, the pilot of a B-17G Flying Fortress of the 321st bomber squadron of the 391st Bomb Group, 1st Bombardment Wing stationed at Bassington, Cambridgeshire.'

He looked up triumphantly.

'What dates are we looking for?'

'The late summer and autumn of 1944.' Mair felt her heart beat faster.

Tomos returned to the entry in the book.

'When the the co-pilot was Lieutenant Henry Gadgett from Trenton, New Jersey, having replaced Lieutenant David Steiner who was killed earlier that year. Lieutenant Peter Hosbach from South Dakota was the navigator, Wiggins ... Cotterill ... Norbert Hayes ... '

'Can I see that?'

There were no pictures of the plane and its crew, just a list of names and dates.

Mair marked the page and turned the book over. The picture of the author showed a middle-aged man with a beard and woolly cap photographed leaning on the remains of an old radial engine. *'Air crashes of South Wales, the Brecon Beacons and the Black Mountains'* was the less-than-snappy title but the book was fat with lists of names of men and aircraft and mostly black-and-white photographs. Mr John Maltravers the author had done his work with love and diligence. Many of the pictures were of wrecks scattered over bleak acres of moorland but in some men in front of their aircraft stood or squatted or lounged proudly showing the aircrew badges on their breasts while others sat on their aircraft's wings or stood by their gun positions or looked down from cockpits some laughing or striking poses with cigarettes or mascots but a few unsmiling, as if knowing that they were marked for death. A few of the pictures were in colour which lent them an uncomfortable immediacy, the faded colours compressing the time since the shutter's click seventy years before into nothing. Some faces were so young as to barely be moulded into their adult appearance. Others were as old as war.

'Sooner or later you are going to have to raise the subject with Mr Picard,' Tomos said. 'It's inescapable.'

Mair silently reviewed the prospect. There was more than a passing similarity between the RAF officer in the picture and Ven who she knew had been a wartime pilot.

'How many people do you suppose served in the air force as pilots during the war?'

Tomos stroked his chin. 'Thousands. Tens of thousands, although the pilot who you think might be Mr Picard is wearing the ribbon of the Distinguished Flying Cross which narrows it down more than somewhat. When you talk to him you could mention his DFC which if we knew when and for what it was awarded would really give us something to go on.'

'That would be an opening gambit, I suppose. And yet ... '

'And yet asking the question will almost certainly raise ghosts that Compton Picard, for whatever reason, would sooner not have disturbed?'

Mair nodded. 'I suppose so. It just seems so sneaky. Compton has never spoken much about the war and it's understood that I don't bring the subject up. I know he was in the Battle of Britain from things he's let slip when something about it has appeared on television.'

Tomos withdrew another book and opened it with an authoratitive flourish. '*The Battle of Britain - The Greatest Battle in the History of Air Warfare*' by Richard Townshend Bickers pretty much the last word on that particular scrap, he said. 'Aircrew who fought under Fighter Command Operational Control July 10 until October 31, 1940, beginning with Adair, Sergeant H. H. and ending with Pilot Officer Zurakowsky, a Pole. If there had been a Picard he'd be between 'Piatowski' and 'Pickering' but as you can see there is nothing.'

Mair stared at the page and its mocking omission. Had Ven lied. Her whole being revolted against the idea. Perhaps he'd been in the battle for only a short time or on its fringes. He had never actually said that he'd flown in the Battle of Britain. Still, a shadow had been cast. She closed the book.

'I don't think I shall be mentioning this,' she said quietly. 'And I'd be grateful if you said nothing. To anyone. I beg it of you.'

It was two in the morning before she went to bed having taken a mild sleeping pill, a whirligig of thoughts having chased each others' tails until arriving at a fatigued standstill. The chemically-induced drowsiness had almost enveloped her when she sat up in bed her heart beating. For as long as she had known Ven, Compton Picard had been the name he had used. She knew for a fact that it was the name on his passport, the one appearing on utility bills and in private correspondence. But he was an author and authors often used made-up names. It must be possible that his real name shed like a skin many years before lay waiting somewhere to be discovered in RAF records. Was that why he never used the wartime rank nor mentioned the decorations to which he was presumably entitled? The thought was like a bridge thrown over the sluggish river of her previous assumptions. Vigorous new notions were now charging across it. Ven might have changed his name for literary reasons but also perhaps to conceal some disgrace. Was it possible that something her father would have no doubt called a malfeasance or malefaction lay at the heart of the matter? Could it have been money? Had he perhaps fallen in with a fast set and pilfered from the mess funds in order to finance an increasingly profligate way of life? She had heard of such things. Sex? Or cowardice? No, surely not that.

As she slipped into sleep pictures of Ven - of Compton Picard - kept coming into her mind. The man was a writer and perhaps expiating some past wrong through his work. She would read his books again combing them for biographical clues. But whatever it was she could, she knew, excuse her old friend. Time and the immeasurable tide of affection, as constant as waves beating upon a shore, expunged all rancour or regret. She settled back down on the pillow letting the thought have its gentle voice heard. What right had she to pry, in any case? The past was the past. What, if anything, Compton Picard had done was between him and his conscience.

And yet the thought accompanied her to the threshold of sleep and some way beyond into her dreams. Ven was in some way connected with the events of 1944 and with the American called Elmeyer and the woman he loved. They had been in Blaendiffaith and Amelia had come to live here towards the end of 1944 and had stayed for some years afterwards. Ven lived in the Rectory which had been Amelia's home and studio. The workings of her mind had brought Elmeyer and Amelia and Ven as they were in 1944 tantalisingly close yet still the door between their time and hers remained shut. It may be that Compton Picard held the key but could she persuade him to turn it, to creakingly unlock the secrets of seventy long years?

Mair emerged from her dreams as from a catacomb in which her deepest emotions had been interred. Most profound of all, sorrow at the loss of her father was reverberating like a Bach fugue played deep within its caverns. The sad practicalities which death entailed had to be addressed that very day.

The food had arrived at the Colliers' and was already being prepared by Tomos and Jane who were chatting and working diligently and therefore best left alone. She would go to the undertaker to view the flowers. If her father was looking down his desire for a huge flamboyance of flowers would far outweigh that for the praises of a minister. Theatrical he would want them, billowing and scented, an explosion of scarlets and blues and a riot of yellows and pinks enough to almost bury the coffin. He would want a good drink to be taken at the Colliers', too. Flowers and fellowship. Only when these two prescriptions were met would old Aneurin Hughes finally leave the company and settle in the plot that would be his until Judgement Day.

As she quietly made to leave Mair noticed the *Daily Telegraph* folded as it had been before at the crossword and placed on the bar near the till.

Eighteen across. Young Tory pedals into low down affair. Young Tory, Young Conservative, YC. A 'low down affair' was a C-List event. 'YC' in the middle of C-List therefore provided the answer.

Mair pencilled in CYCLIST, adding her e-mail address and telephone number in the margin and the words 'I'm getting the hang of this!'

Jane would read it and laugh …

*   *   *

The sky over Blaendiffaith lay still and heavy as a death mask the day they laid Aneurin Hughes deep in the reddish-brown soil.

The village turned out to see the hearse arrive at Mair's door. It was a heavy and sullen day the cloying moistness of the air seeming to deaden sound. Mair found herself wishing that when her time came it would not be on such a day, so oppressive that one's very spirit clung to the earth.

Inquisitive faces and those set with the expression of ritual dolefulness waited but one stood out from the crowd. Jane met her own look with the downward cast of the eyes that is the gesture required of women at a funeral. Mair permitted herself an acknowledging smile feeling herself colouring slightly. With a little curl of satisfaction she realised that Jane must have read the crossword clue.

An undertaker removed his top hat out of respect for the deceased and began to slowly walk in front of the hearse as it set off on Talfan's final journey towards Bethesda Chapel. In sunlight one would have been able to see the tiny whorls in the car's finish where the polisher's cloth had smeared it slightly or the little corners where the cloth hadn't reached but the gloom of the day was such that all light had been sucked from the village and tipped into the blackness of the vehicle, only the flowers around and on the coffin standing defiant against the greyness.

The replacing of the top hat was a signal for the hearse to briefly stop and allow the wearer to mount the passenger seat.

People were going straight into the chapel, anxious for a seat. From the undertaker's limousine which had followed the hearse Mair looked for Compton Picard, but could not see him. When the time came to follow the coffin she did so at the head of a straggle of distant relatives. For all the people of Blaendiffaith standing four deep at the back of the chapel, and crowding the iron-pillared balcony so that it seemed it might sag under their weight, Mair could look at only one thing through the misting of tears. Aneurin's coffin was stood on trestles in front of the baptismal bath in which she had been immersed in the chapel where, upon what she hoped would be a fine summer's day, she would take the same polished and flowered, wheezy-organned and musty route to Eternity.

Tomos sat behind her with a hatted and demure Jane at his side. The service when it began was conducted by a minister she did not know who used the professionally soothing tones of a social worker ... 'Just as Aneurin Hughes protected and guarded us from evil, so we ask the Lord to take him into his everlasting care ... '

Good God, she felt her ire rising, why did these people adopt pious voices and speak in a sanctimonious way already dated a century ago? Her father was a good, old-fashioned copper of mildly conservative views, but why could not the man speak of the love of art that sustained him? And his love of words and the half a lifetime of grieving for his son lost in war? In a few days' time the cleric would probably be talking condescendingly about Talfan, a man who sold drink for a living, a beverage that probably had kept more men sane than it had destroyed. Not that it would matter too much since Talfan's Marxist spirit was hardly likely to be in attendance.

Bethesda's graveyard was at the same time bleak and lovely. A ragged army of grave markers and mossed and ivy-clad vaults topped the rise upon which the chapel stood and marched down to the stream from which since even before the coming of the Christian God the village had drawn life. At a spot overlooking the flank of Mynydd Maen, grim now, but in the summer months alive to the alternate dances of sunlight and cloud. Aneurin's grave had been prepared. Long before the pit had come men had been stumbling over this rabbit-holed and tufted acre to bury the dead. Mair recalled a talk to the local history society about the stone circle that had once stood on a site now occupied by Blaendiffaith but which had been pulled down all except one stone, worn and broken to a stump on the rough patch of ground called The Green opposite the Colliers'. How many times must Aneurin have touched the ancient stone or as a child used it as a goalpost or chalked stumps upon it or used it as 'home' in a game of tag? The lovers Amelia and Elmeyer had surely seen it too and heard the nearby stream's tumbling rush.

She did not cry, not even when the service ended and she followed the coffin out. The pall bearers, stalwarts of Blaendiffaith Rugby Club and of the Colliers' had reached the grave and were now setting the coffin down. The minister was again speaking although of what she did not care to hear. It did not matter. Her father's progress into the infinite would be neither speeded nor delayed by the man's fulminations. Mair found herself wanting to take in the whole scene as if it were a landscape photograph, her eye recording every incidental thing, the shifting of the light now that a wind had begun to disperse the low grey cloud, the little yellow digging machine which stood with its engine running a discreet distance from the grave and Jane, almost lost in the larger scene were it not for the fact that Mair's eye especially sought her out.

And one other woman, old but not in black yet soberly dressed, the cut and quality of her clothes evident even from a distance, wearing a brimmed hat. Mair found herself drawn to where the stranger was standing. The old woman used a stick to steady herself on the rough ground but was straight-backed. It was the woman's posture as much as the face; an erect but not quite haughty bearing counter to the spirit of the age.

People were walking away from the graveside in small groups but the woman was by herself. Mair searched her memory for a compartment into which the stranger would fit.

She found herself approaching her and holding out a hand.

'I'm Mair Huws. I don't think we've met but thank you for coming to my father's funeral.'

The hand that met hers was cool and dry and with a firm press. The quick, intelligent eyes scanned Mair's face.

'Aneurin's daughter? Of course. I can see him in your face. He and I were friends many years ago.

'My name is Amelia Kershaw.'

TWENTY-TWO

THE window still criss-crossed with tape as a precaution against bomb-blown flying glass looked out onto what before the intrusion of a sandbagged guard post with its white-helmeted military policemen must have been a tranquil scene.

Lieutenant-Colonel Edward Smathers watched the MP raise the red-and-white striped barrier with metronomic regularity as large olive-drab military cars entered or left the headquarters of the Eighth Army Air Force, High Wycombe, Buckinghamshire. Many of the cars were British. An RAF one was coming now. The policeman saluted, spoke briefly to the driver, stood, saluted again and lifted the barrier.

This would be his man who rather than go to meet he had ordered to be escorted to his room.

The RAF officer ushered into Smather's office by a corporal clerk was tall and sandy-haired and wearing the uniform of an RAF Wing Commander. Smathers, a professional soldier, thought the Britisher looked ill at ease in the uniform like an actor required to don it in order to play a part.

'Wolfenstone.' The British man offered his hand. 'Percival.'

'Tea, Wing Commander?' There was no salute between officers of equal rank.

'I'd rather have coffee if you don't mind. Your coffee is very good.'

Normally, his WAC secretary would have made coffee but he'd given her a half-day off. Smathers had fitted himself up with an electric kettle for times when his staff were not on call. It had cost a few dollars but there were always ways of acquiring life's little luxuries. He put it down in front of the RAF man who, he noted, wore no flying insignia. A ground-pounder. It should not matter. Plenty of people other than fliers were playing their part in this war but still for the business in hand an aviator would have been appropriate. He was glad he not gone down to welcome the man now sipping appreciatively at his coffee.

On the brown manila folder that Wolfenstone withdrew from his briefcase three previous subject headings had been neatly ruled through. The British obviously wanted to economise on stationery, Smathers thought, the impoverished, mealy-mouthed bastards. He let the RAF man shuffle some papers before almost barking 'You have a man?'

Wolfenstone nodded. 'I rather think we do. Flying Officer Peter Dainty. An ideal candidate I should say.'

Before the other had even sat down Smathers had decided that he did not overmuch care for him. They should at least have sent a flier and not a glorified clerk.

'Dainty, uh? He must have done something pretty un-dainty to qualify for this job. What did he do? Put his hand up your Princess Elizabeth's skirt?'

Wolfenstone went red and plunged his eyes into the file at which point Smathers began to openly despise him. If the RAF man had said something of the kind about Eleanor Roosevelt he would surely have smacked him in the mouth.

'Not exactly that.' Wolfenstone swallowed. 'But he's a pretty rotten apple.'

'A pretty rotten apple, eh?' Almost, but not quite unintentionally, he imitated the visitor's accent. 'And if he volunteered for this job I'd say he's just about the rottenest apple from the rottenest barrel on the Allied side.' Smathers shook his head. 'Yes, Sir. The real son of a bitch.'

He paused. Watching Wolfenstone was like watching a barbecue chicken turning on a spit.

'In a manner of speaking.' Wolfenstone was flushed.

'Then let's have it in a manner of plain speaking. Can this Dainty fellow be trusted to do the job?'

'Yes. He has every reason to do just as we demand of him.'

Smathers sipped his coffee looking hard at the RAF man over the rim of his cup. Smathers prided himself upon being a professional bully and bullies always knew how to sense resistance in their victims. He sensed the worm was turning.

'That's good. Because what we both need is a genuine, five-star, high-octane copper-bottomed bastard who will kill a guy fighting on the same side as him just so he can save his own skin.'

Smathers paused as if appreciating the aroma of a fine cigar, pleased with his choice of words.

'And screw the other guy's girl for good measure.'

Wolfenstone unclipped a photograph and slid it across the table rather more assertively Smathers noted.

'Here's our man.'

It was an official mugshot presumably taken at induction into the Royal Air Force and therefore without background detail that might provide the fragmentary context for a life. In a fraction of a second the camera's shutter had caught a fugitive expression. Shiftiness? Smathers thought. No, not quite that. Wariness, perhaps. And anger. The sort of look a caged animal might shoot at its captors.

'Can I keep this?'

'Certainly. There are other prints.'

'Fine. Because if it's going to chew too deeply into Great Britain's finances I can arrange for the photograph to be copied here.'

The RAF's man's eyes had levelled with his own and they were cold. 'I don't think we need tax your resources. We managed without them until well after the Battle of Britain.'

Touché. Could be there was more to this pale lanky son-of-a-bitch than met the eye?

Smathers went back to the picture, trying to fill in a background. Despite the narrowness of the head, the fair hair and the nose's aquiline profile it wasn't the playing fields of Eton or one of the other Limey private schools that had shaped the features. There was something of the workshop or garage, the fishing boat's wheelhouse or a soldier in the ranks of a regular battalion of the line.

Except for one thing. The eyes. Blue, it said on the description attached to the photograph but to describe them by their colour was like trying to describe a thought by its shape. 'Insolent' Smathers would have said; belonging to a body that outwardly conformed but which inwardly rebelled. Wry. Artistic, even. Bloody unmilitary anyhow.

In the photograph Dainty wore an open-neck cellular cotton shirt and a tweed jacket that looked to be of good quality but also, from the set of the shoulders, one that hadn't been tailored for him and upon which was pinned a lapel badge.

'The lapel pin. What do you suppose it is?'

Wolfenstone took back the picture. 'I haven't the faintest but from what I know of this man I doubt very much whether it's the Boy Scouts.'

Smathers' smile subtly signalled a truce. It just might be possible to get along with this guy, he mused. That was the thing about the Brits. A lot of Americans thought them sly or hypocritical and no doubt some were but he had found that first impressions were almost always misleading. Never take anything for granted was his motto when dealing with the British. Observe and wait. Don't push. Let them reveal something of themselves in their own good time. He'd needled Wolfenstone who had come back strongly and now they were quits.

'Tell me some more about Flying Officer Dainty while I freshen your coffee.'

'As I have suggested, a thoroughly bad lot,' Wolfenstone continued. Born in Northamptonshire where his father did something or another in a shoe factory. Nothing very elevated, a foreman type. Dainty is an only child and seems to have got a reasonable amount of his parents' love and attention although there are those who devoutly wish Dainty had been strangled at birth not least among them the RAF Provost Branch.'

Outside, the red-and-white pole was constantly raising and lowering. If America was so damned good at making things why hadn't it come up with a machine to do the job and send the dope in the white helmet to a fighting unit?

'Your MPs, huh?'

'That's right. Dainty came to their attention early on while he was doing his flying training. Fellow cadets began to report small sums of cash missing. Dainty was stealing all right but there was no proof and he's such a charming blighter that nobody ever thought of accusing him much less give him the barrack-room thrashing he so richly deserved. He always had more money than the others largely due to a profitable sideline in dubiously acquired cigarettes and loaning money at ridiculous rates of interest to those who found their spending out of step with their RAF pay.'

Smathers took a cigar, offering the box to Wolfenstone who declined. 'Some might call that enterprise. Go on.'

'Before I do, it would be as well to remind you of one thing.' Wolfenstone's face was flushed and there was a cold flatness in his voice. 'British servicemen at that rank only get about a quarter of that paid to Americans. We might not be able to pay them well but at least we can protect them from exploitation.'

The rebuke hung in the air for several seconds before Wolfenstone continued.

'All this happened in Canada where Dainty was being

taught to fly under the Empire Air Training Scheme. Off-duty cadets are welcomed into Canadian homes and most do not abuse such hospitality: indeed there are severe punishments for those who do. There is more than a suggestion that Dainty might have taken liberties with the wife of a pillar of local society who was entertaining him for the weekend.'

'Sure sounds as though he was getting entertained all right. Couldn't you have put him on a charge and packed his bags and sent him home?'

Wolfenstone smiled. 'Evidence against him was circumstantial and he lies like an angel. Anyway, he was a brilliant pupil with a psychological profile suggesting that he would be more suitable for fighters than bombers. A loner with a killing instinct.'

'So. How did it play when he got to an operational squadron?' Smathers asked from behind a haze of cigar smoke.

'Brilliantly.'

'I'm not so sure you should say much more. I'm getting to quite like the guy.'

'Your admiration will be dispelled when I tell you that he has been picking Uncle Sam's pocket.'

A momentary silence, during which Smathers looked at the photograph once more.

'You don't say? An international speculator, eh? Perhaps we should invest in him in time for the post-war boom.'

'Either that or have him shot,' Wolfenstone said flatly. 'The evidence that he has been dealing in goods stolen from American bases as well as from British ones is irrefutable. He seems to have built up a string of contacts all over the country and is thought to use a London drinking club called the Limbo Bar as a base. We all know that low-level misappropriation of kit goes on. Your flying chaps are very good at acquiring bits of RAF kit which they prefer to US Army issue, for instance.'

Smathers nodded. 'We turn a blind eye. Your flying boots are far better than anything we have. Men shot down behind enemy lines can cut the tops off to make them look like ordinary civilian shoes thereby increasing their chances of getting the Hell out of it. Your flying helmets are pretty darned good, too. I've got one myself.'

'Dainty's dealing go far beyond a boots and leather helmets or small-time dealing in stolen cigarettes and spirits. Vehicle parts, fuel and oil, wholesale thefts of clothing from military stores, tools and spares are all part of his portfolio. An American flying jacket ending up on an RAF chap's back as a result of some bartering is one thing. Having it stolen from American stores and sold at a fat profit is something else. The materials and equipment that keep Britain in the fight are paid for with the lives of Merchant Navy men who ever since this war began have faced submarines and torpedoes, attack from heavily-armed surface raiders and from the air. The loss of merchant seamen compares with those of Bomber Command or the heavy bomber component of Eighth United States Army Air Force. Take that into account and there isn't a lamp-post in this Realm high enough from which to string people like Dainty.

'Our problem is he's a hero who has had his face splashed all over the papers and set up as the finest example of British decency and fighting spirit. Throwing the bastard in clink would be a public relations disaster. It'd knock morale all to hell.'

Smathers leaned back in his chair spreading his hands. 'Okay. You've convinced me. Dainty's a bastard. Do you want hear about our fellow?'

'If he's worse than Dainty's he's the dirtiest swine imaginable.'

'Worse even than that. He's a communist. Lowest form of damned life there is. Our man is a particularly dangerous sub species of the commie persuasion. He's handsome and well educated and with a great battle record who if we send him home as some kind of hero is likely to give Mr and Mrs Average American notions we would rather they not entertain.

'His crew love him and his superior officers consider him an exemplary airman and officer. The whole fucking world seems to have fallen in love with Captain James Elmeyer.'

Smathers lit another cigar and neatly flipped the spent match into his ashtray.

'This is him.'

Wolfenstone regarded the picture. A slightly petulant mouth surmounted by a moustache prevented the face from being classically handsome. Dark hair neatly contained by an officer's cap, the picture looking as though it had been composed in a studio.

Wolfenstone passed the picture back. 'At a rough estimate I

would say that twenty-five percent of our armed forces have communist leanings and a damned sight more in the merchant fleet not to mention at least half the intelligensia.' His voice was calm. 'I'm sure the United States government has noticed that the Russians fighting and dying on our side are that way inclined themselves. You can't condemn a man because of his political convictions.'

'Understand, Wolfenstone, our chiefs don't see it that way.' Smathers extracted the cigar from his mouth and blew a screen of smoke between himself and the Briton. 'Good American boys with good American values are dying in Pacific swamps, in European foxholes, in submarines and ships and in the air. The last thing they need is some pointy-headed communist telling them that they're fighting for the wrong thing.'

Outside, the Military Policeman was raising the barrier for a three-star general's car. Smathers looked around the room in which everything from his secretary's Remington typewriter to the paper it used had been shipped out from the States. In his mind it all added up to one irrefutable statement. Wolfenstone might be right about the merchant sailors but the war would be won because America was right and had the might.

'Pure industrial muscle will clinch this war,' Smathers said smartly deciding that further elucidation was necessary. 'And that muscle is wielded by tens of millions of workers who are sweating their balls and I guess their tits off too. Trouble is, they don't all have the same idea about what will happen when the war ends. Some of them have heard about communism and how it promises to spread the jam and give a better life for all and are suckered in by it. There are communist sympathisers in the State Department and even, damn it, in the United States Army and there are signs that some of their ideas are taking hold. Without putting too fine a point on it we need a plausible and handsome agitator like Captain James Elmeyer like my ass needs another hole.'

Smathers ran a finger around the inside of his collar. It was a warm, bright day and a Friday. In recent weeks he had taken to going into London and drinking with a clutch of army public relations people and war correspondents. Once, a writer famed for the tautness and manliness of his prose had lumbered into the company and the resulting drinking spree had lasted the weekend, the very weekend he had first heard

Elmeyer's name and even through a fog of alcohol an idea had began to form. The writer himself was a big and heavily-bearded man who reported the Spanish war from the left-wing republic's viewpoint. Smathers had wondered why nobody had thought of bumping off the loud-mouthed bastard. The answer was that the big-bearded man played his life out centre-stage, and was well-connected enough to be able to shift the scenery around with him. He had connections and influence going right up to the White House. Elmeyer, the poor sap, had none of this. Just good looks and courage, a direct way of expressing himself and Marxist ideas which if the plan worked would land him in big, but oh so big trouble.

'Perhaps you would like to look at our detailed proposals.' Smathers slid the file across to the RAF man. Behind Wolfenstone was the desk where Smathers' WAC sergeant usually sat. She'd be off base by now and on the train to London or maybe she'd bummed a ride. If he left soon there would still be time to follow her and meet up in one of their regular watering-holes. Just agree it Percival old chum, old fellow. It was a good, simple plan. Elmeyer would be sent on a flight from Bassington via a waypoint in South Wales ostensibly to check some new radar equipment. There would be a skeleton crew so as to minimise casualties. Somewhere at a point early on in the flight Elmeyer's plane would make a test transmission which would allow a fighter flown by Dainty to locate and jump it. The Flying Fortress would be defenceless since what guns were manned would only have blank ammo. Elmeyer and the B-17 would end up as a smoking hole on some desolate Welsh hillside. It was too bad about the plane but it had to be looked upon as an investment.

'Our bosses have worked out the general policy. It's up to poor bastards like you and me to work out the details,' Smathers said. 'Take the file away. Let me know in, say, a week?'

Another movement of the military police barrier caught the corner of his eye. Bingo.

'Say, Wing Commander. You came by official car from the Air Ministry, I believe?'

'That's right.' Wolfenstone was clipping Elmeyer's death warrant into his leather briefcase.

'Would you mind giving me a lift into London? There's a friend I was hoping to meet up with.' If he moved smartly he'd have time to catch up with his secretary and cut her out from her friends and steer her in the direction of a Bloomsbury hotel where they were known.

Yes, Sir. War was hell.

* * *

At precisely the instant Smathers was being put down in central London Frenchie was pondering what Captain Elmeyer had said. Trouble was brewing like a storm you can't yet see or hear but you know darned well is up ahead. Later, Elmeyer had told him about his interrogation by the two officers. It had spooked him for a while, this first whiff of trouble, but then he'd thought heck, they can't be everywhere and see everything. And business was business. Anyway their business seemed to be snaring commies. He picked up a heavy sheepskin jacket looking for bullet or shrapnel holes and noting that it had been patched twice.

'Flying clothing that's been written off as no good for re-issue is getting to be a buyer's market. Give me a figure,' Frenchie said. The stores Technical Sergeant was an Armenian which he thought must be something like a Jew. The Jews you could trust, even if they did drive a hard bargain. The Italians and the Poles, though, fucking pirates. The sergeant said a figure and Frenchie did some sums in his head. The only time he worked things out quicker was when calculating the deflection needed to shoot down a Messerschmitt.

'This stuff's popular with RAF guys,' the Armenian said. 'With your contacts you'll find buyers.'

'A hundred English pounds. That's as much as I can go.'

'I'll settle for a hundred and ten.'

'A hundred. The offer remains good for an hour. After that it goes down to ninety pounds. It's your call.'

'Okay. A hundred.' The Armenian looked aggrieved. He was the type of bastard who would snitch to the MPs to save his own skin Frenchie thought. Something was up. He could feel it as a spider feels the merest movement on the fringes of its web or as just before a storm when the leaves show their pale undersides and the light has a purplish glow. It was different somehow to other times when danger and discovery had stalked him and he had followed his intuition and laid low for a bit. Maybe he was getting jumpy with too many missions but he didn't think so. Somewhere, something

193

powerful and sinister was gathering its strength and would soon beset them.

Luck Be A Lady was one of three B-17s in the hangar where bigger repair jobs were done. Jacks had been placed under her wings so that the undercarriage could be tested and both inner engines had their cowls off with a crane positioned over the starboard one ready to lift it from its mount. The ship was like an old matron being primped and preened at the hairdressers. As soon as she got out of the repair shop they were to have their photograph taken with her. Army public relations was making a big thing about it. Him, the Cap and Hosbach and all the rest would be in the *Stars and Stripes* and pictures and stories would be sent to newspapers and magazines back home. A week ago he'd bought a natty little camera from a guy who needed quick cash. He'd already tried it out by taking some pictures of the crew standing in front of Luck Be A Lady. A couple of times he's taken the camera to London to take tourist pictures and he'd also taken one of the Cap with Amelia. A couple of weeks later he had bumped into Amelia with the RAF guy Dainty and they'd persuaded him to take a photograph of them together. The pictures had been developed and printed in the base's photo section who owed him a few favours. He'd given the Cap the pictures of him and Amelia and of the crew. There had been a bad momement when the Cap had glimpsed the picture of Amelia with Dainty. Grimly, he had asked if he could keep it and had slipped it inside his diary. Frenchie didn't care for Dainty all that much even though they were doing business together. He'd seen the way the Englishman looked at the Cap's girl. There was trouble up ahead in that direction too, he reckoned.

Still, he'd have to have another picture printed up from the negative to give to Dainty just to keep him sweet. He wondered what the Cap would do with the picture he had of Amelia and Dainty. He hoped he wouldn't brood over it and make himself sick. Maybe he'd stick pins in Dainty's picture.

A couple of men in olive fatigues one wearing a button-neck sweater against the late afternoon chill called out to Frenchie disrupting his thoughts. The luckiest of maintenance crew men had lockers in the hangars in which they could keep tools, working clothes, thermos flasks, newspapers and sandwiches and one of the men had rented his out to him.

Normally, there was a good chance of having the lockers broken into but there would never be any trouble with his. His name was on it and everyone on the base knew Frenchie Hayes, a great little guy unless you got under his skin.

Inside his locker some overalls had been rolled up into a ball. Frenchie liked to wear flight overalls in the summer because they were cool. A peaked olive green baseball cap was hung on a peg and at the bottom of the locker were sneakers and a GI haversack.

The money was bound up in hundreds, each bundle held by an elastic band so he could just grab the amount he required without having to count it out. Not all that long before he'd been handling small amounts, five or ten English quids, maybe. Now it was always in hundreds or even thousands. He was getting big and he would get bigger. Everyone was saying the war would end soon and then Frenchie Hayes, the tousled little dark-haired guy with the cheerful smile who everybody liked would just be one more of tens of thousands of demobilised Sergeants looking for a job.

In a pig's eye, he would.

It didn't take a genius to figure that air gunners without a war to fly to weren't going to be very much in demand. In recent weeks he'd stepped up his trading activities including cutting a deal with the RAF guy Dainty. Nowadays, a lot of the business was concluded without him even seeing the goods just like he'd heard happened on the stock markets. Loaning money to set up transactions, putting sellers in touch with buyers and taking a cut in the middle was his game which had become a game to be taken as seriously as war. More seriously in a way because the war would end but trade would roll on. Frenchie had stopped thinking of his activities as wrong a long time ago. It was wrong that sergeants like him took the same risks as officers but got only half the pay. It was wrong that industrialists who were making fortunes out of war arrmanents without even having to think about risking their asses. It was wrong his little girl was sick. Anyway, free enterprise was the American way, or so he'd been told. That being so, what he was doing was downright patriotic.

They were doing something different about Luck Be A Lady. The plexiglass nose had been removed and something installed around where the bomb sight usually sat. He felt pissed about it somehow. Hundreds of hours he'd spent freezing his balls off four miles above the ground trying to prevent the Germans from knocking holes in the old lady and the grease monkeys couldn't even be bothered to tell him why they were tearing her apart.

'This doesn't look like a routine service. What the heck's going on?' he shouted up at the aeroplane's blunted and vacant nose. A torch flashed as a figure made its way down the fuselage toward him, the light catching a mess of wiring looms, pipes and junction boxes.

'Howdy. Staff Sergeant Hayes, isn't it?' The man wore the two inverted stripes of a Corporal.

'Never mind who the fuck I am. What are you doing to my plane?'

'Don't get so sore, Sergeant. We're just putting in a gizmo that'll make the bombardier's work a bit easier. One more day and you can have this flying scrap yard all to yourself.'

Frenchie muttered something at the flight electrician. Later, he'd check his own turret to make sure the electrics were all right. What was it about Luck Be A Lady that she needed special work done? From time to time modifications were introduced to suit changing tactical requirements but air and ground crews always got to know about it straight away even if it was supposed to be secret. He hadn't heard anything about this. They must have told the Cap, though. He'd speak to him as soon as business was out the way.

Low stratocumulus the colour of congealed porridge covered the sky. Returning to where he'd leant his bike he noticed that he'd left it unchained. It was a small miracle it was still there. There was money to be made in stolen bikes. He'd even thought of going into that line of business himself.

Frenchie was musing on the subject of bikes as the Solitary Cyclist squeaked slowly by, his face hidden by his garrison cap and turned-up collar. Nobody knew where the Solitary Cyclist came from, nor where he went, nor what outfit he came from. A superstition had taken hold that anyone who saw the Solitary Cyclist was for the chop. One guy swore he'd seen the figure just ride through a closed hangar door. The temperature always seemed to drop when the Solitary Cyclist was around. Frenchie didn't believe any of this nonsense but a cold shudder ran through him just the same.

He watched the figure disappear round a corner before getting on his own bicycle and heading off in the direction of flight control.

The Corporal who took the two hundred pounds was a short Arizonan who smiled too much. Frenchie guessed he was one of those groundpounders who liked doing business with aircrew because there was always the chance of the flier being fatally unable to collect. This day the Arizonan Corporal was smiling even more than usual.

'Your ship's got an interesting mission coming up, or so I heard,' the man drawled, buttoning the money into his shirt pocket and patting it. 'They've been keeping it quiet but we hear things.'

'I know about it,' Frenchie lied. 'It's nothing special. I've just been to see the ship. They're always inventing new things to try out.'

'Flying around just testing things doesn't count as a mission though and that's what you guys want, isn't it? To do your missions and get the Hell out of England for good?'

Frenchie decided he liked the corporal even less than usual.

'Even just flying around beats having to talk to people like you.' Frenchie jabbed the shirt pocket where the Corporal had put the money.

'The interest on the two hundred is accumulating as from now and there's something you should know. If I get the chop there will be someone else to collect.'

'Hey, Frenchie take it easy. It's gone all right before. You've never had no damn trouble with me.'

Without further words Frenchie swung his leg over his bicycle and rode off to where he knew he would find Elmeyer.

He did not see the Corporal spit silently behind his back.

TWENTY-THREE

ONE day he would write about this; the tired gaudy chintz covers on the officers' mess chairs their arms hard as a dog's pads where beer and coffee and tea had soaked in and dried, the bitter smell of stale cigarette smoke and sticky rings where pint glasses had been set down on tables from which the varnish had long ago been worn.

Perhaps, Peter Dainty thought, nostalgia would eventually bathe his present actions and surroundings in a golden light. The stale squalor of the mess viewed from the standpoint of thirty years hence would be seen as the carelessness of young warriors for their immediate surroundings. Men who were about to risk their lives in the air didn't particularly care how the curtains were hung. The fear, too, would similarly be hammered from the raw, jagged thing it was into the seamless contours of something suitable for discussion in the golf club or pub bar. 'Yes, I was afraid. We were all afraid in those days,' he would say and it would be a lie. We were all scared fucking shitless would be more like it. Waiting in the warm sun of that hot September of 1940 for the telephone ring that would send them scrambling. Once the wheels had stopped bumping over the grass and had thudded back into the wheel bays fear had been replaced by excitement; the blood was up and he'd once again become immortal. Dainty had flown superbly in those days and fought hard and without mercy.

'If you see one of the bastards dangling from a 'chute let him have it. Jerry can always make planes but he can't find the men to fly them,' he had been fond of saying in those days, generally to shock and impress newcomers to the squadron. By confessing to 'the jitters' he had found it possible to hold at bay the greater thing, the raw, black horror which exhaustion or alcohol could sometimes keep away at night but which crept into his room each dawn, clutching at his stomach and making him physically sick. Each breakfast in those days had been the last meal of a condemned man.

That was during the Battle of Britain four years ago and he had survived. Somehow, in North Africa, flying the slow, rugged American-built Kittyhawks it hadn't been so bad. The ruthless intensity of the Battle of Britain had generally been absent and his instinct for survival by this time well-honed.

Latham the mess steward appeared with the daily papers, distracting Dainty from his memories. He took the *Daily Mail* and threw himself into one of the partially-eviscerated chairs, feeling something hard against his buttock. A half-crown. That was lucky. Another second and Latham would have spotted it. Dainty pocketed the coin with some satisfaction. The coffee he'd ordered arrived a minute later as Dainty was flicking through the news pages. Since the expansion in his business interests he had been taking more interest in what the newspapers had to say. War news still filled most of the rationed newsprint but for several months the coverage had speculated as to the post-war order of things.

Through the open windows came the bark of engines being run up. Dainty summoned Latham.

'Sir?'

'More of this dishwater you call coffee.'

'Coming up, Sir.'

Dainty stayed the steward as he turned to carry out his errand.

'Latham. You're a wise old bird. What do you think will happen after the war, politically speaking?'

Latham had been a Leading Aircraftman for as long as anyone could remember and was widely thought to be one of the most learned men on the entire station and one about whom stories abounded. By different accounts he was a gentleman who having been crossed in love buried himself in the ranks; a university professor seeking obscurity following allegations of gross misconduct and (currently) a valet who had been forced to leave his employment following the discovery of financial shenanigans. On balance, Dainty favoured the latter explanation.

'The socialists will win a general election and form a government. Of that I have very little doubt. I have to say it's not something I relish.'

Latham patted his smooth, straight, black hair in an unconscious gesture humorously imitated by the younger officers. Upon one matter relating to the mess orderly there was general agreement. The utter blackness of his thatch and the Great War ribbons he wore over his battledress breast pocket were not chronologically consistent.

'Why not? It will be the age of the common man.'

'Which is precisely why I do not look forward to it, Sir.

People were quite common enough before the war. I fear it will lead to vulgarity on a scale as yet undreamt of. Every modern war has led to a new coarsening. After the Great War there was grotesque dances and worse music, if you care to call it that. This time it will be motor cars for all, tens of thousands of horrible little houses desolating the countryside and television. The war has seen very rapid advances in what I believe are being called electronics. All this gimcrackery will be directed towards passive civilian consumers the minute the war is over, mark my words, Sir.'

'I mark them well. Sounds pretty good.'

Latham regarded Dainty as he might a puppy that has messed on the carpet.

'If you say so, Sir. I'll get your coffee.'

With the feeling it was him that had been dismissed Dainty pulled a face and shook his paper open at a page of home news and began to read with interest a story about how war production in a radio factory had reached such a pitch of efficiency that it could afford to resume making sets for the civilian market. 'A new technical dimension. Tested in war for your peace of mind,' the advertising slogan read.

'Everything you said is right,' Dainty chirped when Latham returned with the coffee. 'Look at this advertisement for wireless sets but it won't stop there. Pictures and words all in one. Television is going to rule the roost. The newspapers are already talking about how it will spread to cover the whole country.'

Dainty jabbed his finger at the advert.

'A terrible thing of course,' he said in his best sanctimonious voice. 'But what can one do?'

Experience had taught him that it was almost never worth falling out with mess stewards who were in a position to do all sorts of favours for officers whom they had decided to look kindly upon.

Latham's slight bow acknowledged the fact that his superior wisdom had been accepted and withdrew with a faint smile.

The mess was beginning to fill. In an hour there would be a squadron briefing prior to another 'op' over France. Soon the whole caboodle would most probably move to an airfield behind the advancing Allied troops to provide close air support. Suddenly, it seemed as though the rest of Dainty's life was set out before him. He would clamber into his aeroplane and do his job, one that with Allied air superiority was nowhere near as dangerous as once it was. He would treat it like going to the office; flying with the same amount of concentration but with the knowledge in the back of his mind that it would soon all be over. Radios. The advertisement had imprinted itself on his mind. 'Tested in war for your peace of mind.' The trite phrase refused to dislodge itself and he thought of his London lock-up. He would get out of the things he had been dealing in; greatcoats and petrol, tools and boots and tobacco, vehicle parts, canvas, timber, medical instruments and supplies. In another year, when the war was won and the armies and air forces were being demobilised and all their equipment sold off as surplus, you wouldn't be able to give that sort of stuff away. New things were what the punters would be clamouring for; new wirelesses and cars and motorbikes, new sensations and colours with which to cleanse their minds of the memory of the war's unutterable drabness, futility and pain.

Other pilots were making their way to the briefing room. Dainty watched them, leaving his own departure to last. The new additions to the squadron were nervous, some choosing to calm their nerves by chatting too much, others by remaining silent and apart. They would be the ones to buy it if anyone did. In aerial warfare hesitation or over-confidence were habits you often didn't get a second chance to rectify. There were old pilots and there were bold pilots. There were no old, bold pilots.

Dainty drained his coffee and stood. It was time to press on with what was left of the war and which was standing in the way of his making a great deal of money. Radios and motor-cars, gramophones and televisions were what people would want when the wartime spirit of togetherness came apart and everyone awarded themselves a holiday to last the rest of their lives. For an instant Amelia's painting of the ATS women flashed into his mind. He hit the palm of his hand softly with a fist as the outward signal of the moment's vision, determination and triumph coming together. He could see the picture hanging in a cool, spacious room in a villa in the South of France. With their cars, their holidays and their electrical gadgets the masses would be buying the trappings of a life. He and Amelia would live a real life full to its brim. The people might want comfortable reality but would be sold dreams. Okay, so that's he'd be in the market for. When he'd told Amelia he would like to be a writer it was partially to impress but why not? Why not indeed? There was no rule saying that writers wrote because they held high moral principles. He'd dealt out death and been damned near the receiving end. Surely that was worth writing about? Radio and he guessed television when it got into its stride in the post-war world would be hungry for writers and anyway there was nothing he could not do, no barrier that could not be overcome if the prize was the love of Amelia. France would be perfect. Somewhere with a view of the mountains. Amelia would paint and he would sit and watch the eagles soar and write and they would move with elegance in the best of circles.

Latham was going about his business of collecting dirty cups and saucers and tidying away newspapers. Dainty's new resolution required a gesture to mark its importance. He took the half-crown from his pocket and placed it squarely in the middle of the seat where Latham was sure to find it.

An hour later Dainty was back in the air looking down at the French coast towards where the killing would be. Within perhaps half-an-hour he would probably have killed men with the lesser chance someone might kill him.

Wakes of ships streamed below him with other boats and ships nudging the shore like tiddlers feeding at the edge of a pond, queuing at the ports with their cargo of men and machines to be thrown into war's greedy maw. Ten thousand feet below bureaucracies were already being set up. Within weeks of the battle front moving on men in shirtsleeves would be accounting and checking and telephoning and filing and requisitioning and stamping documents as if the bloodiness was a mere administrative inconvenience. Dainty held a theory about war. It was like a wound, stinking and messy at the centre of things but dried and crusty the further you worked out from the bloody bit. Sooner or later, unless you actually died, the crust grew and normality took over as the wound slowly healed. Wars ended by such a slow but inevitable process when men got tired, disillusioned or no longer saw an advantage in continuing and went back to workaday things, the most important of which was making money.

'C flight leader. The Yanks are having some problems

around Amiens. Go and sort it out for them would you? Over.'

Back to today's business.

'Wilco'.

Dainty glanced at his map and identified the co-ordinate before peeling away to the left, the two other pilots in his flight, Preston and Minton, turning with him.

'I think we've found them. Two o'clock,' came Minton's voice. Ahead and to the right he could see a mixed convoy of light armour and trucks. 'They're firing at us already. Not terribly clever of them.'

Had Dainty been a commander on the ground and on the losing side he would get off the road under the cover of trees or buildings and hold his fire hoping that no marauding aircraft spotted him. That way you got to live. He decided to make the first pass just to check it wasn't some nervous and excited British or American gunners mistakenly popping away.

Field-grey. Half-tracks and little Kubelwagens and at least two armoured cars although there might be some others hidden. 'All yours,' he snapped into the radio. No sense in giving the Germans time to organise themselves. Dainty waited until he was clear of the guns and then pulled back into a fast climb. Then he would roll off the top and watch young Preston and Minton be blooded. The German gunners would be sweating and swearing as they brought their weapons to bear on Minton's Spitfire; he could almost smell their breath and their dirty uniforms and their fear; fear which was dispelled by a wild exultation as a long stream of shells spewed orgasmically skywards. All this he saw and felt as the German bullets impregnated Minton's plane with fire. The instant of impact seemed almost orchestrated; a unison of tumbling aircraft and hot curve of flame. Dainty could see the expression etched on Minton's face, a composure that was well beyond fear. The Spitfire went in almost vertically, fuel tanks erupting as the Merlin engine rammed itself ten feet into the ground.

Dainty felt no anger as he kicked his own aircraft round, a cold professionalism making him a part of the aircraft with its arteries of wire and piping, its sinews of metal linkages and the condensed awesome power of its Merlin engine and murderously powerful cannons. Up until this point he had been a mere addition to the aircraft's weight. Now he was the whole deadly point of its creation. He worked from the middle of his back getting the right pressure on the rudder pedals and making his arms and shoulders work the spade-shaped control column and his eyes fix on the source of the firing. Now he was flicking the cover from the fire button his thumb ready to provide the squeeze that would rip whatever farm boy was firing at them to pieces, pulverising his gun and leaving a mother to grieve.

Dainty climbed quickly away, the corner of his eye catching sight of Preston's Spitfire on its strafing run. What looked like a light machine gun spat into action but other than that the enemy had been silenced. After Preston's pass Dainty zoomed over the now-forlorn group of vehicles once more. Nothing. The infantry would clean up any remaining resistance and engineers would bulldoze the torn vehicles into the ditch. RAF people would come and take away what little remained of Minton and his plane. It had been too bad. He'd liked Minton, a fresh-faced sergeant pilot from Surrey, cheerful and willing almost to the point of idiocy. The remains of Minton's aircraft were beneath his own wingtip as he radioed Preston to make for home. It could so easily have been me, he thought. But it wasn't. His number wasn't engraved on the bullet. He had lived yet again to fight another day.

The deep blue-green of the Channel gave out to a lighter blue and then a green-blue rind at the foot of the white cliffs. Minton, poor sod but war was like that, wasteful of young lives and cruelly unpredictable. But there was no point in philosophising. His life mattered and Minton's no longer did was the cold, hard truth of it.

Somewhere below there would be ATS girls on gun sites just like the one Amelia had painted. The thought of the gunner girl with the saucy smile lightened his thoughts.

His own airfield was visible as a smudge of lighter green in the Kent countryside gradually sharpening in a picture of buildings and parked aircraft. Dainty radioed for a downwind join and felt the clunk of his wheels lowering. With barely a glance at the altimeter he turned onto the final leg and lined up for the landing the angle and rate of descent perfect for a textbook three-pointer. Once down he gunned the engine and turned swiftly off the runway so as to let Preston land. The boy would be feeling bad about the loss of his comrade. Weaving occasionally, so he could see around the Spitfire's long nose he taxied to the dispersal savouring the comforting smell of fuel and grass, hot metal and rubber.

Several aircraft, Typhoon fighter-bombers, were taking off as he climbed from the cockpit, stretched and lit a cigarette. They were the bee's knees in the ground attack business built like brick outhouses and each one with the firepower equivalent to the broadside of a naval destroyer. His Spitfire was a lovely machine but designed for fighting and flying at high speeds and altitudes and only pressed into the ground attack role as a stop-gap. She was the one for him, though, his Spit. He'd buy her one after the war if she wasn't blown to tinsel and name her 'Amelia'. The minute the war ended there would be a wholesale scrapping of Spitfires, Lancasters, Mosquitoes and obsolescent Hurricanes. Within twenty years of being sold off for a song they'd be collectors's items. Speculating in aeroplanes would be a long term but sure investment, a nest-egg if the publishers' cheques ran dry.

The airfield had first been used in the Great War as the last hop in England for Royal Flying Corps aviators bound for France. Now there were more buildings and hangers and infinitely more deadly aeroplanes. Small trucks were taking fliers to dispersals and larger trucks and tankers bringing in petrol, spares, ammunition and food. The stale smell of institutionalised cooking assailed his nostrils as he passed a cookhouse outside of which a line of aircraftsmen were queuing. From the hangars came the noise of Merlin engines being run up. And always the sound of aircraft landing, taking off and taxi-ing.

One day he would be nostalgic about it. In stories told to grandchildren the likes of Minton would be cherished comrades who selflessly and without fear gave their lives for freedom. He would speak of his part in war with a quiet modesty. The fear and hatred, overwhelming impulse for self-survival, naked greed and indifference to the lives of friend or enemy would be edited from his memories. Nostalgia was nothing more than hypocrisy plus passing time.

The squadron hut was like a place of work, nothing more. He would not remember in years to come that there was a bright camaraderie, with young men held in kinship with one another by the steely bonds of war although that was the way he would write it because that was the way people expected to read it. Airmen were picking up pieces of equipment, walking and smoking with barely a glance at each other. They might as well be in a factory or a bank. The more edifying view of themselves as a sort of understated elite - 'We were just ordinary chaps asked to do extraordinary things' - would come later as recollections were purged of fear, ambition, greed, boredom, discomfort and indifference.

Dainty's earlier injury had quickly healed and despite himself he'd been eager to return to combat. What was the point in not? he had thought. Time enough for the fireside and the books when the blood was thin and old. Now, with the months of war drawing in, was the time for the last fling of a young man's desire for battle. Ah, such a song he would sing when the time came of triumph, of war and love!

*   *   *

In Dainty's pigeon-hole in the officers' mess was a typed note stating that the commanding Officer wanted to see him at 1430 hours which was in half-an-hour's time. The note's curtness pricked his buoyant mood and replaced it with a chill of apprehension. His fingers fumbled as he shed his flying clothing. Had his criminal activities been discovered? It was an odd thing but he experienced something close to a sense of relief. A condemned man must feel a bit like that, he thought, an instant before the lever was pulled and the trap door crashed open. Fate had played its hand and fear was as pointless as hope.

Snap out of it. Self-pity and doubt were for weaklings. The police and RAF Provost might have nabbed some of the small fry but he'd been as cunning as an old fox in leading the trail away from himself. Probably the Old Man wanted to discuss a routine squadron matter. And yet he could not dispel the feeling of trepidation. Something was wrong. Like a mist that begins as the thinnest of veils and thickens into a dense disorientating fog something was happening to the very air surrounding him. He began to imagine that the other pilots were avoiding him and muttering responses without looking at him, finding reasons to look away as they passed, or at his approach finding a reason to talk to someone else. Steady old boy you're getting into a blue funk. A flight of Spitfires took off somewhere behind him but their roar seemed strangely distant.

The commanding officer's clerk sat behind a linoleum-topped desk littered with files and forms. A girl - the twin-bladed propeller on her sleeve showing her to be a Leading

Aircraftswoman - sat at another, smaller table typing without raising her eyes.

'The commanding officer won't be a minute. Please take a seat,' the clerk said.

No 'Sir' was appended to the request Dainty noticed. Perhaps in the official mind he had already been stripped of his rank and dignity, un-personned and destined for whatever circle of Hell was reserved for people who played the black market. The corporal's uniform looked as though it had been tailored for him and his hair was well cut. After a minute the clerk knocked lightly upon the commanding officer's door and Dainty heard his name mentioned.

'He'll see you now.'

Dainty marched in and saluted and the door was closed behind him. Wing-Commander Noel Bentley DFC, the station's commanding officer nodded toward the seat pulled up in front of his desk. Only then did Dainty see a civilian sat in a corner behind his left shoulder.

'Ah, Dainty.' The Wing Commander looked decidedly nervous. His desk was clear of documents which Dainty for some reason interpreted as a bad sign. 'I heard about young Preston this morning. Bad show. One of my other unpleasant duties this morning will be to write to his next-of-kin.'

'Other, Sir?'

The senior officer made a gesture with his open hand in the direction of the man seated near the door who now picked up his chair and moved it to a position facing Dainty. The man was thin, about forty years of age wearing a brown suit and carrying an attaché case from which he produced a file bound with blue ribbon.

'I will not introduce myself, neither will there be a record of this conversation,' the civilian's voice was flat and cold. As if at a signal Wing Commander Bentley rose. His hands were opening and closing and he was rubbing his thumb against his forefinger, a nervous habit Dainty and others had observed before. The Commanding Officer stopped and half-turned towards him but left the room without a word.

It was the signal for the civilian to occupy the commanding officer's seat. Dainty eyed him with dislike, putting him down as a Whitehall Warrior, the sort that put on a tin hat for Home Guard duties a couple of times a week and thought he was winning the bloody war. He lit a cigarette, carelessly flicking the spent match past the man into the CO's waste paper basket.

'Since we appear to have dispensed with the normal courtesies I'll ask you what the Hell it is you want and to make it quick. Some of us have a war to fight.'

He had intended the words to sting but they had merely sounded petulant. The civilian gave a vulpine smile.

'In which case I shall come straight to the point. You are a criminal, Flying Officer Dainty. A common thief who dishonours his uniform and his service and who, if I had my way, would go the gallows.'

The civilian could give Dainty a good few years but was stockily-built with eyes that were hot and angry and if threatened would give a good account of himself. Dainty felt his impulse to seize the man by the lapels subside. The man saw this.

'Good. We appear to understand one another.'

He lifted a file which had lain to one side and placed it on the desk in front of him.

'I have here a complete dossier on your activities. I'm sure you know what I'm talking about.'

Absurdly, Dainty remembered being summoned before the headmaster when he had made a point of honour in not betraying his fear by swallowing or making some blurted response in a strained and squeaky voice.

'At least you don't deny it.'

The civilian removed a hand that had been resting on the file. 'That would have been tiresome. Just so you understand that I am not playing games with you I have ordered the arrest of sixteen of your accomplices and our American colleagues have pulled in a rather smaller number. There is now little point in your continuing to pay rent on your little Aladdin's cave in Soho which has been cleared of its contents which will be used as evidence at your trial along with a great deal more. We were quite surprised at the breadth of your activities, quite surprised.'

Dainty looked out of the window at the sky without speaking. Suddenly its blue that had enthralled him even since before he had first reached for it in an aeroplane was doubly precious to him. Now that it was to be taken away from him he realised that all he had ever wanted in his life was freedom. To lose life was nothing much. To lose a clear view of the sky was more than he could bear. To stand under a clear sky with

Amelia by his side and be free was all he would ever again ask for. A great tiredness came over him. Wild thoughts of running from the room and stealing an aircraft and staging a crash and then forging a new identity for himself had raced into his mind while the adrenalin was still surging around his veins. Now the fevered thought had ebbed and he sank into his chair.

'Is there anything you want to say?'

Dainty lit another cigarette and summoned his last reserves of bravado. 'There isn't much I can say. I shall be court-martialled and thrown in the brig and then dishonourably discharged. It isn't quite the future I had in mind for myself but there you are. Swings and roundabouts, take the rough with the smooth and all that.'

'We have spoken to your friend, Mrs Amelia Kershaw.' The civilian ignored Dainty's assumed flippancy, watching cat-like as the younger man's face blanched.

'A very talented artist but with some unconventional friends. I seem to remember a pleasing little landscape in the Royal Academy summer exhibition of thirty-eight. I rather fancied myself as an artist at the time.'

The civilian tugged lightly at the end of the blue ribbon. His eyes were intelligent but strangely empty. He too had a killing instinct.

'I expect you know she has a big exhibition in Birmingham very shortly? I find it heartening that our nation's intellectual life is blossoming like a flower after a long winter. However I don't suppose you're in the mood for discussing art, even that created by such a prodigious talent as Mrs Kershaw. I'll ask you instead about Captain James Elmeyer of the United States Army Air Force. Does that name ring any bells with you?'

Dainty had affected cockiness when he had entered the room and now the civilian was mocking him with detached amusement. Secret policemen with eyes like that must look at men being tortured, he thought.

'I can tell that mention of the name doesn't please you,' the civilian continued. 'Nevertheless I shall carry on. Captain Elmeyer is going to be very important to you because he is the only person who can keep you from going to prison for a very long time.'

'I don't understand. Captain Elmeyer and I aren't connected in any way.'

'I see. Then we have obviously made a mistake.'

The civilian flicked Amelia's photograph towards him. Dainty fumbled for yet another cigarette, his hand shaking.

'Elmeyer was never a part of my ... ah ... business activities.' He wondered who'd taken the picture. 'I wish he had been. Then we'd both be in the same boat.'

'You really don't care for him, do you? The funny thing about it is Elmeyer will be buying your freedom. Perhaps even your life.' The civilian was almost purring.

Dainty inhaled deeply, using the time to try and collect his thoughts.

'And just how will he do that?'

'With his own life.'

A pulse was beating and Dainty's lips were dry. Painful, intolerable thoughts of imprisonment tumbled around inside his brain but that part of his consciousness which fuelled the fight for life at any price seized upon an inflection in the civilian's voice and tortured it to extract a meaning.

'I can see you are puzzled. Shall I spell it out?'

Dainty remained silent. He was not going to plead. The civilian had sensed his fear but he would not let him see its nakedness.

'You do realise, I suppose, that we could execute you?'

The sentence hit with physical force. Dainty's vision swam and he felt faint. Suddenly he could smell the prison, sour with boiled food and urine, the cloth bag they put over your head and the sweet, almost hay-like scent of the hempen rope as it was placed about his neck. Then the rush of air and the falling and ... blackness.

The civilian was again talking but the words were distant, as if heard in a dream. 'Death by hanging is not something I imagine you would welcome, but it is a very real possibility and shall I tell you why?'

Dainty replied hoarsely. 'Yes.'

'Two weeks ago at a naval shore establishment in Scotland a soldier fatally stabbed a guard while trying to make his escape after stealing from a warehouse. The man was questioned in a manner which I imagine was quite robust.'

The civilian extracted his own cigarettes from his jacket pocket and lit one without offering the pack. He sat back, smoking slowly and studying Dainty, moving slightly in his chair so that he could get a full length view of the man before him. Like an executioner sizing his victim up for the drop,

Dainty thought.

'The soldier will of course hang.'

'Trials are one thing. Hard evidence is quite another.'

Dainty inwardly cursed the waver in his voice.

'I suppose you have some?'

'My dear fellow credit us with some intelligence,' the civilian said smoothly. 'The soldier was a common little fellow from Glasgow with a police record that would take from now until Doomsday to read out. He had no idea you even existed and I'm sure his sordid little person was unknown to you. After some fairly muscular questioning he told us the name of his contact and so on up the chain until we got to you.' The civilian paused. 'So you see. The murder can squarely be laid at your door. Even if you are able to bear the idea of your own death you might spare a thought for Mrs Kershaw who will have plenty of time to mourn your passing from the solitude of her Holloway cell.'

'You ... bastard.'

A fist lashed out, catching Dainty on the temple. Hot tears came to his eyes. The civilian's expression was that of one prepared to kill.

'Not what I like being called by scum like you. You are an accessory to murder which took place on Government property under circumstances that were detrimental to the war effort. I can give it you chapter and verse but you can take it from me as far as you are concerned a long prison sentence is the best you can hope for.'

Engines were being run up somewhere on the squadron dispersals and a flight of aircraft were taking off. Absurdly, the station band was practising in a nearby Nissen hut. Dainty sat dazed and drained.

'Perhaps you might like to know the alternative to such unpleasantness.'

The civilian lightly drummed his fingers in time to the band's music as Dainty dabbed a the cut.

'Which is?'

'Ah, good. I see you are a little more receptive. Which is that you return to the business you know best, killing people by shooting them down.'

Dainty let out a hard laugh. 'If you want me to carry on killing Germans why waste time playing games?' He made a last attempt to simulate anger but felt only a cold helplessness and bewilderment. The civilian stopped drumming.

'Killing the enemy is something that soldiers, sailors and airmen do, not thieves and accomplices to murder. Since you have disgraced your service you will not be surprised to learn that your Distinguished Flying Cross has been rescinded and that your name obliterated from the official record. After leaving this room you will not even have a service number. It's all been for nothing, Dainty, absolutely nothing. You will never be able to tell your kids what you did in the war and even those who knew you will turn their backs on you for the despicable criminal you really are. But even that's not enough for me. There is one last job to do before we throw you out like so much spoiled meat.'

'Tell me. Get it over with.'

'You must shoot down an Allied plane. An American B-17. At the controls of which will be Captain James Elmeyer.

'I don't understand .... '

'And you never will. You will shoot down a perfectly flyable B-17 of the United States Army Air Force which has Captain Elmeyer at the controls and carrying a skeleton crew. The aircraft will be unarmed. A nice, easy job tailor-made for a callous and corrupt bastard like you. You will be briefed and debriefed by one person who will not be me after which you will never refer to the matter ever again. Since it is pointless asking you upon your honour as an officer and a gentleman I shall merely remind you of the consequences of a loose tongue.'

'If I do it I'll be free?'

'Free from prosecution yes, assuming your criminal activities are brought to an end.'

'The way you put it suggests some kind of penalty.'

'Oh there will be, but not imposed by us. You will be able to spend the rest of your life going over the few minutes in which your canon shells tore into Elmeyer's plane and it's falling from the air. Your radio will be set to the Fortress's wavelength so you'll be able to hear the screams and curses of those who survive your gunfire in the last minutes of their lives.'

'And if I don't do it? Send an innocent crew to their death?'

At the beginning of the interview the civilian had pulled free the piece of ribbon with which the file had been secured.

Now he dangled it from his finger, the end knotted into a noose.

212

TWENTY-FOUR

A thunderstorm rumbled in the distance as Frenchie wheeled out into the flat countryside and pedalled toward Bassington. Cumulonimbus was piled high, its peaks painted by the sun but its base fringed with the ragged curtains of heavy showers. He pushed harder against the pedals and within twenty minutes was passing the outlying cottages and the little car repair workshop.

Just outside Bassington's bank were railings against which he leaned his machine before chaining it. Bicycles were like gold dust. No passing GI who didn't know it belonged to Frenchie Hayes would think twice about riding it away or making off with it in the back of a truck or Jeep.

Inside a single light with a plain celluloid shade emphasised the bank's bare functionality.

A thin-faced blonde girl sat behind one of the two grilles. A tiny electric fire with one bar switched on was behind her. The place smelled of England, dusty and cold. The customers' side was empty apart from himself.

'Mr Pelham will see you now, Sir,' the girl said with a slight delay before the 'Sir' because she could see his sergeants' stripes. Frenchie caught the glance and thought to Hell with snooty England.

He had expected the business with Mr Pelham to be drawn out but it was quickly completed. He'd pulled out the money and put it on the table and said what he'd like done with it in the event of his death. When he saw the wad of notes the manager's attitude changed and when Mr Pelham, a tall man with thinning sandy hair, called Frenchie 'Sergeant' he made it sound like some sort of general. He offered Frenchie a cup of tea who said at first that he would prefer coffee but changed his mind because he'd heard that English coffee tasted like a mix of acorns and powdered horse shit. A little tray with a pot and two dinky cups and saucers and what looked like a sauce boat with milk in it were brought in by the girl with the electric fire who seemed to be the only clerk. Mr Pelham drank his tea daintily and talked of various ways Frenchie could invest for the future. Frenchie liked the idea that there might be a future other than as an unrecognisable cinder in a burnt-out Flying Fortress. Forms were signed and Mr Pelham counted the money with the required professional air before rising from his seat, proffering his hand and steering Frenchie towards the door.

The English were no different to Americans when it came to money, Frenchie thought. All this stuff about class was bullshit. Class was money plus a few years. The girl looked at him more respectfully when he left risking a shy smile.

The first heavy spots of rain were hitting his face making his eyes sting as he stopped at the guardhouse to show the MPs his pass and then rode on to the motor pool where there was a Sergeant he needed to see. After that he had some more money to collect. He would put that in the bank too. Before he'd come to England Frenchie had never been in a bank. He tried to imagine what happened to his quid bills once they had been smoothed out and put into drawers. They got sent to a bigger bank and somehow got sent out as business collateral but like homing birds flew back into his account only this time plump with interest. Make enough dough and you could live on the interest. The bank had given him a little book with the amount he had put in written into it. Several times an hour he took the book out and looked at it; an almost unbelievable sum, more money he guessed, than he could ever earn in the air force even if he got to be a captain, and the interest would make it bigger ... he did some sums in his head ... Holy Smoke! Before Luck Be A Lady's last combat mission he'd get all the rest of his dough that was in the locker and that was owed to him and get it in the bank. Two washed-out bank workers and a crummy electric fire it might be but it was the entrance to a glittering cave heaped will all sorts of unimaginable treasures, a repository of dreams for him, his wife and little girl.

Luck Be A Lady was being towed out of the hangar tail-first, a sudden shaft of sunlight lancing through the cloud and striking the ship on her divided windshield. You could always tell your own ship even at a distance and there was something special about Luck Be A Lady.

Once tomorrow's training flight was over she only had to be lucky just one more time. Only once more did he have to climb into his F-2 electrically-heated suit and sit there waiting for some Kraut to come and try to shoot his ass off. Then the rest of his life could begin. The things he knew in life, Frenchie decided, added up to a lot of little things. He knew how to shoot straight and the fact that James Elmeyer was the finest guy he'd ever met and that he'd learn a lot from him in the years to come. He loved his wife and kid and he knew how to make money but that was only a really little thing if you didn't know how to make people happy with it. There was only one big thing to know which was how to survive. Everything depended on that.

*   *   *

Two days later Frenchie had made another large deposit in his account at Bassington's bank and the work to Luck Be A Lady was finished. They were ready for the flight.

Hosbach the navigator had been briefed and was already busy with his circular slide rule laying the true track and then allowing for magnetic variation and for drift. Just by looking at the chart Elmeyer could tell that it would be about two nine-zero True for the first leg to the RAF air station at Valley in North Wales then one eight-zero to their next turning point on the Bristol Channel and then zero seven-five for home. They wouldn't actually land at Valley which was a stop off for bombers being flown over from the States. That was a plus. The airspace would be crowded with rookie crews. Mike Wiggins, the bombardier, had been taken away and given a short course of instruction on the new equipment shoehorned into Luck Be A Lady's plexiglass nose. It hadn't been much of a course Mike had said, which was fine with him so long as they didn't want them to fly into action with the new gear. If the air force wanted to waste its time and dollars having them fly up and down Britain with a piece of equipment they hadn't been properly trained to use that was pretty much up to the air force but personally he'd prefer to get the final combat tallied off.

From his memory of the way South Wales had looked on the road atlas they'd taken on their trip to Blaendiffaith, Elmeyer guessed Luck Be A Lady's track would pass within a couple miles of the village. Maybe he'd get a glimpse of it in its cleft in the mountainside which would be enough to warm and cheer him for the rest of the routine flight. He would be flying with a slimmed-down crew; Gadgett, Hodgson, Mike Wiggins, Hosbach, 'Sparks' Cotterill and Frenchie who had been briefed to fly in the rear turret to test a separate modification to the gunsight. Frenchie had been slightly picqued that this modification had not required him to attend a special course but he was a sergeant and maybe not important enough for them but so what. He could buy and sell the bastards.

While it was still dark the group had flown off on a mission to the Ruhr. Elmeyer had got up early to see them off as they flew towards where the sun would rise. Cotterill had griped that if Luck Be A Lady had been down to fly they would be taking off on their last combat mission but Hodgson had countered that the target was known to be heavily defended by flak sites so not being detailed to fly was a damned good thing. Maybe their last mission would be a real stinker Cotterill had said but Hosbach countered it could just as easily be a milk run and so the inconclusive argument went as they assembled their flight gear. Frenchie looked his guns over and viewed the automatic gizmo that had been fitted to them with some distaste. All had gone through their checks with no great haste.

'A great day for sightseeing.' Elmeyer called for a radio check. Yet something was making the fine hairs on the back of his hand prickle as it flicked over the mixture and pitch controls and closed over the throttle lever waiting for the hollow, hacking sound of number one engine as it fired up.

Luck Be A Lady smelt warm and comfortable like an old horse in her stable. There was reassurance in the human scent from the grimed seats and from the flight clothing of the crew, the dust and warming Perspex and braided wiring, the thin oil used by the instrument mechanics and the vacuum flask of coffee from which Cotterill was taking a quick cupful.

It would be cold at the height they had been instructed to fly but not cold enough that he needed to wear an electrically-heated suit. Elmeyer tucked the ends of Amelia's green scarf into his A-2 leather jacket and zipped it up all the way. Lieutenant Henry Gadgett, a new man on the squadron, was co-pilot. The man responded to Elmeyer's orders and went through his checks but otherwise said little. Gadgett's name had made the men smile when they had first heard it because 'gadget' was Army Air Force slang for a cadet pilot usually thought of as the lowest form of aviation life. He'd ridden the joke with a self-deprecating smile and faultless work.

Elmeyer taxi-ed Luck Be A Lady to the runway threshold

and waited for clearance to take off. When it came he pushed the throttles forward, feeling the screws winning their purchase on the air and pulling Luck Be a Lady forward to rotation or take-off speed. It felt good to have such immense power under his hand. Without her load of bombs Luck Be A Lady would spring eagerly into the cool blue of the fall morning like a Labrador puppy jumping into a pond. He smiled as he switched radio frequencies to the Tower and followed the instruction to line up on the runway and hold.

'Okay back there, Frenchie? This is like a day out at the seaside for us.'

'For you, maybe, Captain. Me and Lieutenant Wiggins got to fool around with this new equipment.' And, he could have added, the thick wad of money he hadn't had time to put into the special account he'd set up and which was uncomfortable in his pocket.

'Pardon me. I thought this new stuff they put in the plane pretty much looked after itself.' Normally Elmeyer was strict about use of the intercom but the uneasiness of a few moments before was evaporating with the crew's banter. Frenchie was right. All he had to do was fly the plane. He hadn't given much thought to Luck Be A Lady's modifications until she was climbing to the altitude required for the test. The gyroscopically-balanced Norden bomb sight was an instrument which interacted with the flight controls effectively letting the lead bombardier fly the plane whilst laying the bombs onto the target but nothing to do with the guns. But perhaps they'd re-routed the power feed or made the bomb-sight more stable when the guns were firing and recoiling which explained the need for Frenchie to be aboard. The briefing officer had said that at some point during the flight they would be approached by an Allied aircraft. Wiggins would do his stuff and calibrate the new equipment then all they would have to do was fly the rest of the course and come home.

'Two six nine magnetic, Skipper,' Hosbach's calm voice came through. Navigators, Elmeyer sometimes thought, should be required to develop a bedside manner as a part of their training, like doctors. Nothing was as re-assuring when holes had been shot in the plane which was flying with one prop feathered and the gas running low than to hear Hosbach's grave voice giving a new heading. The guy was as calm as an airline stewardess announcing that coffee would soon be served. He sure had been lucky with his crew. The ship deserved her name but it was the men who had flown her who made the luck. You didn't have to like them all that much. Just trust them.

Flying involved contradiction. You had to be relaxed and easy on the controls but at the same time vigilant, alert to events both in and outside the ship. Pilots who were alive to every sound, who could understand not only the sparking of plugs, the workings of servoes, the pressures and currents which drove the instruments but also the capability of his crew.

Elmeyer was satisfied with the details and was himself on a kind of watchful autopilot. For whatever reason the word 'lambent' was chasing through his mind summoned there, he imagined, by the clear coldness of the air. Something he had noticed about himself over the last few months was that he was constantly playing with words; setting new ones into sentences and rolling them around on his tongue. Some had even made it to the margins of flight notes or in the diary he always kept with him. Oftentimes he would just open the diary and look for a page in which Amelia's name had been written in pencil, savouring his recollection of the meeting as he might savour a rich and heady perfume.

'RAF Wyton to starboard. Our first way point,' came Hosbach's voice.

Whenever anyone mentioned the RAF Elmeyer felt a sharp and bittersweet stab. He had tried to analyse the pain and in a moment of ruthless honesty had concluded that in some perverse way Dainty was necessary to Amelia and himself. Dainty was the Devil - charming, and amoral - who had to be faced up to and overcome. The question was where and when would the showdown come? At the crackle of the intercom he shifted his thoughts back to the mission.

'Permission to check my guns, Skipper.'

'Go ahead, Frenchie,' and then quickly 'Negative. Hold it.'

A small shape was climbing fast from the direction of Wyton now receding from their starboard beam. The fighter aircraft displaying British roundels took up a course parallel to Luck Be A Lady's but two miles away.

'Okay, Frenchie. Do what you have to. Just watch out for our little friend.'

The hammer of the twin Brownings made the Fort tremble. In battle the sound often led to a liquefying of the bowels but today with its feeling almost of holiday the familiar noise, antiphon of war and death, had an almost carefree chatter. Elmeyer was superstitious enough to think that the aeroplane felt it, too. Free of her usual burden of bombs and guns and full crew the old bird was flying like a lark.

And yet something was not right.

Elmeyer could hear the whining of electrical servo motors which drove the gun turrets and the beat of the perfectly synchronised engines and feel the air as it slid by under Luck Be A Lady's huge wings. All was as it should be. And yet a thin sliver of panic was making his back sweat and his hands tremble on the control yolk. Chuck it, Elmeyer. He rebuked himself. Just fly and relax. This is one mission you don't have to think about too much. You're still spooked by the interrogation and thinking about Dainty. Just keep your mind on your damned job.

'Captain to tail gunner. Keep an eye on the fighter tagging along. Maybe he'll make a visual signal.'

'Roger that Cap. But if he's the intercept we've been told to expect won't he make a radio call?'

The RAF fighter should have made a call by now just as Frenchie had said but the briefing had been vague. He had been told only to fly an accurate course and let Mike Wiggins take care of the rest.

'Captain to bombardier. Is your new toy all set up, over?'

'Affirmative but nothing is supposed to happen yet. It's way too early in the flight.'

Only someone who knew Mike Wiggins well could have sensed puzzlement.

'Okay Mike. Keep me posted.'

'Hey, Cap, did anyone say anything about my ammo feed being stuffed with duds? Over.'

'Negative Frenchie but you must have checked the goddamned ammo?'

'I did Cap. Point five-0 caliber M1 rounds with tracer. What I got here is blanks. How the hell did that happen? I was sure ... '

'Okay Frenchie. I'll kick somebody's butt when we get home but even the most suicidal of Krauts isn't going to be flying this far West over Britain in daylight. You'd better move to the upper turret where you can keep a better lookout.'

Elmeyer felt the movement as Frenchie pulled himself from the tail guns past the empty waist gun positions and into the mid-upper turret. A hacking whine of the servo-motors indicated that he was carrying out his task of quartering the sky. What he'd said about Germans having been chased from English skies which was true did nothing to dispel Elmeyer's sense of unease. For the higher-ups Luck Be A Lady didn't need her defensive weapons was one thing but why go to the lengths of substituting blank ammunition? The fighter which couldn't be anything other than the intercept they had been briefed about wore friendly marking but what if they had been black crosses? And another thing. Why had there been no radio contact?

The skyline behind them to the East was steadily darkening. Gadgett, sitting in the right-hand seat pointed his gloved hand ahead and below where the fighter shadowing them since Wyton had re-positioned.

'Cotterill. Try raising our friend again. Keep trying.'

Ten minutes later Cotterill's voice came in again.

'Nothing, Sir.'

This wasn't SNAFU - situation normal, all fucked up. Elmeyer moved his shoulders feeling a prickling of sweat. Whatever else the crew mustn't sense his funk but something was wrong and whatever was in store for them wasn't by way of a practical joke. Their inability to contact the fighter might - just - be put down to simple oversight but Frenchie was too methodical not to notice his ammo had been switched. And the British plane shadowing them … he couldn't say it was sinister because the fighter had remained at a safe distance without even the suggestion of a threatening move. It was just … strange. Two or three times the British plane had moved close enough for him to be able to see the pilot. Sun glinting on the smaller aircraft's canopy and the fact that its pilot had his oxygen mask clipped into place meant the face could not be made out but he would have expected a friendly wave, or maybe the fighter peeling off to play around at buzzing them or fool around with aerobatics to pass the time. But nothing.

The day had started with a high, vaulting sky. Now, skeins of mist were snatching at the propellers and streams of rain flowed back from the split in the windshield. It was colder and dark enough for Elmeyer to remove his sun glasses.

'We'll go up a couple of thousand feet and get above this crud,' he said to Gadgett at the same time as moving the throttles forward and putting back pressure on the yoke and seeing once more the fighter now only a few hundred feet away. Apprehension was turning to anger. The clown. The damned stupid, ignorant clown, getting in that close when they were flying on instruments and without radio contact.

The fighter was on Luck Be A Lady's starboard side away from Elmeyer's seat.

'Anyone. Get his serial number. When I get to him I shall personally rip his balls off.'

'Negative, skipper.' Gadgett had been watching the aircraft for some time.

'A British Spitfire but with no markings to show his squadron. Pretty damned strange, huh?'

Strange or sinister?

Events of the last weeks and days tumbled one over the other in Elmeyer's mind refusing to settle in any order or pattern. Frenchie and his black-market activities? No. The MPs would pull him in and throw him in the stockade somewhere in the West of England where offending US service personnel were sent where they would probably beat the crap out of him but nothing so elaborate as this; the radio and the guns and the strange and threatening airplane. None of that. It was to do with him. All about him. The roughing-up from the anti-communist bloodhounds followed by the casual way in which he had been released back to flying duties should have put him on his guard. There had been no threats of further interrogation or prison or demotion. The absence of menace he now realized was in itself a threat.

*   *   *

Though gaps in the cloud Elmeyer could see grey hills bare and veined with streams. By his rough calculation Luck Be A Lady was no more than twenty miles from Blaendiffaith. Beneath the layer of cloud the village would be going about its day; boiled white sheets flapping and snapping like sails in the wind, Talfan the socialistic pub keeper serving the first pints of the day to miners coming off shift, the gossiping, laughing, bickering, birthing, dying, raw little village with its pit and its

221

common grazed by ponies, stone walls and rusting sheds and kindly bobby and most of all the little room at the Colliers' Arms.

'How much longer are we in the air, Hosbach?'

'Two hours twenty skipper'

In a little over two hours the big wheels would be coming down and he would be lining up on the runway at Bassington and then they would be assigned to their last mission and that would be that. He would relegate Dainty firmly to the past and Amelia would be in his arms and their future together would stretch before them like a golden plain.

Only then did he know for sure it was two hours he would never see. This was his last moments.

He felt no surprise.

In the part of his brain far deeper than memory or even consciousness he knew this was how it would be.

Frenchie trained his useless guns on the fighter. Maybe, he thought, the bastard would make a move when he saw the heavy-calibre Brownings fix on him. He swung the guns round and felt the bulk of the wallet in his back pocket. He now wished that he'd cycled back into the village and put it in the new account he'd opened shortly after making a will. He'd felt good making a will. There was money for his wife and kid and a bunch left over for Amelia and the Cap if he got killed but Cap survived. The legal arrangements hadn't been all that easy but a British lawyer who used the Limbo Bar had returned a favour.

His guns were on the British plane which had maintained position. Shit, if he didn't have dud ammo he'd have popped off a few rounds just to make the bastard hightail it. What the heck was the matter with the limey sonofabitch? Couldn't he see the big white stars on Luck Be A Lady's side and didn't he know what a Flying fucking Fortress looked like? He thumped his gun's breech in frustration.

Elmeyer had decided to say nothing to the crew.

Just let it be quick and merciful.

Gadgett looked at him quizzically but that was all. A primal sense of foreknowledge had already answered the question his lips would never utter. Hosbach, working on a fix, was silent. Wiggins was fiddling with his new gear. He could not see Frenchie but wondered whether he also knew.

'Cap ... Jim ... It's going to be fine.' Frenchie came in. 'I'm here. We're together, aint we?'

Frenchie then, knew too.

A thudding sound came from somewhere aft.

The assassin wasn't taking chances. Elmeyer reckoned he must have been told about the duds.

All right, if this was how it was to finish. He wanted to hear death as it stalked him, not through his headphones but in the real, high, cold impersonality of its chosen arena. He pulled off his flying helmet to be assailed by noise, the roar of the Cylones and the vibrating, pounding of the airframe and now a puncturing sound varying in pitch as the bullets tore aluminium, steel and flesh.

Everything, when the moment came, happened so slowly.

Something entered his body making it jump in his harness except it didn't hurt hardly at all and a dullness was spreading and then he was hit again. Light flashed along the port wing and Luck Be A Lady's nose rose as she began stall out. Elmeyer tried to make his hands reach out for the yoke but they were powerless. Gadgett, lolling in his harness, had a hole punched in his chest. He thought back to Steiner. Maybe being co-pilot wasn't so lucky. What a stupid thing to think. Perhaps he could get some control. Elmeyer tried to force the nose down and pile on throttle in a textbook stall recovery but it was no use.

He grabbed a handful of throttle and with all the strength left to him got the nose down until Luck Be A Lady seemed to be level although with the artificial horizon and bank indicator smashed or obscured by Gadgett's gore he could not be sure. It was now much darker and colder but suddenly there was a clear lighted opening in the cloud and he could see what he was sure was Blaendiffaith pinned to a bright patch of mountainside and from somewhere, mysteriously, Amelia was coming towards him and he knew then the question every human asked had already been answered.

TWENTY-FIVE

AMELIA Kershaw.

Around whom Mair had built like a stage set an image of the village and Elmeyer and the events of seventy years before only to dismantle and rebuild it in her mind until she reached the point of doubting whether there was any essence or any one particular truth to discover.

And now here before her the living truth.

Mair took in every detail of the woman's appearance, the lines on her well-bred face, the stitches on her superbly-cut suit and the fine grain of her black leather shoulder bag, but most of all the eyes into which she read humour and pain and defiance. Would this oracle made flesh speak or maintain the silence of many long years?

All else around her melted into the background. The people chatting in small groups or making their way back to the Colliers' had now become the shifting scenery and Amelia Kershaw the luminescence holding centre stage. She stood without any assistance or sign that she might be tired.

'Thank you for your condolences. My father was old, and had had a good life. It was so good of you to come. I had no idea ... '

'That I was still alive?' Amelia said with a faint amused smile and then a slight pause.

'I had a little difficulty in finding you. Your name isn't spelt the same as your father's.'

'I spell it the Welsh way. One of those gestures a person makes. Wales is a very special place for me.'

'I understand that. I would have done the same. I wanted to put down roots here even though the soil is not mine. There was a time I lived here you know, for a year or so immediately after the war. I believed that if you cannot exorcise a ghost you might as well make yourself comfortable in its presence.'

They walked together following groups of mourners towards the Colliers'.

'I thought about Aneurin a great deal over the years', Amelia said when they had reached the pub. 'He was such a gentle man and so cultured. In London it is easy to appear cultured. Here, unless you have a real love of art you will always appear a fraud. People do not have so many affectations. I like that.'

Amelia Kershaw paused to sip her Scotch. In the lift of the head that showed off the line of a jaw and the set of a nose Mair saw her beauty.

'I didn't see Mr Dainty among the mourners.'

Dainty. The word hit Mair with a physical force, emptying her of breath.

'They hardly knew one another. Ven ... Peter ... keeps himself to himself. Truthfully, I think most of the villagers are a little in awe of him although I don't know why that should be. He's a sweet old man.' The words came gushing out, betraying her nervousness.

'I wonder if he still has the painting I gave him long ago.'

'He has several. What is it like?'

'It's of some servicewomen on a beach in the South of England during the war. I gave it to him as a deposit on the place where he's now living. It's a long story. I shall tell you it later, although events of seventy years ago might not interest you.'

'He cherishes the painting. Do you intend to meet him?'

'Naturally, now that I'm here.' The old woman placed a hand, freckled with the years but the fingers long and straight, on Mair's arm. 'Although I don't want you to think that I came here to see Peter. I knew your father during the war for a few months which were the most deliriously happy of my life. Just coming back here brings back such memories. The Colliers' hasn't changed as much as I'd feared. I thought it might be one of those ghastly gastro-pubs by now. I wonder if the room James and I had is anything like it was.'

'James ... Elmeyer?'

'Yes. You know something of those years, then?'

'There are so many things I would like to know,' Mair said after a while. 'But you've come a long way and I expect you would like a rest. Afterwards we could talk some more.'

'A rest, yes. I drove myself all the way from London, you know, following the route I took with James during the war. Of course there wasn't anything like so much traffic in those days, although I do seem to remember a rather amusing incident with an army convoy.' The old lady's eyes lit with amusement. 'I shall go to my room and read and then, after some supper, go to bed. Tomos, Talfan's son has promised me the room James and I had. Do you know, I think I can remember Tomos being born.'

'Do you intend to stay for Talfan's funeral?' Mair asked.

'Oh, yes of course. I am glad in a way those old friends died such a short time apart. That way there is little time for one or the other to grieve. Now I must rest. In the morning we'll have a nice long chat.'

Amelia Kershaw stood, signalling the end of the conversation. Surprising herself, Mair pecked the old woman on the cheek. An old hand sought hers and gave it a squeeze.

'You want to know everything, don't you, about what happened all those years ago? I expect it's the policewoman in you, or perhaps the romantic. You are very like your father.' The grip was surprisingly tight. 'It's a common obsession with the young and you are young compared with me. The old know that there are some things which are best left unrevealed. The truth, in my opinion, can be daunting and rather hurtful.'

The old lady patted Mair's hand once more before turning towards the stairs.

Mair's night was spent in the company of her father's wraith. In the bright of a new morning she made her way to the Colliers' where Amelia was already downstairs taking breakfast.

When it was over the old lady extracted a cigarette from her pack and lit it with an ancient and battered Zippo lighter with almost ritual grace.

'Would you like to see?' Amelia saw Mair looking at the lighter and held it out to her.

Mair weighed it in her hand. Heavy deposits of carbon had built up around the flint and wick and there were minor dents in the body.

'James gave it to me. Actually, I suppose I stole it.'

'It was a bit mean of him not having it engraved before he let you steal it, wasn't it?' Mair said, injecting a lightness into her voice at which Amelia smiled.

'What can be etched on a piece of metal that can't be engraved upon one's heart? We used to give each other little things. I gave him a green silk scarf which Frenchie got for me. Frenchie was his gunner. I can see Frenchie, too, sometimes. They were very close, and Frenchie had a daughter in the United States who was very ill.'

Mair's hand moved to a small shoulder bag she had brought with her. Should she show it now? By the time the question had formed her hand had already made the decision.

'Was this the scarf?'

She lay the neatly-folded object in the older woman's hands, which began to shake. Slowly, with tears forming in her eyes, Amelia Kershaw raised the scarf to her lips and kissed it.

'I can see him wearing it now,' she murmured. 'Oh, so many years ago. I don't think it's even been washed. It still smells of oil and sweat. And there's dried blood on it.'

She looked at Mair. 'His blood.'

The blood of James Elmeyer linking the living woman who sat before her with the cold, dead scraps of metal which still lay up on the mountainside. Just as her father's spirit had come to her in the night, Mair now felt Elmeyer's presence. The dying Talfan had told her that Elmeyer was or had been a communist. Did that mean that he was an atheist whose soul was denied the solace of Heaven? The thought of his spirit forever haunting the bleak moor where his mortal life had been snuffed out made her miserable.

'The scarf was sent to me after my father died. Together with these things.' Mair went back into her bag again and withdrew the diaries and photographs. Amelia put on her spectacles and took up the diary but her eyes were misted and she shortly put it to one side.

'Perhaps I'll read it later, although it seems wrong to read someone's diary even after they are dead. But these ... ' She picked up the pictures. 'I've never seen them before. That's me. And there's James and there's Peter. Frenchie took the pictures so far as I can recall. My, how handsome they both were. James and Peter never met, by the way. How is Peter? Very old, of course, but is he well?'

'Physically, he's outstanding for his age. I wonder though whether he is easy in his mind.'

It was said with the very gentlest of inflections. For a fraction of a second Mair thought she saw puzzlement in Amelia's eyes.

'Old age has its comforts, but also I am afraid, its anxieties. There seems so little time left in which to make amends for any wrong we may have done. Later, perhaps you will take me to see him.'

The door to the breakfast parlour creaked open.

'There is no need, Amelia,' Peter Dainty said. 'I have come to see you. It is a meeting I have both feared and longed for. Let me kiss you.'

Gathering up her bag but not the scarf, the diary or the photographs Mair quietly left the room.

TWENTY-SIX

MUCH later Mair went to the Old Rectory where Peter Dainty was sipping whisky in hand gazing into the fire. A mist formed by the cold air creeping down the mountain had obscured most of the village. The old man was like an ancient god alone in his kingdom of clouds.

'It must have been wonderful to see Amelia after all those years.' It was a question rather than a statement.

'I wonder why she hasn't visited Blaendiffaith before? She knew you were here and that my father and Talfan were alive. It seems strange.'

Dainty's hand shook as he lifted the whisky tumbler to his lips.

'I am surprised that you've come to see me.' The voice had a bleakness she had never before heard. 'I should be a pariah, shunned and positively hated by Amelia Kershaw for all time.' The whisky bottle which only uncapped the day before was now three-quarters empty. Peter Dainty was drunk.

'You see, I killed James Elmeyer, I killed the man she really loved.'

Mair set herself on the arm of his chair and laid her hand on his forearm.

'Ven ... Seeing someone for the first time in many years can be unsettling ... '

'Sit down Mair. In your chair so that I may see your face.'

Mair sat where so often before she had sat while they chatted sometimes far into the night.

'I killed James Elmeyer, Amelia's lover, as surely as if I'd drawn a pistol and shot him through the heart. Every detail of his execution and that of the men flying with him is etched on my brain and will be until I die.' He took another gulp of whisky. 'And probably after that.'

The silence which unlike so many other silences between them was without peace lasted a full minute.

'It was all a very long time ago,' Mair said at last.

Dainty's smile was bitter and the look in his eyes was one Mair had never seen before; their fading blueness an ocean of anger, regret and pain: 'So it must seem to you but to me it's only yesterday. I shudder to think how greedy I was greedy for cars, thrills, money and women. I had been working the black market in a big way making so much money that I was able to buy this very house, for cash, the idea being that Amelia would buy it from me by instalments. That never happened, the painting of the bathing ATS girls was a deposit although I didn't ask her for one. Dried spittle had formed at the corners of his mouth. His face, neck and cheeks were like parchment and stubbled. For the first time Mair was conscious of his being very old.

'I'm a husk of the man I was in those days when I thought I was a demigod. I had a Distinguished Flying Cross pinned to a bespoke tailored uniform and there was nothing I couldn't do including winning Amelia from Elmeyer by fair means or, as it turned out, foul. Ah, yes. Cool Amelia. A woman whose ambition reflected my own. There was you know a certain ... cruelty ... about her which was an aphrodisiac to me. We were like a pair of young lions each exulting in the other's virility.'

The evening had grown cold and dark, and the only light was from the fire. Mair drew her cardigan about her, intent upon Dainty's words.

'And then something went wrong,' he continued.

'I hadn't learned that the longer a chain the more likely to have a weak link. A Glasgow thief who was one of the poor bloody foot soldiers in my operation was disturbed while stealing from a warehouse and killed a naval policeman while trying to escape. They got him and he was hanged which I must also add to my moral overdraft. Anyway that was just the loose thread the authorities needed and when they tugged hard enough the whole lot unraveled. My God how many times I've wished I had paid the price then. What happened next ... with Elmeyer ... was to haunt me for the rest of my life.'

A log cracked and fizzed sending a hot fragment onto the old spark-pitted carpet sending up a smell of singed wool.

'The only way to describe it is a deal with the Devil. The secret service knew of my illicit activities and blackmailed me. In exchange for shooting down Elmeyer's plane I would keep my life and my freedom if you can call it that.

'When the dirty deed was done I was stripped of my rank and decorations and my name deleted from military records which is why you won't find the name 'Dainty' in any roll of honour of those who fought in the Battle of Britain although that's when I won the DFC. I suppose there might even be a couple of chaps still alive who would remember me although I could never approach them. The shame, you see.'

The old man put a hand to his forehead spilling whisky into his lap. Mair moved to the side of his chair and placed her arms around him. He was frail, terribly frail. 'Oh, Peter. It was all so very long ago.' He shook his head, resuming the narrative in an even voice, a confession delivered clearly and slowly as if in evidence to a court.

'I can't remember if I actually hated Elmeyer. I suppose I must have done. We never came face to face even though we used the same London haunts. Amelia was good at keeping her eggs is separate baskets. Through the black market I knew one of his gunners nicknamed Frenchie who was with Elmeyer when their plane went down.

'The actual killing business was over in a minute. There was no reason for Elmeyer to expect an attack from a friendly aircraft. I think his guns might have been removed because there was no returning fire. She was a sitting duck. It wasn't as though I had been trained to feel hatred for anything that fell under my guns but I was insanely jealous and that grips you like a cancer and eats you away from the inside. I watched the bullets punch into the Fort and fall from the sky. I had orders not to follow her down.'

A log fell in the fire sending sparks up the chimney. The only sound was the ticking of the big mantlepiece clock. The painting of the ATS girls hovered on the edge of the firelight the central figure's smile now seeming for the first time to have a mocking quality.

'I never saw Amelia again. To this very day I don't know for sure that she knew what I'd done although the Limbo Bar which was her favourite drinking den was a hotbed of gossip so I wouldn't be surprised. Out of sheer funk I never went back there. I would have been a pariah even in that moral cesspit. '

'And all those years after the war. Until now?' Mair softly put in.

'I tried to console myself with the thought that I'd been used as a sort of sharpening stone she used to hone her love for Elmeyer. She buried herself in her work and became famous as she always knew she would. For a while marriage and my own work provided a passable imitation of happiness. But now ... '

The tears of old age gathered and fell. Mair took the glass from Peter Dainty's hand and placing a rug around his knees and a guard around the fire crept silently from the room.

TWENTY-SEVEN

DESPITE the earliness of the hour Peter Dainty was up and dressed smartly in cavalry twill trousers, polished brown shoes and tweed jacket and with a stick.

'I'm ready to climb the mountain,' he said.

She would remember the composure of his face. It was as though his youthful courage had surged back to fill an aged frame.

'Will Amelia be coming?' he asked.

'Of course. Tomos is running us all up in his Land Rover.'

'It's a marvellous day for it. Will you fetch me some flowers to take?'

His voice was thin and soft, almost a sigh. Flowers, Mair thought for her father and for Talfan - and for Elmeyer and his doomed crew seventy years dead.

The last of the stars lingered through fans of cirrus cloud which were the first outriders of rain to come as the Land Rover bumped and swerved first through beech and pine and then onto the bare mountainside towards the ancient mound known locally as the Tump near where the wreck lay.

Amelia sat next to Peter Dainty and was silent but her eyes and the minute movements of her face were a moving map of emotion as the car lurched upwards along the bracken-flanked track.

When the time came for them to go on foot Mair helped the old woman down, holding her elbow as they moved towards what remained of B-17G Luck Be A Lady.

Two of the huge radial engines lay nearby, the alloy casing and fins whitened with age and the ferrous metal parts fused into a rusted mass. A piece of airframe, sheeps' wool caught on its jagged edges, wagged stiffly in the wind. A third engine lay some distance away. The fourth, Mair concluded, must have sunk completely into a boggy patch. Four miles overhead an airliner unzipped the sky with its contrail. The moor, wreckage and the airliner and the chattering flight of a bird was the here and now. There were no ghosts. Wherever the men on the Flying Fortress were it was not here. Amelia turned away, her eyes moist, but whether from the wind or thoughts of long ago Mair could not tell.

An hour later Mair and Amelia were warming themselves

by the Colliers' fire. For months Mair's thoughts had turned around Luck Be A Lady, Amelia, and the two young men who had loved her. She had become fascinated by the minutiae of history, the uniforms and the blackout, the sour smell of ruptured drains in bombed cities, daily orders which sent fearful men into the air and the aeroplanes themselves, everything bound up with the grim industry of death. But all of it secondary to the three central characters one of whom now sat by her side.

Now the final seal. The question she must ask.

'When my father died he left me as well as the diary and pictures and green scarf a very great deal of money. I wondered if you knew how that came about?'

Jane Staunton had served them coffee. She could hear Tomos's cousin's cheerful voice coming through from the public bar. It was a voice of this world, of the present, and she hoped of the future.

'Do you know I can't honestly say.' Her voice was light as if Mair's question were of only passing concern. 'Well, not for sure.'

'Frenchie, James' gunner, worshipped his skipper who he usually called Cap. They were devoted to one another in a way men sometimes are. Frenchie was something of an entrepreneur which would be the nicest way of describing it and kind to me because he wanted James to be happy.

'It's possible that having heard of Aneurin and Blaendiffaith and all that it meant he sent your father money as a sort of back-up fund to make sure I would be well provided for if anything happened to James. When I failed to return to the village your father did an eminently sensible thing and invested the money in his own name.'

But it couldn't have been like that. Surely not.

Elmeyer's blood was on the scarf which meant it must have been removed after the crash almost certainly at the same time as the diary and photographs. And her father had been in charge of proceedings following the crash and must have entered the tortured remains of Luck Be A Lady. Had memories of his dead son, the brother Mair never knew, gone through his mind and had he perhaps hoped to send the diary and pictures to Elmeyer's relatives who in the end proved untraceable. As for the money perhaps it had been dislodged during the crash and just lay there ... There was no answer. She would never know for sure.

'Are you all right, dear?'

Amelia's question snapped Mair back into the present. 'You look as though you've seen a ghost.'

Ghosts. A lot of the story was about ghosts, Mair thought, ghosts unable to tell all about the world which had been theirs. The truth in limbo.

'I think I know what might be bothering you. Would it hurt you for me to speak of it?' Amelia asked. Mair looked into eyes which were gentle and direct giving no hint of anything about to be withheld.

'Your father was the first to enter the wrecked aeroplane, or so a Mr Parr-Gruffydd who had been a Home Guard officer told me after the war had ended. Aneurin was the last to set eyes on what remained of James Elmeyer and Frenchie and the others. If ... if anything was found other than the scarf ... Let's just say it found its way to the right person. Luck is a frolicsome blighter and when it turns up you must wrestle it to the ground. Luck Be A Lady was true to her name.'

'Were you ever told about how the crash happened?' This at least Mair had to know. A catspaw of rain pattered against the window.

'In no great detail,' Amelia said at last. 'Why should anyone bother? I was married to somebody else and Frenchie the only person I knew who was closely connected with James died with him. Later I was told they were on a test flight during when something went wrong with a new piece of navigational equipment and they flew into the mountain which was shrouded in cloud. James is buried at a military cemetery near Cambridge and Frenchie next to him. Blaendiffaith, by sheer chance, happened to lie under Luck Be A Lady's flight path. There was an enquiry of sorts or so I was told but it was war-time and they were just one crew among hundreds. For a long time I was grief-stricken to the point of becoming unbalanced, haunting the places where James and I had been together and touching the things I had seen him touch. I even reached up to stroke the nose of the fox over the bar because its glass eyes had once looked down at James or so I convinced myself.'

'And Peter Dainty?'

'I never saw him until now. He was a sort of counterbalance to James Elmeyer, ruthless where Elmeyer was thoughtful. I loved James but I needed the spice of Peter's callousness. With

James dead he became ... ' Amelia shrugged. 'Dispensible. That sounds cruel but women as well as men are hardened by war.'

By a trick of light the planes and angles of the old woman's strong and linear face began to soften giving a glimpse of the woman Elmeyer had loved and Dainty had craved.

Peter Dainty was near at hand and would soon be joining them. Amelia, at the centre of her thoughts for so long, was sitting by her side. In the Colliers' Arms where Amelia and Elmeyer had loved so voraciously and so joyfully the spirit of the dead American airman seemed summoned as if from the walls that had once resounded with his voice and laughter.

They sat in silence for a while.

'Have you ever been in love?' Amelia asked. 'I hope you do not consider that an impertinent question.'

'I have been in love and I hope to be so again.'

'That's good. Well, I shall go to my room now. I shall see Peter in the morning and then I shall go home. It's late in my life and I don't suppose I shall ever see Blaendiffaith again. Goodnight my dear.'

The old woman offered her cheek, which Mair kissed. From Peter Dainty she had learned the secret of Elmeyer's death and it would be a secret she would take to her own grave. Amelia had long ago settled on a version of events which it would be pointlessly cruel to dispel.

As for Peter Dainty, they would go on as before. He would remain Ven, her friend. What men did when they were young could be expunged. Peter Dainty had expiated his guilt on the rack of long years. Now, please God, let his suffering be at an end.

Life was for the living.

Jane was humming a tune as she stooped behind the counter on top of which lay the *Daily Telegraph* folded at the crossword that had one clue stretching across two unfilled lines.

Sung by a not-so-Blue Angel? (7,2,4,5).

Mair filled in the empty spaces.

Falling in Love Again.

The rain had let up and through the window she could see a last beam of the setting sun striking the mountain near where the remnants of Luck Be A Lady lay scattered.

Something made her open the page and glance at the date .

It was October the Eighteenth. And as she put down the pen the bar clock wheezed out the quarter of an hour past six.